FROM GEEK TO GOD

95,014 words

1,021 Paragraphs

40 Small chapters

509 Total short pages

Writer, Eddy V. Parisi

Email;

fromgeektogod@outlook.com

FROM GEEK TO GOD

FROM GEEK TO GOD, The novel

There is a wide range of genre in this book. You will find fantasy, fiction, non-fiction, romance, action, humor/comedy, some geeky nerdy stuff, Christian and some mild erotic.

Brief description about this book. After high school he went on a road trip that is unbelievable and bizarre, but true. Later in life gets in an accident and has a yellow brick road type of journey where he meets characters and has an outer body experience, there he learns about life and life after death.

ABOUT THIS BOOK

Based on real-life experiences. I am not sure how to define this book because the first 60% is true, but I had to combine a fairy tale to the characters story to deliver the main message.

Tommy has a heart of gold, he is a funny class clown and has odd childhood encounters in S. Calif. After high school he went on a road trip that is unlike what you can imagine, unbelievable and bizarre, but true. After that he fell in love and had to get a job. With no education and great luck, he bluffs his way into a high paying job, there he finds his inner-genius and makes worldwide developments. Soon enough he is a master Geek! This eventually causes him loss of love and the ability to be social. He gets in an accident and has a yellow brick road type of journey where he meets characters and has an outer body experience, what happens after that you must read to find out!

NOTICE: We are all humans and do the same things, we have habits and bodily functions, it's how God made us. Please read this with a realistic attitude about the content in this book, some things might make you blush, and some things are strong content and hard to believe but they are true. I try to be modest and speak in a way most people should not be insulted but I told the story exactly how it is. There are many misspelled words on purpose to simulate speech, so please do not police the grammar or spelling. Hopefully it delivers a powerful message in the end. If you ever leave me feedback or a review, please leave a good review based on I am not a professional, I would rather not have a review then to have someone write a bad one, and please, if you leave a review, I ask that you do not retell the story like some people do, that ruins it for anyone wanting to read the book, please leave me a small review saying it is good enough to read. Thank you so much!

INDEX

LET'S MEET TOMMY

The summer of 1963 in southern California. It's early in the morning, the Sun is shining and the temperature is perfect at 74 degrees. In the background you hear the hottest group to ever hit the U.S.A., the Beatle's, and they are singing one of their 5 top hits on the radio, "And she loves you yah yah yah, she loves you yah yah yah, and with a love like that, you know you can't go wrong."

Mom is looking around the house for 4-year-old Tommy and can't find him, she ends up looking outside in the backyard and there he is. Glancing across the yard she sees him holding Digger, their Jack Russell terrier. She can see the dog's tongue going crazy. He's vigorously licking his lips and swiping his tongue across his nose like someone dabbed peanut butter on it. Mom yells at him, "Tommy, did you just do what I think you did? What did I tell you about doing that to your dog?" And there is Tommy laughing at the dog as it struggles to lick his giant booger off its nose. Somewhere in time Tommy discovered this odd deed as a form of amusement. Probably not a good way to introduce Tommy and not what you wanted to hear this early in the story. Hey, don't judge him, he is only 4 years old and I know he isn't the first little boy to do something weird like that, keep reading it's not as bad as you think. Tommy is different than most kids but has a big heart and is a very lovable little guy. Hugging comes naturally, and no person is exempt from being snuggled with. When mom takes him to the grocery store he always finds a way to win someone's heart. He usually smiles while he glares into a person's eyes as they walk by hoping to catch their attention, but what always gets mom in a conversation with a stranger is when he blows a kiss at them or winks at them, yes, a four-year-old winking.

I am fast forwarding into Tommy's life in elementary school. Tommy loves life and enjoys every minute of his day. He walks about 1 ½ miles to school every morning feeling the comfort of the great California weather and admiring all the fruit trees in the yards of houses he walks past on his way. He always makes time to sneak a treat from a different tree each day and has found other streets to go to school, so he can get different types of fruits from the trees on those streets. Some days he kicks his way to school on a skateboard, other days he pedals a banana seat bike with a sissy bar, and other days it's just too nice to ride anything, so he walks.

In the 60's there are so many cool cars to see since that is the most exciting time in automotive history. As he walks to and from school he has one car he passes every day that gives him a huge thrill, he sneaks up on it, opens the door, beeps the horn and then he runs. It's a 1968 Plymouth Road Runner. "Meep-meep" it sounds like the cartoon character on TV, which is how Plymouth purposely made the car from the factory. Thank goodness the owner thinks it is cute and doesn't get mad, how could he, he is proud to hear his car go Meep-meep. One thought I have is back then cars did not have alarms, what if the cars back then had alarms that used the horn like the cars do today? You're in the parking lot at the mall, and there it is, Meep-meep! Meep-meep! Meep-meep! It would be kind of hard to take a car alarm serious that Meep-meeped at a burglar, what do you think?

This time in Tommy's life is so fun, after school its grab Digger and off to any one of his good friend's houses to play, usually it's a variety of sports since Tommy is naturally athletic and loves sports.

At that time a toy company introduced what would become the biggest selling little toys ever, Hot Wheels. How great it was to collect them and challenge friends to a race them on the amazing plastic tracks that kept the cars in line while gravity pulled them down the hill. There were Camaros, Chargers, GTO's, El Camino's, even a Road Runner, too bad the Road Runner didn't have a real horn to blow.

Tommy had a group of friends that loved to climb trees. It was amazing to see how high up in the trees they would go. So many times, they would come across a bird's nest and just sit and watch the little babies as they chirped for food.

During the summertime, there wasn't any time for friends unless they are at the city park. The park is where it all hangs out and so does Tommy. Every day is an adventure walking to the park. California in the 1960s is a safe place; his biggest fear was not bad people it was crossing the fast-moving highways to get to the park. Now that he made it to the park, the fun begins. There is a huge Olympic size swimming pool where he is jumping off the high dive and chasing kids around in the water.

On the weekend at the park, it's a huge party. There is an amphitheater where they have the battle of the bands and all the Hippies are hanging around in big circles listening to the band music while passing a joint around the circle followed by a bottle of wine. The hippies welcome Tommy as he runs around the circles blowing bubbles for them and they are laughing at him as he dances and does funny tricks with Digger to amuse them. On the way home, he stops at a house called the 'Love House.' The Love House is a place sponsored by Hippies where anyone, any race, and any age is welcome to visit, live there or just hang out. When you look around the room, a lot of kissing and hugging, pot smoking and music. Peace, Love, and Rock-N-Roll are the theme. This is a lot for a ten-year-old boy to be around but some way he just seems to fit in everywhere he goes. One day when leaving the Love house, he bumps into a girl named Dianna walking down the street, she attends the same elementary school he does. He says, "Hi Dianna", she replies,

"You just come out of the hippie house?" He said, "That's not a hippie house girl, that's a love house." She thinks this kid is off the chart at his age all alone walking out of what seemed like a scary place to her.

One day after school he bumps into her again walking home the same direction and caught up to her, and after talking to her they figure out they live one block away from each other and walk home together. This

becomes a daily event now as they become good
friends and walk home together almost every day. One
day typical adventurous Tommy felt they should cut
down a different path through an alley and try a new
route. As they are walking he noticed a strange tall
bush that has an opening, it's like some kind of
entrance. Tommy said, "Hey Dianna look it's a
hideout, let's go look inside it." They walk up, and
Tommy sees something, "SHHHH! Be quiet," he tells
Dianna. They peak in and to their amazement, there
are two teenagers in there kissing but unable to see all
they are doing they notice their pants are down and
they are wrestling a ritualistic type of dancing thing
and that was too much to understand. Neither Tommy
nor Dianna can move at first, they are watching and
spying on this guy and girl. They both very quietly
back up and tiptoe away. No one will talk for about 5
minutes of walking then Tommy just can't hold back,
"Dianna, that guy was sticking his tongue in her
mouth."

"That's not all they did, that was really weird," Dianna said. Nothing else was spoke the rest of the walk home. The next day they were walking home about to pass the weird bush, they just look at each other and without saying a word sneak up to it like they are 2 navy seals about to take over an enemy compound. Peaking in they find it's empty, no action here today. Tommy grabs Dianna by the hand, walks in and now they have this mysterious fort all to themselves. Tommy starts talking to Dianna, "Hey, what do you think those people were doing yesterday?" Dianna said, "Looked like she was biting his tongue from the way I could see what was happening. Tommy's reply, "Well he was sticking his tongue in her mouth, but it looked like he was punching her belly with his belly, whatever it was she sure liked it." Tommy gets the wild idea they need to try what the other people were doing and talks Dianna into biting his tongue. After a few times taking turns of this stupid unimpressive tongue biting what do you think happened next? Well, to make this part of the story a bit shorter and less descriptive, they ended up exploring other things while alone in there and learned a couple things about the facts of life on their own. This became another new daily event for them and that bush hide-out was one great place to do the deed, now we know why the other two people used it.

Now here is something hard to believe but unfortunately happened. Tommy was home one day with his stepfather while his mom was gone. The stepfather told Tommy to go take a bath and clean up for supper. Tommy the fun-loving little guy he was went to take a bath and played in the bathtub. To Tommy just jumping in the tub splashing and playing was as good as a full bath, he got wet and that solved the problem. He got out, dried off and then told his stepfather he was done. The stepfather took one look at him and said, "Your hair isn't even wet!" Tommy thinks nothing of it. The stepfather grabbed Tommy by his arm and walked him down the hall to the bathroom. "Fill that tub up and let's do this again!" After the tub was full Tommy jumps in, the stepfather came in and took a glass and scooped water into it. He poured water on Tommy's head then applied some shampoo, then he scrubbed Tommy's head. "Now let's rinse your head off." This seemed to be going fine then Tommy noticed the stepfather did not reach for the glass to rinse his hair but pushed him back then dunked Tommy's head under the water. This would have been OK at first but about 5 seconds into this Tommy is trying to sit back up. The stepfather is still holding him down. Tommy is struggling to get back up and this big grown man was still holding him down. About 20 seconds later the stepfather lets him up. Tommy is gasping for air and can hardly breathe from holding his breath and all the water passing by his mouth. The stepfather asked him, "Do you see how this works?" Tommy still trying to catch his breath said nothing. Must have made the stepfather mad by not answering, the stepfather pushed him down again and dunked his head under the water keeping him down till he was just about to give up and then he pulled him back up. The stepfather asked again, "Do you see how this works?" Tommy is scared and crying and still gasping for air at this point, with a shivering small voice he could barely get it out and said, "Y-y-y-yes s-s-sir." The stepfather threw a towel at him and left the room. This was the first odd encounter he had with his stepfather and he did not understand what happened, but this was the day that made Tommy fear this man.

One day when Tommy was in school he discovered a girl named Kelly. Kelly has freckles that covered her face and she is the first girl he ever seen with freckles. He makes his way over to her at the playground and starts talking to her. She is so cute! That's all he can think about, she has long straight brown hair and clear pea green eyes, she is a beauty! Trying to get this girl to like him he kept bugging her till she gives in and she finally let him in her world, now at recess he hangs around with Kelly. Kelly is not as advanced as Tommy in the boy/girl thing since Tommy has already been there and done that with Dianna. He started working on her to let him show her something.

Tommy finally persuades Kelly to skip recess with him and go back to the classroom. They sneak back there, and Kelly has no idea what is about to happen. Tommy told her she was going to do something with him that was really cool and talked her into going in the closet. In the closet was lunch bags, backpacks and basic school stuff. You could smell the peanut butter and banana sandwiches which were popular back then.

When they get in the closet, Tommy is already lifting her skirt. "What are you doing?" Kelly asked. "I am looking to see if your thing is like Diana's."

"What does Diana have?"

"She has lips with a hole on the middle. Do you have one or not?" Kelly was not sure what this is all about but trusting Tommy let him finish. He inspects it real good and believe it or not the way he is touching and rubbing it, to Kelly's amazement this is turning her on already. He convinced Kelly at this point to let him do what he did to Dianna.

Sure enough, this worked out well because they did this several more times. So, what is going on here is Tommy has discovered sex, and yes sex is good! I am sure you must have figured that out by now. I don't know why any kid this age gets to be involved in sex that early in life, but Tommy was getting it. To go one step further with this sex thing, Tommy and Dianna were walking home from school one day with a girl named Marsha, she is one of the neighborhood kids. Tommy and Diana told Marsha they knew something she didn't and wanted to show her. Marsha is three years older and couldn't wait to see what these second graders thought they knew. To demonstrate what they knew they stopped on the way home to do a little show for her, they went into this area with a trash dumpster because it was surrounded by a wooden fence. Tommy and Dianna pull their pants down and showed Marsha what they knew. Marsha is flat out amazed. Tommy told her he would do it to her if she wanted to try. Sure enough, Marsha went for it. She lifted her skirt and pulled her undies to the side and Tommy did it.

He noticed something was different about Marsha, she had hair there. He asked her why she had hair there and she said, "I don't know, it just grew there." Later in life Tommy figured that out anyway.

A few years go by and as time passes Tommy is more athletic and playing with girls and experimenting with sex is fading out. For whatever reason Tommy is a natural athlete and good at sports. Southern California is a great place to be in athletics since the weather is perfect all year round and offers a lot of time to play outdoor sports. Tommy can do most sports very well, he tries all of them and loves most one of them. Baseball is his sport of choice at this age. The first year he played he got MVP in his league and the team got second place trophy.

TOMMY GETS BAD NEWS

~ 15 ~

Tommy's stepfather came home one day and has a sit-down meeting with the family. "Everyone gather around, I have a decision to make and need to tell all of you. Either I stay working and we move out of state or I lose my job and that might mean we lose our house". Tommy's mother asks, "What are you talking about?" The stepfather told her, "The Company has laid-off 200 people; I am spared if we move where they have a job opening and get a 20% raise for going. So, as far as I am concerned we are moving."

Tommy is listening to all this and is heart broke, and he is sad about this. Later when the time came to move, they are packing and just about to take off on their cross-country trip and he can't find Digger his dog. "Hey Mom, I can't find Digger." Mom replies, "Tommy, he was outside last night and when I called for him he wouldn't come in, he is probably next door eating with Mr. Wilson like he does every day at lunch." Tommy went next door and Digger wasn't there. He walked down the street calling, "Digger, here boy." Walking and calling, and no Digger. Coming back down the alley behind a house he sees a fluffy little pile behind a trash can from next door, fearing what he hopes is not Digger, he walked up to it and there is Digger, laying on his side. He went up to Digger and tried to pick him up and Digger was stiff and hard, he was dead.

Tommy screams and starts crying. He picked Digger up, carried him home and put him on the porch. Yelling, "Mom, dad, Digger is dead." Mom and stepdad come out and already know this scream is real with some meaning behind it. They get out to the porch and seen the dog lying stiff, no words needed to be said, the picture was enough! This is not the way to leave town, they console Tommy and finish getting ready for a long sad trip across country with they're heart broke from Digger passing away. The Stepdad asked Tommy's mother to go to the hardware store and get a shovel, so they can bury the little dog. When mom left the stepfather grabbed Tommy and walked him to his bedroom.

"Tommy, you were irresponsible! You did not take care of your dog and he died. You need to be punished." The stepfather made him turn around and take a spanking. He started swatting him with a belt. Normally someone who spanks a child gives a few swats, but this man whipped Tommy's behind for almost three minutes and that is an eternity when it is a constant thrashing. Tommy took a severe beating ending up with bruises from the back of his knees to the middle of his back. He never told his mother that happened for the fear of getting beat again. He did not know why this man went to this extreme to hurt him, but now he has even more fear of him and this set off what would be the beginning of many times to come.

They gave Digger a burial behind the house, step-dad spoke, "Here is where you came into this world, this is where we first brought you into our family to love and share our lives with us, and here you will stay left behind, even though we will be miles away you will always be with us in our hearts." What kind words to come out of such a vicious animal, in the meantime stepdad is giving Tommy a very strange look. Tommy couldn't help but feel like stepfather had something to do with Digger dying.

Time has finally come to make the move, before Tommy had to get in the moving van he ran to say his last good-bye to Dianna. The family jumps in the moving van; Tommy is crying and hating this whole episode of leaving Cally. When they are passing Dianna's house, Dianna is waiting outside for them to pass standing there with a sign she made especially for Tommy. As they pass by she is holding the sign up, reading what it said as they passed, it read, 'I am going to miss you, Tommy I love you.' All this did was add insult to injury, the last thing he needed is to be reminded he was never going to see her again and is going to a new place where he wouldn't know anyone.

TOMMY STARTS HIS NEW SCHOOL

Tommy moves with his parents to Pennsylvania. What a culture shock, East coast kids are so different. Walking to school is crazy, by the time he gets there his toes and fingers are frost bit from the icy weather. Mom greets Tommy when she gets home from work and asks how his first day of school went.

Tommy said, "well, first I had to go to the nurse's station to get my fingers and toes thawed out, then a big brute named Zeek wanted to be friends with me, so he introduced himself by punching me in the stomach. Then later in the day I was trying to hold back but I couldn't and accidentally farted really loud in the class which made everyone laugh at me. Then my shorts fell off in P-E and I wasn't wearing underwear and some kids got to see where the fart comes from. Then I had this amazing pretty girl walk up to me and what I hoped was going to be her saying "hi" to me, instead, she pointed at her nose with a wiping motion and then pointed at my nose saying, "You got a booger on the end of your nose." Certainly, an embarrassing day, but with all that said I had a great day at my first day of school Mom."

Fast forward, more odd moments coming up. We are going into junior high school where he reaches puberty and his urges are driving him crazy. In class he is observing the girls growing breasts and staring at their legs in the short little skirts they wear and sometimes getting a peek at their panties which arouses him. This is where he found out he can't control his mid-section. He got up to sharpen a pencil and noticed a few kids laughing and pointing at his crotch. It's a tent, so easy to see he is erect. How embarrassing this was! Don't judge him, it happens to most teen boys.

He is still walking to and from school and learned he is one of only 2 boys that walk home the direction that about 8 girls are going. No problem for Tommy, he gets to know the girls and makes friends with all of them. Eventually, he gets to know them better, and in a sexually promiscuous way because he has plenty of time and using his kissing wisdom he learned early in life with Dianna at the bush hideout he mesmerizes them with his lips.

His raging hormones are causing him to act like a predator, he puts on a splash of cologne, a tank top muscle shirt and a pair of sunglasses, and he is ready to go. This guy is a lady-killer, he makes sure no parents have made it home from work yet, then after school he goes visiting all the girls one at a time at their houses. He kisses them and shows them new things they should never know. He became popular with all these girls, they are so excited to see him when he knocks on their door. Most of the girls know he is traveling around visiting the other girls, but who cares, when they get their turn they are satisfied! He is in demand for his skillful kissing and the after-school service for the young ladies. It's freezing outside, what else can you do?

He could easily persuade all these girls into having intercourse sex but being the gentleman that he is, he just teases them by going so far and keeps them yearning for more, sooner or later they will get anyway.

His favorite house is the Browning's. Why? The Browning's are three sisters, 12, 13 and 15. All three sisters are in love with Tommy and have no problem sharing him as if he was a rooster in charge of hens; here at the Browning's house, he gets 3 for 1 unlike at the other girl's houses. One of best days he can remember is when the Gainge twins came to visit the three Browning sisters. Tommy was there on one of his daily after school extravaganzas and guess what happened? Yes, all five got the Tommy special! Tommy is one busy young man. Again, it's freezing outside, what else can you do?

A different day after school a guy named David asked
Tommy to come over to his house and play football.
Tommy is excited to meet some of the other guys in
the neighborhood he has not met, he wastes no time
to show up and make himself known. Tommy not
quite the biggest kid out there has not much
advantage to kick butt, but he gets in the game and
sure enough not one kid can tackle Tommy. He bobs,
weaves and he swerves, and sure enough scores
several touchdowns. All the kids are cheering him on
and starting to really like this guy. The kids are taking
a break to grab some water and catch their breath.
Tommy is pacing the yard with vigor and energy
waiting and coaxing the kids to bring it on, "What are
you stopping for, I am just getting started."

While these kids are resting Tommy is fake
quarterbacking throwing the ball in the air to himself
and catching it. He ends up tossing the ball into the
next yard. He runs over to get the ball and there is
something incredible, in the window, he just dropped
his mouth open and could do nothing at all! Tommy is

frozen in amazement. What did he see? The absolute most beautiful thing on the planet ever! He asked himself, 'My God, who in the heck is this?' This is heaven looking right back at him, it's Holly Barber. WOW! Where did she come from, where has she been all this time? In the meantime, all the kids are yelling "Tommy come on we are ready." Tommy is all mushy and weak after seeing this amazing little sweet thing. He gets back in the game. The kids are throwing the ball at Tommy and he keeps missing. All that superhero sports biz suddenly is gone. David runs up to Tommy and asked him, "What happened, you were Superman 15 minutes ago and now you are Blunderman?"

One of the other kids jokingly yells out, "He must have seen Holly." They all start laughing. Tommy looks over and said, "Is that her name?" After that, he never heard another word these kids said, he just started walking away till he got to her doorstep and knocked on the door.

Hollies dad answered the door and asked Tommy what he wanted. Tommy asked for Holly and dad called her to the door. She got there, and Tommy looks at her and starts babbling nothing that makes any sense, and here is what he said, "Hi am I Tommy, I seen you football as I was playing look at the ball while I looked back and you wanted to meet you so I, I... I... sorry, I can't remember why I knocked on your door, I think I better come back another time," Holly just stood there next to her dad and looked up at him confused. The father looked down at Holly and said, "OH boy, this is where it starts." Yelling at Holly's mother in the living room, "Honey I think we need to start keeping Holly in the house more, another boy noticed her and came to the door, and he was speaking all flabbergasted with more of that blubbering speech crap like the other boys do."

Tommy got home later than normal and is greeted by stepdad. He had a look in his eye and Tommy knew something was wrong. "Tommy, why are you home so late? You know you have a 4:30 curfew!" Tommy already knowing this is not good because this is the 'I am about to beat your ass voice.' The stepdad took Tommy to his room and for about the twentieth time took a belt and started whipping Tommy's butt and again bruising him with dark strap marks.

The next day Tommy is at school, walking to the cafeteria and spots no one other than Holly walking past. Absolutely no female on earth has her face, her hair is long and has these round curly things that hang on both sides of her face, and those eyes, yah, those eyes! She is the one! No more visiting the usual crew of girls around the neighborhood, she will be his new target. Tommy walks over to David's house after school, no one answers. Pacing David's driveway for about 20 minutes David never shows up. Sure enough, he glances over at Hollie's house and she is looking out the window at him. Tommy is so overwhelmed by her beauty and he just cannot get the nerve to go talk to her. He starts heading home, rounding the corner he hears a door slam, he looks over and here she comes his way walking her cockier spaniel. Forced to pass her she walks by and as they are passing she said Hi. He cannot believe it, she said Hi! He looked over and all he could think to say is "Nice dog." She replied, "her name is Corkey."

That's all it took, they started walking and talking and found they had too much in common. Weeks go by and Tommy is in Love, she also cannot help but be in love. Tommy has been holding back and one day after school they end up at Tommy's house and no parents are home. Tommy wastes no time at all and plants the big one on her, they kiss like they are never going to stop and hours on end this kissing is now an obsession. Day after day they meet after school and this kissing becomes all kinds of other things. These 2 are basically inseparable now and almost like a husband and wife, and only they know about this, no other kids nor their parents.

After making the transition from West coast to the East and he is now comfortable with all the new kids and the surroundings. Tommy is waiting at the bus stop that he never went to because he really enjoyed the walking to school but the last couple days were too cold so that day it's ride the School Bus.

Tommy is waiting in line with some other kids. Ronny, one of the neighbors was behind him. Here comes the Bus. Ronnie was always first on the bus until today because Tommy got there first. Out of nowhere with no reason or idea why, as Tommy was stepping up into the Bus, Ronnie decided to kick Tommy square in the middle of his butt while he was entering the doorway of the bus.

Ouch! That hurt! Tommy felt this pain shoot right through the middle of his butt and could hardly stand up. Ronnie yelled at him and told him that he was always first in line and to get out of the way. Tommy the nice guy he is turned and said: "I am very sorry, but I was first, so I am going on in first." While Tommy was turned around talking to him, Ronny was feeling a bit powerful because he got away with kicking Tommy in the butt, so he swings and pops Tommy in the face with his fist. He was thinking this was going to be an easy bully moment and then he would just get on the Bus and everything would go on as normal, but Tommy never said one thing after getting punched. With split-second accuracy of getting hit, Tommy jumps out of the doorway and tackles Ronnie to the ground clearing 4 more kids out of the way. Punch, smack, pop, hit, bang, punch, smack, pop, hit, bang and a bunch more like an outraged Gorilla. Tommy beats this kid's butt really bad, bad enough that his face was unrecognizable.

Tommy hops on the Bus and Ronnie ran home. When Tommy got home from school that day, Ronny's mom was at the door with Ronny, and when Tommy saw Ronny, his face turned white as a ghost. Ronny was black and blue from the top to the bottom of his face. She asked Tommy, "Well, what do you have to say for yourself young man?" Tommy apologized and told her,

"He kicked me then hit me, I just couldn't help myself." Ronny's mother asked, "Is this true Ronny?"

Looking at Tommy looking right back at him, he knew better than to lie, "Yes Ma'am."

"Then you tell Tommy here that you are sorry!" Ronny apologized. Tommy was a gentle spirit. He never hurt any person, nor could that have been his intentions. He felt terrible. After that a few weeks went by and they started talking and became friends.

Somewhere deep inside Tommy had a rage developing that was the equivalent of what happens to the Incredible Hulk when he gets mad.

The next week a boy by the name of Darryl Scoggins heard about Tommy beating up Ronnie and approached him at school, "Hey punk, do you think you are tough?

Trying to be a jokester Tommy said, "Yes I am Ruff and tuff and able to blow down little pig houses." Tommy thought this was funny and laughs because he didn't know Darryl and assumed this was a weird friendly approach to get a conversation started. Darryl was not there to make friends or to be funny. Darryl heard about Ronny getting the beat down and felt he was a bigger badder boy than Tommy and told him he wanted to fight. Again, he doesn't think this guy is serious and replied, "I already did fight, I sniffed your mother's butt and had to fight for fresh air, Ha-ha-ha!" Not a second passed, Darryl popped Tommy on the head. Just as this happened a teacher walked up, not knowing what happened the teacher thought this looked like a mutual fight, so she sent both of them to the principal's office.

After explaining to the principal this kid Darryl started it, and Darryl lied telling him Tommy started it, either way the principal did not care at this point and sent both to after-school detention. After school is here and it's time to go to detention. They are in the class sitting without the ability to talk and kept glaring at each other. I am sure for Daryl it was him thinking how he was going to beat Tommy's butt. And for Tommy, probably thinking why he got in trouble for this kid's actions. For whatever reason, the after-school detention teacher got up and left them alone in the room together. Darryl wasted no time and told Tommy not only was he getting punished by the school, but he was going to be punished by him after detention. Taunting him he kept repeating, "You are so getting it boy!"

Tommy was doing all he could to avoid Darryl's punishment thing and tried calmly and patiently to avoid that kid, but that did not stop him. He was way bigger and very intimidating. Darryl walked over to Tommy and pulled his hair. Tommy warned him, "I really don't want any trouble." Darryl did it again, and Tommy told him, "stop that crap or else," This time Darryl smacked Tommy on the back of the head and that was the last thing Darryl remembered. Tommy jumped out of his chair and tackled Darryl down to the ground and pounded on his face, ratta tat tat like a jack hammer! Darryl screamed over and over for help. They struggled and rolled around a while till they ended it underneath a table where Tommy had no more room to swing his arms. Tommy finally let him go.

Tommy can't believe this, "What the heck?" He got into another fight. Tommy has some new thing going on. When he gets hit a couple times he becomes violent, and describing his reaction again, he is like the incredible Hulk! What's happening? He is taking out revenge on these kids for payment of actions done to him against his control. Later in life he realizes he was taking out his frustrations on them from getting beat so bad by his step-father, hitting him was releasing built-up anger.

3 weeks later in class, once again when the Teacher had to leave the classroom for a while, another kid took advantage of this time. Kenny Gerrard walked up to Tommy and said, "I hear you got lucky."

Tommy not sure how to reply to this just kept quiet. Kenny said, "You better answer me, boy!" Tommy just sat there and said nothing. Kenny literally slapped Tommy across his cheek with the palm of his hand. The slapping sound was heard all the way around the room, the whole class became silent to pay attention to this.

Tommy's face was stinging bad, he asked him, "What the heck was that for?" Kenny told him that when he asks a question it better be answered, or you get slapped. Kenny said again, "I heard you got lucky, you little girl." Tommy with a stinging face and a bunch of embarrassment said: "what does that mean?" Kenny told him that he heard about Tommy beating up Ronnie, then Darryl, and that makes him lucky.

Darryl was his friend, "If you mess with Darryl, you mess with me, but the difference in me and Daryl is you won't be lucky, little girl!" Kenny reached out and slapped the other side of Tommy's face. The room was so quiet, all the kids were looking, and Tommy is so embarrassed because the slap brought tears to his eyes. Kenny meant business, he took one more slap at Tommy. From the embarrassment and pain from the slaps he received he jumped up like a Raging Bull and pushed Kenny. Looked like he knocked him about 4 feet away, Kenny flew backwards to the window then Tommy leaped at him and held him with one hand around his throat against the window and punched and punched and punched him and would not stop.

He started swinging both arms and he punched him unmercifully for almost 1 minute nonstop, which in a fight is endless. Kenny is bleeding from his nose and from his lips, the boy's eyes were puffed up to the point they were almost closed. No other kid had the courage to break this up and some actually cheered Tommy on because he patiently put the bully off at first.

Finally, a girl in the class who was terrified by the fight started crying so loud Tommy snapped. Tommy backed up and Kenny's face was red all over and he was crying like a waterfall then Kenny ran out of the class.

What do you think happened after that? Tommy's parents got called into the school. The school defended Tommy because they uncovered the fact he did not start the fights. What the school was concerned about was the severity of the outcome,

Tommy wasn't just winning the fights, he was damaging the kids. After hearing about the fighting the parents went home and had a talk with him. Later that evening Mom went to get a few things at the grocery store and guess what happened? Tommy's step-father found another excuse to whip him. I guess the fact Tommy was not picking the fights and was only defending himself was not OK with step-dad.

Tommy is now becoming well respected by almost every boy in school who was normally somebody to fear. After He finally became adjusted to the school and to the neighborhood and now he has this beautiful girlfriend, here came all these bad ass bullies putting the moves on him. When would this end? Well, the answer is this, Tommy went to meet Holly after school to ride the Bus home. Tommy is about to board the Bus and was happy, he is about to ride home with miss beautiful. He got to the Bus and before he could get in the door a boy named Kevin taps him on the shoulder. He turns and smiles, "Hi there, what can I do for you?" Kevin never said a thing, he punched Tommy in the ribs and yanked him out of the bus's doorway. Kevin yelled at Tommy and said, "You are one ugly little sissy and I hate ugly little sissy girls."

Then Kevin took his foot and squarely kicked Tommy in the ribs right where he just punched him. Tommy is gasping for air. He looks up and there he sees Holly looking out the window of the Bus. The astonished look on her face said enough. Just as he was about to turn and walk the other direction, kick, right in the other side of his ribs. Kevin had been in Karate for 3 years and he knew how to get a hard landing kick in real fast! In a split second he was turning purple with fury, but if he would have been a cartoon character he would be the Incredible Hulk turning green.

Holly kept looking at him, he was in pain, and he is very embarrassed. With all the rage he has ever felt in one single second Tommy leaps out as Kevin is taking his next swing at him, before Kevin can connect, he tackled him by the waist, picked him up and body slams him to the ground like he was a 2-pound bag of ping pong balls.

This totally surprised mister Kevin. Tommy wrestles his way around to pinning him down, and with both hands swinging pounded and pounded and pounded the living crap out of Kevin.

A huge crowd surrounded them. After a real 2 minutes, Tommy can only see black and red on Kevin's face, this was not from red marks of hits from his hands it was blood and immediate bruising. His face was already blackish and blue underneath the red bloody mess. Tommy stopped and stood up, Kevin just laid there as if he were dead. Tommy did not realize he had just about killed this kid. He looks up at the Bus and all he could see is Holly crying, but for some reason, it was not because she was scared for Tommy, he could tell by the look in her eyes it was because she was afraid of him.

The next day Tommy is at lunch, a huge crowd of guys walked up to Him, and the way this looked sure enough he knew he was about to get his ass kicked by a mob of haters. The biggest guy in the group walked up to him first. Tommy was about to get up and take off walking the other way before this got nasty, but before he could get away the biggest guy said, "Hey are You, Tommy?"

Tommy answered, "Yes I am. Why are you asking? Are you getting ready to jump on me too?" The guy said, "Hell no! Why would I do that? No way would I want my ass beat like you beat Kevin's ass!" Tommy is stunned by this guy's statement, he looked at him thinking he was joking and really read for a fight. Tommy said, "He left me no choice! The same thing applies to anyone else that attacks me. Now are you looking for a fight?" The guy said. "I really am serious when I say no one in this school will ever mess with you again. Kevin holds the state Black Belt championship in his age group and has won 2 titles."

Then he went on to tell Tommy, "no one has ever fought him and won outside of the ring. Kevin has been the biggest bustard school bully we have ever known, and everyone hates him because he beats everyone's ass for no good reason but to show off." The crowd of guys all started reaching out to shake his hand and introduce themselves. At that point Tommy could see he would be able to finish the year with no more trouble.

Tommy felt a form of relief he never felt before, but to him, this did not mean what the crowd figured it did, they thought he was filled with pride. Tommy just wanted to be left alone, to be able to go to school with no troubles and be friendly. Winning fights was not what counted in his life, it was about having fun and living life peacefully. As for Holly, she really was afraid of Tommy, in her mind he could turn on her and hurt her one day. She didn't know the real reason he becomes so violent when he fights, and the fact Tommy only fights back after he has been pushed beyond his limits. After that day she would never talk to him again.

TOMMY MEETS EDDY!

Now we are about to embark on the crazy high school days. This is where Tommy meets Eddy. Tommy has been using his energy to become more adventuresome. He was entertaining the girls in junior high school, but not in high school, he spends more time riding dirt bikes and competing with his friends. Most weekends you will find Tommy in the woods camping out where he can ride his dirt bike and go hiking. One of Tommy's closest friends he has known since Junior high school, Doug, is usually hanging out with him. Doug is a very nerdy geeky guy that is the polar opposite of Tommy, he is more relaxed and technical to the T. Doug loves making things faster, so he spends his time tweaking dirt bikes engines for higher performance. This is good for Tommy because he gets to spend his time testing the hard work Doug spent tweaking the motorcycles. How? Racing and rapping out the motors and pushing them to their limits. He redlines the motors rpm's as far as they can be revved without blowing them up, at the same time he is jumping hills and making new trails.

Doug is in Mr. Pucciarelli's drafting class, this is where he meets Eddy. He's a real outlandish guy ready for trouble and a good time, in a fun way! Of all the places he could sit he gets parked right behind Doug in Pucciarelli's class.

Eddy just moved there from North Carolina and does not know anybody yet but has no problem meeting people. The first encounter Doug has with Eddy is when he blasts a huge fart in the middle of class. Does that remind you of anyone? Doug, the super reserved guy that he is cannot believe what he heard in the middle of class from the new guy. Usually, it's Tommy farting, so this is not new to him because Tommy already introduced this type of class disruption years ago in the English class. Tommy continued getting away with blasting gas everywhere since the teachers never reprimanded him, but no one else was ever that bold and now, here is this guy doing it!

Doug turned to look at Eddy using his best evil-eye, wanting to send him a message of non-approval and disgust, but sure enough, when he turned to give the evil eye, he sees that Eddy is already looking right at him. With a big smile from ear to ear, Eddy said, "That would be the eggs I had for breakfast big boy, possibly the spaghetti my grandma cooked, or it could have been a bunch of air escaping that I swallowed." Doug takes that as an attack, he is mad now and about to say something to him, but Eddy is extending his hand out for a handshake and introduces himself, "My name is Eddy, glad to meet you in such an awkward way," thus spoiling the evil-eye to put Eddy in his place.

Doug has been dealing with Eddy daily and all his obnoxious antics. The first day it's loud passing of gasses, next day, it's getting whacked on the back of the head with spitballs shot out of a straw, and another day it's getting the chair pulled out from underneath him before he sits down on the seat. Eventually, after Doug has had many interruptions from him, he is starting to like him, he and Eddy became friends. Doug looks forward to his crazy class clown events watching him take turns antagonizing other students in the class.

It's Friday night and we are at the High school dance; KC and the sunshine band is the sound coming from the auditorium where students are dancing and hanging out. The song is 'Shake your booty', "Shake shaka shake, shake shaka shake, shake your boodie, you can do it…"

Lights are spinning around the room; strobe lights are flashing like it's a real disco club. Eddy is there and has a date with one of the schools hottest looking girls ever! Tommy and Doug are walking in the entrance; they strut in the door like they own this place walking like John Travolta in Disco Fever. You can only imagine, it's as if the Bee Gees are playing in the background," You can tell by the way I use my walk I'm a lady's man, no time to talk…"

Doug seen Eddy who is fuming mad at a distance. He walked over to see what's up. Doug asks, "What's up Eddy?" Eddy is going one hundred miles an hour cussing, flexing and twitching with emotion and he said, "That stupid girl has some nerve! I went to get her a drink, my date. I started talking this other girl from my math class for about five minutes, I look back where I left her, and she is gone. When I looked over at the exit there she is, walking out with Mike the big stupid rotten school bully, apparently, she was jealous of me talking to the other girl!"

Doug looks at Tommy, "By the way, Tommy, this is Eddy, Eddy, this is Tommy." Tommy is looking at Eddy thinking this guy has a different kind of look, a bit strange but cool enough. Eddy looking at Tommy thinking something similar. Tommy has never met Eddy before but got an ear full of stories from Doug too many times about his wild antics. Tommy is eager to find out more about this Eddy character. Here is this nutty guy Eddy that he has only heard of and now he meets him during one of his worst moments and feels there might be some excitement about to erupt. After hearing this story Tommy is pulsing with an energy that you cannot imagine. Eddy mentioned the fact that she did him wrong and should not get away it. Tommy is eager to match Eddy's intensity, he quickly suggests they go do something about it, "hey buddy, I know we just met but I hate to see that happen to you. I have an idea, you want to let her know she did you wrong, right? So why don't we go visit her house?"

"No, that wouldn't prove anything! She would open the door, say hi, then make an excuse why she left and that would make me a loser!"

Tommy wasn't talking about a social visit. "No, I do not mean visit to say hi, what I meant was visit her house with a special treat!"

Ok, now this Tommy guy is off his rocker! Not only does he want to visit but he wants to take her treats?

"Excuse me but taking her something good to eat is not what I think is getting a point across to her for doing me wrong!"

Not understood, Tommy was talking about a different treat. "Taking her something to eat, and taking something you eat to her house, are two different things! What I have in mind is, let's take some eggs and go egg her house, in the morning she will have to clean it up and that will start her day off the way she ended your night!" Eddy willing to do anything to get back at her is more than ready to use this guy's energy and act. Eddy is not sure about this Tommy guy, a guy he doesn't even know, and their first-time meeting is instant action, and at a risky level. But, here is the start of what will be a lifetime of never-ending friendship, and with many outrageous stunts to come. Doug will not have anything to do with this feeding eggs to Helena Deckers house and runs off, "seeya later gators."

They jump into Tommy's used mail delivery Jeep, Tom puts in his cassette of, 'Rock and Roll part two' by Gary Glitter, back then it was a popular college fight song. If you don't know it Google it or YouTube it and think that song in your mind while reading this part of the story. They are cruising now, listening to the rowdy pump-up fight song, and the sound of drums pounding and electric guitar blasting loud, and so loud there can't be any talking on this ride because they can't hear each other. The music is pounding, drums beating and guitar blasting, repeating over and over.

Adrenaline is pumping hard, this music is cranking up louder and escalating the mood, their hearts are pumping hard, and they are driving to the grocery store to get eggs. The music was turned up so loud people were staring as they pull up to the store. Pumped up to the max, they must get these eggs!

Now we are back at the school parking lot. They jump out and are walking to Helena's house, Eddy's ex-date lived 2 blocks away behind the school auditorium. While walking, the fight song they were listening to, Rock-n-Roll, is still ringing in their minds.

They don't to talk to each other from the excitement they feel and knowing what they are about to experience, and the fact they hardly know each other. They approach Helena's house and stand across the street in the darkness watching every movement around them. Silently watching to see if any neighbors might be looking and watching for cars that might be coming by. Tommy never once having any fear grabs the first egg and launches this thing at the house. Eddy reaching for an egg gets pushed aside. Tommy grabs both 12 packs, ran up to the house and starts whipping these eggs one by one as if you were watching a cartoon where the arms of the character look like a spinning circle. All you can see is his arms heaving and eggs blasting out of his hands. What seemed like 20 minutes was about 10 seconds.

They take off running simultaneously after the front door creeks open, its Mike the big school bully. He comes barreling out the front door and without saying one word starts running after them. Tommy stopped just before they get back to the school parking lot,

"Hey Eddy, I dropped my Jeep keys." Too late, Mike had been on their butts like a cheetah chasing a rabbit and is standing 15 feet away.

Mike said, "Do you happen to be looking for anything that resembles this?" Tom looks at him and mike is holding the keys up dangling them. Tommy said, "That's right, just throw them here and we will be out of your way buddy." Mike laughing sarcastically throws the keys on the ground and Said, "You want them back come over here and kick my ass!"

Tommy is shaking in his boots because no way is he a fighter. He had some previous experience but now he is a little older and a lover, a fun guy, a crazy lunatic, anything but a fighter. Well, Tommy looks at Eddy who is still mad about this brute taking off with his date. Eddy is feeling powerful with Tommy by his side and tells Mike "You can't kick Tommy's ass, you stupid dork!" Mike heard all he can stand and walks up to Eddy with the intent to kick his butt. He is just about to grab him, Tommy seen this coming and without any delay walks up to Mike and touches Mikes' shoulder.

Mike looks over at Tommy and said, "What? You have the balls to touch me? You will pay for touching my shoul..d..." All you hear is BAMM!!! Before Mike could finish saying shoulder, Tommy punched him square in the jaw. Lights out. Mike is lying there on the ground completely knocked out. Eddy is speechless. Tommy picks his keys up, shaking his hand because it's stinging from the blow he just gave Mike and said, "Hey Eddy, you feel like going to Denny's for some eggs?" Eddy is looking at him like he is crazy and replied, "I know you are you joking but that was good timing with the delivery! Shouldn't we call an ambulance?" Tommy said, "No way, then we would have to explain what happened. He will be fine. Look at him just lying there, he is so much nicer when his mouth is shut, and he can't bully people."

Then they jumped into Tommy's old mail jeep and went to Denny's to eat had egg-n-cheese omelets.

Tommy was not joking about eating eggs, what a night to remember.

Time passes, and this new friendship is booming. Tommy and Eddy hang out all the time and are having the time of their lives. It's Friday night, Tommy and Eddy are downtown walking the beat where all the High school kids are running the streets with their Hot-Rods. Cars are jacked up in the back by air shocks and looking weird but at that time it was the fad. The cars are circling 5th Avenue coming back down 6th avenue. Racing each other light to light and beer drinking everywhere, all eyes are steady watching to avoid the cops. Music is blasting out of every car and people are yelling at other friends as they pass. The older High school kids are throwing beer bottles out the window to underage high schoolers, so they can catch a buzz.

Tommy is constantly doing something to capture everyone's attention. He is at the corner about to cross the street and the light turn's red to stop moving traffic. He leans over and gets on his hands, then he walks across the street on his hands in the crosswalk thus getting the attention of everyone at the light. People are laughing and cheering him on and he steals the show. Why aren't Tommy and Eddy circling the block like all the other kids in a car? The answer, mail jeep! This is what Tommy owns at the time. It doesn't attract very many girls and unmistakably doesn't scream out, look how sexy! It can't outrun anything, and it's a lot like a Rolls, a Rolls-Kinardly. It rolls down the hill and kinardly go up the next.

Tommy and Eddy are getting anxious as they watch all the commotion around them. Tommy told Eddy, "How are we going to meet any girls if we can't ride alongside of them?" Eddy's reply, "Why don't we hitchhike and when we get picked up we can spot chicks as we pass them, and then get our ride to pull over or drop us off so we can talk to them." The next thing you know they are hitchhiking around town getting picked up and dropped off, and can you believe most of the cars that pick them up are girls? Getting picked up by girls and hanging out together made this the best idea ever. Who would have thought you would get more girls without a car?

A car passed by while they were hitch-hiking and one the people in the car recognized them, so they stopped and picked them up. During the time they're riding in the car one the guys they know gets the idea to light up a joint and smoke it. Everybody in the car including Eddy but excluding Tommy are puffing and smoking on this joint. Tommy doesn't smoke cigarettes nor is he willing to smoke pot because he doesn't know what it would do to him. One the guys asked him to take a puff, Tommy simply replied, "I am happy, I feel extremely good I don't need anything like that for me to feel good." But un-benounced to Tommy, as he's riding along in the car guess what happens? Tommy catches a buzz for the first time in his life. The driver put an eight-track tape in, back then needless to say they only had 8 tracks or regular cassette players, CDs weren't thought of yet. The tape in the tape deck is Steppenwolf, and the song playing is 'The pusher man.' Eddy laughs at Tommy because he knew he was high. Tommy is silent and motionless and just staring into space like he is tripping. The music is blasting, and the tunes are fitting with the situation because the words to the song, 'The pusher' go like this,

> "You know I smoked a lot of grass....... You know I popped a lot of pills......... you know I seen a lot of people walking around with tombstones in their eyes......"

After about 20 minutes of riding around in the car with these guys, Tommy develops the munchies. Tommy told Eddy he felt like it's time to exit the car and they got dropped off at the jeep. They are hungry and have nothing to eat, and neither guy is near their home where parents cooked supper and neither one has any money. You could hear Tommy's belly squealing with noises and he asked Eddy, "How are we going to eat if there isn't any money to buy something with?" Being creative and frugal, Eddy has a good but bad idea, "Let's dine and dash!"

"What's that?"

"It's when you go to a restaurant and eat, then when you are done, and no one is looking you run out the door without paying for your meal." So, there it is, Tommy and Eddy plot their first time dine-n-dash. Pizza, at the all you can eat buffet is where they end up. They start by getting 6 slices each, slide the cheese and toppings off 3 pieces and put it on the other 3 making it a double ingredients piece. Yummy, their bellies are full after eating about 15 pieces each.

Watching intently with anticipation, they are monitoring the employees and waiting for them to be preoccupied so they can pick a time to run. When the time was right they ran towards the door. I guess Tommy was nervous, he had clumsy feet suddenly and trips himself directly into the counter directly in front of the cashier. The cashier yells at Eddy, "What the heck is going on?" Eddy Yelled back, "A mouse jumped out of the wall on me and my friend!" The cashier loudly asked, "Mouse?" And next thing you know the people eating by the register stand up looking around to see where this mouse is. By this time Tommy is back on his feet and out the door, and Eddy is trailing on his backside. About 3 blocks down the road Tommy yells at Eddy, "Wait, we are missing one huge thing here!"

"What's that?"

"My Jeep! It is sitting back there in the parking lot at the pizza shop." OK, now what? How do you run away and not think to jump in the car you took to get there? All that excitement and no one thought about the escape route? Now they are walking home unless they go back to get the Jeep.

So, they walk back, Tommy is feeling guilty and figuring the worst is about happen which is the police will be waiting for them.

When they get back, they don't see any police. Tommy being the good guy he is figures he needs to make this right. He went into the pizza shop looking for the manager. When introduced to the manager he freezes up, and all he could think to say to the manager was,

"I ran outside to chase a car that drove by, I thought it had my missing dog in it so I couldn't stop to pay for the food, when I got halfway back I realized I dropped and lost my wallet while running. Now I have no way to pay for my supper, but, I will be glad to work it off if you let me."

The manager laughs at him tells him "good story! I do not believe you but since you had the courage to come back and tell such a stupid story I am going to let it go this time and you're off the hook, but you need to bring some customers back here that will spend money with us. By the way, your friend mentioned something about a mouse, was that anything to do with your stumbling act running out the door?"

What good luck, on their first dine-n-dash they goofed up and didn't have to pay for the food or their mistake. I say first dine-n-dash because this became a trendy thing now, not for survival but for an adrenaline rush.

They have been going to many High School parties that are out in the woods. Doug comes to these outdoor parties in the woods with his four-wheel drive Dodge Ram. His Ram is the rock climbingest, hill jumpingest off-road truck anywhere in town. Doug has this thing decked out with all the goodies, extra stiff shocks, a lift kit, exhaust and traction controls just to name a few things. Doug is not a drinker, but he sure has a blast waiting till people get tipsy, then he piles them in his Ram to go adventure climbing in the darkness wherever this beast of a truck will take them. They climb rocks and jump hills in the dark while people are bouncing out of their seats and their heads are spinning in circles buzzing from the booze. Doug laughs his butt off watching some of them get sick.

Tommy and Eddy are having too much fun! Here is a list of typical things they've been doing. Hitchhiking around town, attending outdoor parties, off-roading in the dark, Friday nights they go downtown to watch the hot rod racing while meeting tons of girls, dine-n-dashing, hiking in the mountains, camping, 25-mile walks for cancer and anything that creates new adventures! They wake up every day looking forward to what new adventures are waiting for them, or maybe it's better said what they will turn into crazy adventures.

A few years later when Tommy and Eddy get out of school they are working hard and loving life. Construction work, it's the easiest job to get and the job of choice since you can start as a laborer with no job experience, just a strong back. Being a laborer made them develop muscles and they got bigger and stronger from picking up steel and carrying it around the job-site. The good thing about this work is they get physically fit while earning a paycheck.

They are going to Disco clubs, dancing and meeting lots of fine-looking women. Tommy has become quite a dancer from going out to the clubs and spending so much time on the dance floor. He spends several hours on the floor shaking his hips and spinning with all kinds of dance moves. One night they met a couple of wealthy girls and were hanging around with them.

The girls wanted to introduce them to what they considered a good time, so they take the guys to a new type of dance club. This time in life was good and people are becoming liberal. One of the new wave crazes going around is hanging out at the Gay disco's watching drag queens perform dancing to the latest hot tunes and snorting anything you could get up your nose like pop-its, cocaine was raging, and people blew marijuana in your nose with the joint backwards in their mouth calling it a shotgun.

When Tommy heard they were going to this so-called queer club he automatically seen this as an opportunity to have some extra fun. He told those girls to show them their closet. One girl asks, "What do you need in there?" Tommy Whispers to Eddy, "Since we are going to a crazy place like that then let's get crazy ourselves, let's dress up as women and drive those little gay guys wild and crazy." So, Tommy said, "OK ladies we need to try on some clothes, whatcha got?" The women went with it and got them some dresses. This took guts because both these guys are 100% macho men.

This night was one for the history books, when they told all their friends what they are about to do everyone showed up for the outrageous night of weird fun. Of course, the first thing you see when walking in is a group of Drag Queens performing Y.M.C.A. by the Village People. All the gay guys in the club spent hours hitting on them. To fin off the gay guys, Tommy would tell them that Eddy was his bitch and Eddy told them Tommy was his stallion.

They went as far with this gag as to slow dance with each other and when the music sped up Tommy spun Eddy around completely out of sync with the music like it was a polka dance. The gay men in the club love them and become friendly, and they kept buying rounds of drinks while they hang out and raise hell. Eddy's brother showed up and when Eddy introduced him to the guys that were hanging around with them, he introduced his brother like this, "Gentlemen, I would like you to meet my big sister," the gay men laugh their butts off appreciating the humor. This place was grooving, the music was hot, the people were fun, and everyone had a blast. At the end of the night they score big with the girls that took them there and those girls probably never met another couple of guys again like our two guys.

TWO MEN AT WORK

The guys have been working at a construction site as laborers for a good while now. By far, they are the hardest working guys on the job and everyone loves having them as their helpers. Although these guys are hard workers, the real truth is these two are not attempting to work hard, they are in a contest to outdo each other.

When Tommy walks by he is carrying 2 steel rods on his shoulder and looks at Eddy when passing saying with his expression, look at how much I am carrying, now top that. Eddy has without any doubt learned all of Tommy's facial expressions, and he knew what Tommy was thinking. The next time you see Eddy he has three steel rods on his shoulders, and he makes double sure to walk right past Tommy and gave him that glare to make sure he understood he did not outdo him. This is a daily exercise, neither has to say a thing, it's automatic that this contest always exists, and not a battle but an extreme pleasure to see who can outdo who at the highest level.

One day they were sent to work upstairs at the building they were working on. The job foreman left the two guys alone, and their task was to hang the drywall along the inner edge of the wall. It was about 150 feet which is at least a 6-hour job for most good Sheetrock hangers.

They started at 8 and were done by 12:00 lunchtime. When they got back from lunch, the foreman told them when they get done with the first wall the next thing was to load the sheetrock into the second floor and to start the other side of the room. Well, needless to say, they were already done with the first side and started off grabbing sheets of drywall and carried them upstairs. The foreman was watching them and came over asking, "What are you doing? I need the first wall finished, I said load the room after you finish the first side!"

Tommy replied, "Hey man, we are doing exactly what you asked us!" The foreman said, "NO you aren't, I told you after you finish the first wall and I need that done by 4;00." Tommy said, "But it's done man, what's your problem bro!?"

The foreman is losing his patience and demanded that they do what he said. After a minute of all this babbling back and forth the foreman followed them upstairs, and when he saw that the wall was already hung he was amazed. "What the heck? How did only the two of you get that much done?"

"We don't play big boy, we came in here to work, and that's just what we do!"

Then Tommy points down at his feet and starts singing the song from the early 60's called 'These Boots Were Made for Walking" by Nancy Sinatra. Changing a couple of the words he sang this, "These Boots were made for working and that's just they'll do, one these days these Boots are going to work all over you!" Her version it was worded, "these boots are going to walk all over you."

The foreman said, "O.K. then, doing that much work in that short of a time is very impressive, but that song, terrible!"

Another day while they are working a group of motorcycles pull up to the job site. The guys driving them get off and walk over to the foreman and start talking. Eddy yells over at Tommy, "Hey boy, guess who those guys are?"

"Dunno?"

"They are Satans Demons!" Satans Demons are a notorious storm trooping hell raising biker gang that was a big terror back in the 1960's and still ride in very large packs sometimes clogging up highways and streets with 100's of motorcycles. "What? Do you think they are here to kill the foreman?"

As it turns out the Satans Demons are not the old storm trooping rebels that raise hell and throw wild parties full of drugs and sex fests like the older ones from years ago. These guys still ride in packs but became more responsible citizens that hold legitimate jobs. Not all bikers make money dealing drugs or weapons.

This spawned some big interest in the two guys since they've never been around any real Gang type bikers. The first time the bikers and Tommy have any interaction is one day when the Electric foreman asked the guys to come over and help. The guys went, and he had them pulling wire through electric conduit. This is very labor-intensive work, but you know if Tommy and Eddy are doing this it is done way

beyond the ability of any one on the job. They are
pulling this wire through the pipes; the Demons are
Journeymen Electricians and are over seeing this
portion of the job. They are making the connections at
the panel while Tommy and Eddy are pulling it to
them. After about two hours of this both guys are
developing blisters. Eddy walks up to the Electric
foreman and told him that they were getting blisters
and needed gloves. The foreman seemed to be on
some power trip and told Eddy that he needed to get
his own gloves and the company did not furnish them.
Then he said, "You need to quit your belly aching and
get back to work or your fired!" Wow! What a rude
man! Tommy overheard this and walked over to the
foreman and told him, "Hey buddy, you see these
blisters? These hurt and are not making me laugh, I
suggest you help us find some gloves and do it real
friendly like or me and you are going to have a
problem!" The foreman laughed and told Tommy he
better watch his mouth. Well, about that time Lugg,
one of the Satans Demons overheard this and walked

over to the foreman and said, "I think there is something wrong here and I'm not diggin it man!" The foreman replied, "Yeah, I know what you mean, these two weenies are crying like two snot sniffing babies about their whimpie little baby fingers being sore."

To the surprise of the foreman, Tommy and Eddy, Lugg said, "No you shithead, you have the problem, these guys work harder than anyone I ever seen and deserve respect, beside the fact, you are supposed to use the gas engine puller to pull that size wire and you have these two using their hands!!"

Turns out the Demon hated this Electric foreman because a while back when he was an apprentice that foreman was rough on him too. He was always a bastard mean guy to all the employees. This was clearly unexpected to Tommy and Eddy because they figured this Demon was coming over to give them trouble also but instead he defended them. Later that day on the way home Tommy asks Eddy, "Did that really happen? I mean did that Demon actually defend us?"

"Yep! Seen it with my own eyes." About 3 or 4 days into this the Demons, Tommy and Eddy were becoming good friends since they were working together and developing respect for each other. At lunch Tommy spends some of the time entertaining these guys with jokes and does crazy things like backflips and walking on his hands. One day Lugg invites the guys to come to his house for a party the Demons are having on Saturday night.

It'd Saturday night and they went to Lugg's house. They pull up in the van that Tommy is driving now, and sure enough about 100 motorcycles line the street. They walk by several long-haired bearded guys wearing blue jean vests branding the Demons coat of arms.

This is real intimidating, the Demons hanging out in front yard are looking at them like they are trespassing and need to be prosecuted. They get to the door and Tommy said, "This looks like a regular house." Eddy replied, "What did you think, he lives in a compound?" A guy came to the door and asks, "what the hell do you need man?"

"We are here to see Lugg, he invited us." The guy turned and yelled, "Lugg, you have 2 guys out here saying they need to see you man." In the background you can hear the song playing by Steppin Wolfe, 'The Pusher.' This was a hardcore song, the words are like this, "I said God D, God D the pusher man" (Using D word instead of spelling out the word), it's the same song that was playing the night Tommy got high inhaling the second-hand smoke from the guys that picked them up hitch-hiking downtown a few years earlier. Lugg walks up and said, "Hey man, it's cool! These are my work buddies, come on in guys, grab a beer and when someone hands you a joint take a toke and party on!"

As the night went on they drank some beer, listened to nothing but hard rock and roll groups like Steppin Wolfe, AC/DC, Motorhead, Thin Lizzy, Alice Cooper,

Led Zepplin, Deep Purple, Pink Floyd and many more, all which were hard rock bands back then.

Eddy smoked all kinds of pot while Tommy was in a place he had never been before, this was like some scene from a movie. They watched and listened the whole night, come to find out Lugg was a high-ranking officer for the Satans Demons and nobody, but NO Body messed with Lugg! He told everyone there that Tommy and Eddy were his friends and not a single biker there gave any trouble to either guy.

Lugg walks around and kisses any woman he wants. He tells someone that he wants a certain thing performed and the people do it with no resistance and giving total respect to this guy. Tommy is curious about the vest that Lugg wears and asks, "What does T. C. O. B. mean."

Lugg tells Tommy, "When you look around several of us have that inscribed on our vest, that's a special honor, it stands for; Took Care Of Business. When you took care of business you performed a very specific duty for the President of the Satans Demons. Generally speaking, you killed a rival gang member or someone who needed to be put down from interfering with another Demon. As you see I have 5 lines after mine meaning 5 times I took care of business." When they left the party that night they had a sense of power that neither one ever felt before, it was though they wanted to go start a fight and tell their victim you better not mess with us, we are friends with Lugg! Several months went by and Tommy and Eddy had great work relations with Lugg and his small group of other Demons that worked at the construction site. They went to several parties at Lugg's house and kept in touch a long time, even years after the job ended.

THE GUYS TAKE OFF

One very cold day they are at work, it's 23degrees, and Eddy is hating the cold temperature and was whining and griping non-stop about how ridiculous it is to have to work in that kind of weather. Tommy is not bothered by the cold and was jabbing all kind of jokes at Eddy.

"Hey Eddy, did you know it is so cold that; Pickpockets are sticking their hands in strangers' pockets just to keep them warm!"

"When you milk cows today in this temperature, you get ice cream!" "Police tell a robber to freeze, and he really does,"

"Illegal Mexicans are sneaking back across the border." "Enough Tommy! I am too cold to hear your stupid cold jokes." "Eddy, why don't we hop in the van go for a ride and get warm?" "Sounds good to me Tommy boy." "Eddy, I mean let's go for a ride to some warm place, like Florida!" "Yah, right on Tommy."

"I am walking to the office to quit and get my last paycheck Eddy, You with me?"

20 mins later Eddy is looking at the job foreman walking alongside of Tommy, as they walk up to Eddy

the job foreman asks Eddy, "I hope you aren't quitting too, I need to finish this job this month and I need your labor to finish it." Tommy jumped in his van and drives up by Eddy while he is talking to the foreman and rolled the window down, "Hey boy, there's an empty warm seat over here with your name on it. Well?" There it was, he is ready to take off! Tommy looks like a madman who is about to start spinning in circles like the Tasmanian devil. The boss is across the way pleading with Eddy to stay while the motor of Tommy's Van is getting revved every 4 seconds prompting Eddy to go. Eddy cannot believe what's going on here. Looking at crazy Tommy and shivering, "Oh what the heck! Seeya boss!" And there begins the road trip. With the wind in their back and the road in front of them they plop a cassette in the radio and play some music. Knowing Tommy now can you guess what song he plays first for this road trip? Steppe Wolfs "Born to be wild!" So here it is,

"Catch-em out a runnin, Head out on the highway, looking for adventure in whatever comes our way, I like something lightning, messin with wind and this feeling that I'm under, like a true natures child, we were born, born to be WILD! We can climb so hi, I never want to die." Somewhere down the road they put in an AC/DC tape in memory of Lugg. Guess what the song was? "I'm on a highway to hell!"

Driving through North Carolina they stop off at this old girlfriend's house of Eddy's and spend the night. Tommy gets the pleasure of spending time with Sherry's sister while Eddy rejuvenates some old sparks with Sherry. After a great night of hanging out and eating good home cooked food, they get up and notice the temperature is getting warmer there.

Energized by the nice weather Eddy tells Tommy in a joking way they should cut the roof off his Van and make it a custom convertible van without a retracting convertible top. Well, Eddy not thinking about how off the chart Tommy is, turns his back to him to go say bye to his old girlfriend, and when he is returning to the van there it is. Do I need to tell you what is happening, or do you already know what is taking place here? There is Tommy, tin snips, a hammer and a face full of crazy! He is pounding a hole in the roof and cutting the metal with his tin snips. "Tommy, what the frikkin heck are you doing?"

"You said you wanted a convertible Eddy, didn't you?" "Holy bahjesus Dude! Tommy, you have lost your mind?" The girls are laughing because this was something they never expected to see. They start taking pictures of this crazy event. I wish we could go back and find those sisters now, so we could see one of those pictures, and pictures of what a young crazy Tommy looks like cutting up his Van while young Eddy is staring at him realizing this guy has no limits. They left those girls with a never-ending image of what a crazy guy Tommy is, and the guys, they never forgot that weird episode.

Now we fast forward to the guys entering Alabama. Can you guess what cassette Tom slides into the radio this time or do I even need to say it? That's right. Lynard Skynard's, 'Sweet Home Alabama.' They sing along with the song, "Sweet home Alabama, where the skies are so blue, Sweet home Alabama, Lord I'm coming home to you! Yah Yah!"

These guys are killer, no one or nothing can stop them, and they are on a mission, a mission to get the most out of life. With all the power of 2 super heroes these guys are making way to some place warm and fun. Driving down the highway looking as crazy as they are, the roof is off the van, and people are looking and laughing at this hillbilly looking duo. Early one morning they are passing a state highway sign for a national park. "Tommy let's go there and see what it looks like." Not a problem for big bad Tommy, he exits and here they come, adventure diary is about to get another big story. They travel down the roadway to another sign reading; State waterfalls park. They follow it till they get to the park area and as they pull up to it they are in amazement of how beautiful it is. "Eddy look!"

"Wow! Tommy this looks like a paradise, I feel like I just entered Heaven." They walk down this path for what seems like forever, finally they come up to the main site and there it is, gushing down the side of this small rocky mountainside is a slow-moving waterfall. It's spraying a fine mist over the side of the small mountain and all over the place beneath it. What a nice treat, after all this driving they stumble across this paradise. Now what? Well, these guys cannot possibly get in trouble here, they are the only two around for miles. Looking around taking in all this beauty they realize that's basically all there is to do. "Eddy, we been driving most of the night, all around us are these giant flat rocks so big we could play full court basketball on them, what do you think about catching up on some sleep and us taking a nap right here in this amazing place for a couple hours?" Eddy replies, "Let's do it boy!" Of course, Tommy with his crazy ideas had to add to it, "Since we are the only 2 people here why don't we nap nude?"

"Well Tommy, only you would think of that but what the heck, I never did that before so let's do it." They grab a couple sleeping bags, throw them down on the rocks by the water's edge, lie down on them and drift off into sleep heaven. A couple hours later it's about noon time. Eddy never really was able to sleep good in the sun light, and now he is becoming aggravated, he is dreaming that he can hear people making noise and talking. He is opening his eyes and barely able to see because the bright sun is shining down on him. He finally gets the mind control to force his eyes open and make himself wake up. Looking around the rocks where they are lying down, he is amazed at what he sees. "Tommy. Wake up boy! Tommy, Wake up man!" Nudging Tommy and poking his ribs finally gets the sleeping beast to acknowledge him. "Dude, can you see anything?" Tommy still sleepy eyed trying to get his vision focused looks around and he is also shocked in amazement at what he sees. No, it's not a pack of wolves, no, not a big hungry bear either. No type of threat that could cause any physical pain. All around this rocky formation that at the beginning of this day was a deserted place left exclusively for these guys is now what Eddy thought was a noisy dream. As far as you could see, there are people everywhere. Yes, people walking around talking, laughing and making noise. Eddy is wishing he was dreaming this and is wide awake now and it was actually happening. Why couldn't it have been wild animals that inflicted pain on them? No, it had to be pain from embarrassment.

They are sitting there butt naked with all their junk exposed and obviously the only 2 people there naked. They are embarrassed at the highest level. They are looking around at all these people and for whatever reason not one single person ever looks their direction. They are walking by sightseeing and some people are in the water swimming and splashing around like it's nothing at all.

Tommy looks at Eddy and said, "Uh, I guess we are invisible? Where the heck did all these people come from?" Come to find out the park does not open till 11:00 O'clock and they went in without permission early. I guess if anyone would take the time to read the little signs they would clearly know not to enter the park till normal hours.

Tommy jumps up and stands there. "Hey Eddy, look, no one will look at me." Big enough for everyone to see, Tommy can't stand the fact these people are acting as if they do not see him. Tommy shouts out, One Two, One Two. Eddy looks up and there is crazy man doing jumping jacks, about the same picture you can imagine in an army boot camp. Things are flapping and smacking in a place not to mention, I guess we could have called it flapping jacks.

O.K., Eddy is not about to let Tommy steal the show and falls into place, now its double flapping, double popping and smacking in places not to mention and what a sight that was to see. A minute passes and Eddy takes the bull by the horns. "Hup two three four! Hup two three four," he starts marching forward stomping his feet. Tommy falls in behind and starts singing very loud with spirit the 1964 Manfred Mann song, "There she was just a walking down the street singing" and Eddy immediately joins in, "Do wa diddy diddy dum diddy do," Simultaneously they both continue marching like they are inline in a military exercise and very loudly yelling out, "clapping her fingers and shuffling her feet, singing do wa diddy diddy dum diddy do, She looked good, she looked fine and I nearly lost my mind! Before I knew it, she was walking next to me singing do wa diddy diddy dum diddy do."

This is a scene from a movie with Bill Murray and John Candy called 'Stripes.' Hopefully you can see that movie one day and then you can get the just of why they already knew how to fall into place and start singing the tune they sang.

OK, now everyone in this place is looking. Everyone is starting to break out of their shell, not able to hold back some people are laughing and suddenly several people who thought this was a ballsy move and supported it started singing along with them, and the next thing you know almost the whole place is alive with some people laughing, some staring in amazement. Like I said, this is all hard to believe and it's so bizarre this whole story could actually happen to anyone, but it did, and that's why I am writing this book, I had to tell this story.

Traveling a little further south in Mobile, Alabama. Tommy and Eddy are driving through the city and decide to look around. They were shopping in some of the stores and talking to different employees asking things about the city, and what might be fun to do, and where is a good place to eat, etc... Not able to find any answers that struck their fancy, Tommy wants to hear some music hoping he could go dancing. He is thinking hard what else they could do to have fun.

Well, they were walking down the street eager to do something exciting and there it is, Le Silhouettes! It's a strip club, yes, with naked dancing women. Do not get the wrong idea, Tommy could care a less if he sees a naked woman, it's the unknown experience that's about to happen Tommy boy is excited about. They walk in as if they are the owners and sit right up front by the stage. Tom extends his legs out and puts his legs up on the dance stage with his feet resting at the edge. The dancer comes up and straddles his feet with her version of sexy dancing trying to seduce him. Tommy wiggles his finger with a motion to come closer, she does and bends down to see what he had in mind, he whispers in her ear. She laughs and after she is finished dancing on stage, she hurries over and

sits between them. Eddy asked her, "What did he whisper in your ear?"

She replied, "He told me that when I was straddling his feet that I should not be offended if something happened. He said it was making his toes hard and he wouldn't be responsible if his toes did something they shouldn't. I thought he was corny as heck, but he is kinda cute, so I come over to find out more about this hot looking cornball."

This place was dragging with boredom and only a few people in the joint. Tommy is getting this bug to dance and asks the stripper if she would dance with him. She told him that this would make the boss mad and she better not. What does Tommy do? He gets all the strippers to come by the stage, and he asks them if they are doing any good, and most of them replied how slow the night was and no money was being made.

So here is what Tommy came up with. He ran up to the DJ and requested a song. Then He jumped up on the stage, and next you hear the Bee Gees song Saturday Night Fever,

"You can tell by the way I use my walk I'm a woman's man, no time to talk."

Then He does his best John Travolta dance as if he was Travolta himself. Spinning and wagging his hips he moves from side to side performing for these stripper women. They are in awe of him and love it. They laugh and cheer him on like it's a contest. The next thing you know it's the women wanting some action. They are going crazy yelling at him while he dances, and they persuade him to take his close off. As if that was hard to do. He slithers to the edge of the stage and the women that could get to him started throwing dollar bills at him. There you have it,

Tommy's first stripper gig, a male dancer. He got to do something probably no other man had ever done up to that point and the women got a special treat that night. Believe it or not, later we come to find out the owner of this club had the best time with Tom doing this, and by the reaction the women had to him wiggling his stuff for them the owner started one of the first male strip clubs. He called it, Cheval de Garçon, and it was so successful he eventually shut down the female strip club and opened several more male dancing clubs around the state.

After leaving the strip club and feeling energized with fulfillment, they are ready to call it a night. Tired of sleeping in the van they are sitting on the side of the road in the downtown area. They are talking and thinks it's such a nice night why sleep in the van. So, they park the van by a bus stop, walk over to the bus stop benches and each grab one and lay down. About an hour into this the local night duty police officer shows up. The officer informs them that they are violating a city ordinance and need to leave. Tommy and Eddy are both pleading with the officer to let them stay and explaining to him they have nowhere to sleep. The officer tells them to leave or go to jail. Uh-oh, wrong thing to say. Tommy looks at Eddy with those gleaming eyes and said, "I've never been to jail, how bad can that be?" Tommy turned to the police officer and asked him, "Will we be able to leave in the morning or do we have to stay a few days if we go?"

The police officer said to them, "You are not committing a felony, it's a misdemeanor and you will be able to leave first thing in the morning." Tommy told Eddy, "Hey that has to be way more comfortable than these wooden benches, plus what an adventure this could be. I'm going, are you going with me?" Eddy replied, "Of course, why would I ever miss this adventure?" To the back of the police car they are placed, and away they go!

Here is what makes this funny enough that this had to be told in this story. Google or research the Internet about this movie scene you are going to read about here. If you never heard of it, then go watch this clip that I tell you about at the end of this next part.

It's the Richard Pryor and Gene Wilder movie called Stir Crazy. While riding in the Police car, Tommy has this fantasy suddenly of walking in the jail and acting out the scene in the movie. He asked Eddy, "Do you remember the scene in Stir Crazy when Richard Pryor and Gene Wilder get arrested and are walking in the jail cell?" Eddy replied, "Of course I do!"

"Will you do that with me when we walk in the jail cell?" Eddy said, "Without a doubt buddy, that will be something we will never forget!" The officer overheard this conversation and said, "I saw that movie and that was so funny. I bet neither of you has the balls to do that." This officer sure did not understand who he was talking to. They organized who would do what when they entered the jail cell. They get there, and the officer walks them in the jail and back to the jail cells. Going in the door to the cell block they are bobbing their heads and with a strutting walking motion. Tommy starts off simulating the scene and said nice and loud, and pardon some of the language here, it's straight out of the movie, "If you bad they don't mess with you," while walking past the first cell doors. Walking past the next couple inmates Tommy said, "What up Holmes, yah, yah!" Now we're entering the cell that they will share with the other inmates. Tommy and Eddy are still bobbing and strutting in the cell doorway and Tommy said, "We bad, that's right, uh huh we bad, don't want no shit either." Eddy's turn, he said with a stern look and a huge smile on his face, "That's right." Then Tommy said, "No shit, don't take too much shit, we just don't take no shit." Eddy walking in right behind him said, "Damn right, no shit!" Without a doubt, this movie was very popular for quite some time before they went to this jail, and everyone in the jail immediately recognized this scene and busted out laughing, and for the rest of the night everyone was cutting up, joking around, and had a fun time at the jail that night. So why is this funny? After you watch the movie and see this scene, then you will understand. The movie is Stir Crazy,

scene; "That's right, we bad, we don't take no shit."
Actors Gene Wilder and Richard Pryor.

TOMMY AND EDDY MAKE WAY TO FLORIDA

After spending some time Alabama, they find
themselves drifting over to Florida. The first stop was
finding a beach and exploring the scenery. They end
up finding a little town and make way to the beach.
The first thing they notice is the water is clear and
tinted blue. What a beautiful sight, they decide to take
in the beauty and lay down by the water and rest.
After resting on the beach by sunbathing they leave to
see some of the town they are in, Clear Water, Florida.
They are walking down the street and came across a
brand-new Lincoln Mark VII. At that time in life these
were as high class and expensive that a car could be in
the world of cars, and you were somebody big if you

drove this special luxury car. Back then, the bigger the car meant more luxury, and this is a big car!

Eddy walked up to the guy who was getting out it. Wanting to start a conversation about the car he asks the man, "How can you drive that car mister? I mean what do you do for a living, you must be rich, I just want to know what type of job pays enough to buy a big car like that?" Proudly the man replies, "I make a lot of bucks!" Eddy asks, "Well, what do you do?" The guy replies, "I am a Pro-ball player for the Pittsburgh Pirates and it pays big dough."

Well, there you have it Eddy, Pro-Ball players get to drive nice cars. Tommy is very excited because this sport is his favorite sport and immediately he recognized this guy, his name was Willie Stargell, he played for Pittsburgh Pirates and after living in Pennsylvania Tommy spotted him with no problem. He is curious and asks, "Why you here in Florida? Are you vacationing?" Willie replied "No, its try-outs and almost all MLB teams have camp here every year, and this place is where we practice, scout new players and pick our newest players.

"How do people get to try out?" He said, "You sign up and then they start a process of elimination, if you make it past the first round you go to the next and then the next till you make the team or get cut." Guess what? Tommy was on his way. He is laughing at Eddy and said, "I can't believe you did not know who that was, that was Willie Stargell, and he is a famous baseball player. The next day he gets to the try-outs and signed up for the Pirates. The recruiter asked, "What position would you like to try out for?" Tommy told him he will try out for the third base position since that's what he played in little league baseball when he was younger. The first day they run Tommy through the try-outs, he is catching and whipping the ball like nobody has ever seen. The infield coach came up to congratulate him and told him to make sure to be on time tomorrow, so they can take a better look at him.

The next day, Tommy is on time waiting his turn to show off his athletic skills. For 6 Hours he is running, catching and throwing. The coach came up and told him, "We certainly are enthused about your athletic abilities, you made the first cut and it looks you are the best rookie third baseman we seen in this pack of try-outs this year. See you tomorrow."

At this point Tommy doesn't even care, he isn't trying out to be a baseball player, it's an adventure and he wants to show off his athletic abilities and see if he can make the team like him. 3 weeks later Tommy was told to go take a one week break and in 3 days they will decide if he makes the team and then they will contact him with the final news. He actually made the final cut, when the team Manager is trying to get Tommy to come in for a contract negotiation he can't find him, he has no home or phone, his home is just a Van that rolls from town to town. Tommy left an address and phone number where his Mom lives. What happens now? Tommy is back on the road again and never knew he made the final cut till he made it home after this road trip, when he got home he went through his mail to find the letter they sent asking him to get a manager, so they could set up a negotiation and sign a contract.

After the try-out episode, Tommy and Eddy are rolling on the road and getting hungry. Looking at their financial condition not so good they become desperate to get some food and Tommy plots this scam to grab a meal the easy way and guess what they do?

Pulling up on a Burger King they get out and here is Tommy's plan, Tommy goes inside to the line to order and Eddy waits by the door outside, when someone's order is coming to the counter Tommy signals with a hand gesture and then Eddy has to come in, grab the bag as if it's his order and go outside to the gas station next door and hide behind the dumpster.

Here it comes, Tommy signals, Eddy swiftly moves in, grabs the bag and walks through the door, when he goes outside, all you see is the backside of his body and he disappears. At this point, Tommy acts like he is in a hurry and changed his mind and walks out to the van like he seen nothing. Tommy pulls up to the gas station next door, Eddy jumps in and is ecstatic.

Tommy asked, "what did we get buddy?" Eddy replied, "A feast!" Apparently, this meal was for a family, it had 6 hamburgers, 4 orders of fries, 2 orders of onion rings and 3 apple pies. This was a good stop, no one tripped, nobody got caught, and a nice filling meal paid for by some unsuspecting family.

In conjunction with not having money for food, here comes the matter of they do not have any money for gas. Tommy asks Eddy, "What the heck, we didn't do a very good job managing our cash, what are we going to do?" Eddy replies with the obvious, "Rob a Bank!" Before Tommy could open his mouth and jump on another adventurous opportunity, he followed through with, "JUST KIDDING! What I meant to say is let's get a job somewhere, so we can make money and get back on our feet here."

So, Eddy having the most hands-on work experience got busy looking and found a construction site where they are building a large warehouse facility. He walked in, and with little effort landed 2 labor jobs building enormous tool bins.

About a month into the building portion of this it's time to stock the bins with tools. Tommy is looking at this situation one day and realizes that each individual size of tool comes in a large box. The tools are stocked in the bins till full, and that leaves hundreds of tools left over in each box that are not accounted for.

In Tommy's world, the question is, why would you waste what can make you money. And, he concocts a plan. Each day they are to walk in the building with a lunch pail that weighs about one pound, when they leave each one weighs about 10 pounds. Can you figure what the extra weight is when they leave each day? Several weeks later, the laborers' portion of this job is almost over, and the guys are supplied with a couple months' worth of saved up paychecks and hit the road.

They get to the next town and see a Pawn shop. Tommy immediately stops and tells Eddy, "this is the time to see what the big bonus paycheck is from our recent job." Eddy asked, "Don't you mean Pay off?" Tommy just nodded yes, and they went into the pawn shop. They tell the counter person they have tools they want to get rid of. The guy at the counter told them this was a good time to sell the pawn shop tools because the next town over was building a giant warehouse, and there was a bunch of construction going on there. He went on to tell them, "Right now tools are a hot commodity," no pun intended.

They carry the tools in, and the pawn shop guy was gleaming with anticipation. Looking at the tools they brought in he made it clear those are the new Snap-on brand and they are the best tools made in the USA. Joking he asked, "where did you get so many of these new high dollar tools, you rob a tool manufacturer?" Tommy and Eddy look at each other, and both looked like they had seen a ghost, moving onward they close the deal and sell the tools making a few thousand dollars and were financially set for many more adventures to come.

PAY FOR THE FOOD, YOU HAVE MONEY NOW

Tommy and Eddy are driving through this town and spot a little diner that has a flashing sign reading, 'Best Down-Home Country Cooking!'

O.K. it's chow time and these guys are starving. Tommy told Eddy it's time to relive some old dine-n-dash. "Eddy, I think tonight we should feast, then dine-n-dash."

"I know you are playing with me!" "No way man, I am serious!"

"Tommy, we have plenty of money, we can pay." "I know we can, but this place looks like a real challenge, look, there's a cop sitting outside in the parking lot, c'mon man, let's do this!" Eddy can see Tommy is pulsing with vigor. "Eddy let's have some fun and eat some Down-Home Country Cooking at this place and take-off." "O.K. then let's do this!"

They park the van a block away and walk down to the diner. These two guys are sitting down to the best meal they have had in several months. Yes, this food is really good, and Tommy is already rationalizing about the next meal to come after they are done here. "Hey Eddy, what do you think about splurging here and let's go for a double meal deal?" Eddy replies, "What the heck are you talking about?" Tommy is plotting a feast here. "I mean since we hardly ever know when we are going to eat food this good, why don't we eat a couple dinners, and stockpile our bellies so we won't be disappointed for a while?" Of course, this makes total sense to Eddy, Tommy could sell him poop on a stick and make him think it's a Popsicle, so it's on! The waitress comes up and asks if there was anything else they would like, possibly dessert. "Yes! Me and my buddy would like another round of this awesome food." The waitress double checks and asked them if they are actually able to eat that much, and after some convincing, she brings another meal to them. Meanwhile, as she tells her manager how funny she thought it was that these two young guys were about to eat their second meal, the manager starts looking at the scene and becomes skeptical. The manager was watching very closely from the cook station where he can see them, but they can't see him.

As Tommy and Eddy are doing the stop, double-look and listen routine to get ready for the sneak off and run episode, the manager is convinced these two are suspicious. Tommy is looking ahead the direction he can see, Eddy is looking ahead where he is able to see and as they are winking signals to each other they finally hit the right signal and up they go to the door. The manager yelled across the room, "Hey you two! Where do you think you are going?"

Stunned like a rabbit who is about to be pounced on by a bobcat, Tommy yelled: "Run Eddy!" Eddy takes off running. 10 feet on the other side of the door, this time Eddy trips and falls, and the next thing you see

Tommy is tripping over Eddy. He looks like a mix of a gymnast and a flying ballerina gracefully flipping and twisting reaching about 6 feet in the air, on the way down he looks like a Polar bear falling out of the sky from being slammed into by a Semi. While he is doing this acrobatic flipping thing he manages to land on the restaurant manager's car parked right by the door. Too bad for the car, Tommy is a big guy and his big butt made a nice sized dent in the car's hood.

As he is looking out the restaurant window and approaching the front door here comes the manager. He can see this train wreck as it's happening on his way to the front door. After watching his prize 1958 MGA show-car getting slammed with Tommy's big butt he is very angry.

The restaurant manager takes off running after them. What luck for Tommy and Eddy, this restaurant manager just so happens to be an ex-college track star and former state champion Boxer! He is in very good shape. When Eddy and Tommy get up, they see this crazed man coming at them like a swarm of angry bees. Tommy never said one thing he just sprung up off the car like an Olympic gymnast and zoom, bye-bye, off to the races.

Eddy looks up at Tommy and seen nothing but Tommy's back disappearing like a cartoon character shrinking. Eddy gets up, takes off running behind him, and they can hear is the manager yelling out, "I can run a full hour at top speed, so you better stop now!" They are running like they are being chased by the Bulls in Spain. They both stop gasping for air, just as they think they finally got away, they look back and there he is, the manager, he is running like a finely tuned Ferrari coming in hard and fast and just about to catch them. He is shouting, "I have a Black-Belt in Tai Kwan do, and am going to show you how a 2X4 feels when getting cracked by my foot." They start running again and figured it's time to split up. Tom hooks a right, Eddy thinking quick diverts the manager to a backyard in the neighborhood, he found a shed and hides in it and waits for a while. Several hours later they meet back at the Van where they had it parked. Tommy told Eddy, "Boy that was a trip! Get it?" Eddy is still shaken up, "Yeah, you're so funny, when I tripped, and your big butt tripped over me you stepped on my wrist and I can hardly move it." Tommy replied, "Sorry buddy, but you were already down, and I tried to go over you but when I tried to jump over you my foot already had a grip on your wrist, well, it made me trip harder and then you see what happened after that." Eddy laughs, "Yep, that car never knew what hit it." Tommy adding to the moment said, "After all that running! I am hungry, what do you say we grab a bite to eat?"

THE GUYS STOP TO CALL HOME

The guys are driving down the highway and decide its time to check in with their parents, friends, and family to see how everyone is doing. For anyone too young to have seen one, back then they had coin deposit phone booths all over the place to make a phone call. Cell phones were only an imaginary thing that would be in the future. They stop at a mall and go in to use a phone booth. Tommy said, "How do you purpose we call without enough coins to keep adding into the pay phone? We can't call collect our parents won't go for that and none of our friends can accept a collect call because their parents won't go for it."

Eddy's stepfather worked at the telephone company and told him a secret. If you ever need to make a phone call and have no money, you tell the operator you want to bill it to a third party. When they ask who to, you give the number to a home know won't answer, that way they cannot verify if it's legitimate. Also, you can look in the phone book and pick a random name and use their number.

So, they spend a couple hours making phone calls billing to some poor sucker that never knew he was going to get a huge phone bill. When Tommy and Eddy called Doug, he did not have good news for them. He told them there was a group of guys that had become angry with him and beat the crap out of him. Doug was always a very soft-spoken guy, very friendly and would do anything for you if you asked him. This was way out of touch with anything Doug should have to experience since he is a truly good person. Doug went on to tell them what happened. Driving home from work one day his mother accidentally cut off this scruffy mean guy. He followed her home. When she stopped and was getting out of the car the guy went up and pulled out of her car by her hair, he then threw her to the ground and yelled at her, "You stupid old B! You better learn to drive or you're going to get killed!"

Doug heard the commotion from inside the house and ran out to see what was happening. When he got outside, he saw his mother on the ground, and the guy was getting into his car and drove off. His mother told him what happened. Doug recognized the guy that threw his mother down. He had an idea where he lived and as soft-spoken as he was, he looked this guy up and went over to his house. He got to the door where the creep lived and knocked on it. The guy opened his door and asked, "Yeah man, what do you need?

Doug never said a thing, he swung in the door and punched this guy square in the jaw and told him, "The next time you throw someone's mother to the ground you better think twice!" Well, obviously this did not go over well with the crazy jackass that threw Doug's mother to the ground.

The next day Doug leaves to go to the store for motorcycle parts and noticed this car following behind him and there was a carload of guys in it. As he is driving, he notices the car getting closer trailing a half a car length behind and it's obvious this car was pursuing him.

After the next traffic light, Doug went to pull away and the car full of guys pulled in front of him and cuts him off forcing him to turn right. Doug is getting mad now, he rolls his window down and balled up his fist out the window at these guys. He yells at them, and while he was yelling he got a dead square look in the eye of the driver and seen it was the troublemaker he punched for throwing his mother to the ground that day.

The car swerves at Doug now forcing him off the road. Doug stops and starts to roll up his window but it's too late, the group jumps out and opens his car door. They pulled him out of his car, one by one they take turns punching and kicking him.

What made it unacceptable the guy who initiated this trouble in the first place could have left it at a good butt kicking, but instead, he had to take a couple extra kicks to Doug's head knocking him out and causing a 2-week stay at the hospital. It took a month before Doug could hear or see normally from the kicking in the head.

Tommy was mad! He was ready to drive home right then and there to go take care of this. He asked Doug to tell him who it was. Doug answered, "I don't know his name, but do you remember the day when we were around 13 years old and we were at the park playing basketball, and that kid who lived by the court kicked that white dog in the stomach for walking on the court? Do you remember how everyone got mad at him?"

"Yeah Doug, how can I forget that butthole!"

"That's him, he lives up by the drugstore now in the green house that always has a bunch of cars around it." Not good news, "Sorry to hear this Doug. Has he given you any more trouble?"

"No way, I am afraid to walk out my door, my mom told me he deliberately drives by our house very slow every other day and throws a beer bottle on the lawn and stares at her as if daring her to say something. Tommy is fuming mad and ready to kick ass, he has known Doug since 7th grade in school.

Tommy said, "Eddy, time to turn this road trip around, we have business to take care of!" Eddy thinking about this replied, "Hey, why do this ourselves, I have an idea, can we try something my way and see if it works?" Tommy ready for anything said, "This better be good!"

About a week went by and they called Doug back and again using the third-party billing for a free phone call. Doug's mother answers the phone, "Hey Tommy good to hear from you!"

"Can you let me talk to Doug please?" "You bet, he has been pacing the floor to talk to you." Doug picked up the phone with an extra excited voice and he said, "Tommy, you will never guess what happened. I heard what sounded like thunder coming down the road, I looked out my window and these bikers pull into my driveway and are halfway down the road. My heart started pounding with fear, I had no idea what was happening. I figured the troublemaker found more trouble makers and came back to massacre our house. And sure enough, that bastard troublemaker came to my door with this big biker dude, I figured this was it, and my life was over. I didn't notice at first but when the really big biker dude began talking I could see the biker was holding him by his hair like he was his little bitch. The biker guy also had all those guys that beat me up with him, and behind them was about 60 of these other bikers. To my surprise the guy went on to tell me and my Mom that for the next year those guys who beat my butt would be coming by every week to mow our lawn, clean our yard, wash our cars, and when they were done they better knock on the door and say they are sorry and thank you for letting them serve us. Also, they will do anything extra we asked them, and do it gladly with thanks for the privilege to serve us. Then he told us the guys had to pay us $50.00 a week for the privilege to work for us, and if they missed paying one time that he and the biker gang would be back to readjust the little punk's memory of what they were supposed to be doing. Then he pulled the guy into the front yard with all the other guys who beat my ass. The biker guy and all his biker buddies beat the crap out of them. The last thing you saw was the big biker guy kicked the piece of crap troublemaker in the head and said, "this kick is for Doug's mother punk!" Then he kicked him in the head again and said, "This kick is for kicking Doug in the head!" Well folks, here is what really happened. Eddy had the idea to call their old biker buddy Lugg, the Satans Demons leader they used to work with who liked them. Lugg gladly T.C.O.B. but no one died! Come to find out later Doug started riding with the Demons and they prospected him, which means he was on probation to join the gang. That would be a time when the Demon's would watch Doug to see if he had what it takes to be a member and sure enough a few months into it Doug became more aggressive and confident and was chosen to become a Demon. As for the trouble maker, he and his friends made good on their obligation and never missed a week.

TOMMY AND EDDY MEET 2 CRAZY GIRLS

After hearing the wonderful news from Doug these guys headed west and cherish life each day without a single care in the world. They lived life like they were immortals above the earth in heaven. They are traveling through Louisiana admiring the miles of beautiful countryside, and as they are about to leave the state, they come to a little town called Lake Charles. On the other side of the bridge they notice what appears to be a small beach. It looked like there is some Bikini action over there. So, they decide to take a pit stop and see what this place has to offer in the way of some adventure.

They pulled up to the beach area, and before they can get out of the van, 2 of the most beautiful girls they ever seen walked up and asked them for a lighter to light their cigarettes. "Say baby, yo be gatta light foe my my smokes?" Tom looked over at Eddy and said, "Get a load of this, they have a sense of humor." Eddy is laughing because what Tommy meant is by the way they walked up, they looked like playboy bunny models but the girl speaking sounded like she was from the ghetto. But in-the-hood girls don't look like these paper white little lovelies, they couldn't possibly be serious enough to talk this way for real.

So, Eddy with his minor acting skills played along and answered speaking with a ghetto accent and said, "Yo sayxie Hoe, what kindah fiyah ya needs to be lighten yo smoke wit? I be a fiyah fightah (Fire fighter) and nomelie puts outs dah fiyah but can be make an exceptions to light up yo fiyah baby gearrl. I can be do dis wit my lip up nex tah yo lip or be doin it wit my finga tip rubbin yo fine booty all up and down wit oil. Now which one I be gonna do tah ya baby gearrl?."

(In English) "Hey sexy bad girl, what kind of fire do you need to light your cigarette with? I am a Fire fighter and normally put out fires but will make an exception this time to light a fire. The way I can do this is by rubbing your lips with mine or rubbing your body with lotion. So, which one do you prefer?

One of the girls replied, "Yah dat aint be gonna happen, ya aint got dah right kinah cah so sticks outchah lightah and be lighten my smoke foo." (In

English) "No, that's not going to happen, you don't drive the right kind of car! So, just give me a light you fool."

Tommy said, "You guys are so cute, and that act with the ghetto talk is definitely a great way to break the ice." One girl replied with, "What yah dumm ass be meanin? Who dat you speaken at wit dat we ghetto talkin shit?" The guys are just about rolling on the ground in tears because they are so fine and yet funny at the same time. The other girl said, "Lookit deese two foo, they think we be some kinah (Kind of) back woot (back wood) ret (red) neck." Tom laughs again and said, "O.K. your killing me I can't stand anymore, talk right so we can get to know each other." After several minutes of this back-and-forth ghetto talk the one girl finally explains and said, "We be coon ass!" Eddy finally gets the fact that these girls are not trying to be cute and asked her, "What the heck is a coon-ass?" The one girl told him she was not sure where the word came from but people in Louisiana are Cajuns. Some of the decedents of the old slave days mixed dialect with French settlers and speak a mixed slang that's passed down from generations of people, those that speak with the slang are 'Coon-Ass'. But, she was sure it didn't matter because that's just how they talk.

After spending time with the two Cajun cuties, they got to where they could understand this strange weird ghetto white girl talk.

Sparks were flying and all of them wanted to get to know each other better so they spent a few hours in the sun walking the beach shoreline and telling each other about their funniest life adventures. Later in the day the guys went over to one of the girls' house to hang out. Those girls cooked a tasty Cajun dinner and ultimately, they had a great southern cooked Cajun meal made by the two Coon-Ass cuties.

After dinner Tommy walks in the restroom and notices a pair of what looked like stripper G-string panties laying on the floor. It was overwhelming, instantly it was exposed to Tommy that he has a fetish. He likes panties! Without any delay he picked these up dreaming to himself that these must be the Blondes panties! Yummy! She had to be the one who wore these it's her house, and if she did, they must have her delectable body stuff on them. His fascination to touch them brought him to ecstasy in the thought of these panties caressing her special spot. He is now sniffing them and putting his nose in the very center of them, and he is gleaming with lust and flying high to a place he has never been before until this moment. It's around 2 minutes into this fantastic experience of sniffing and fantasizing then out of nowhere Tommy heard, "Oh my Gott! What dah hayle (hell) you be doon (doing) Foo?!?"

Tommy is in total shock embarrassment. The girl had opened the door to see what was taking so long. His heart is racing from being startled with the surprise of her catching him. He responded, "Well, I noticed your panties on the floor, and they were so sexy and hot looking. All I could imagine is your exquisite body rubs these things with your, well, you know, your thing.

Anyhow, I could not help myself, it was just my way of getting to know you as good as I could without being where these things are when you wear them."

She turns red laughing and is struggling to breathe from laughing so hard. She laughs so loud and gasped so hard it caused Eddy and the other girl to come running in to find out what the heck is going on that's so funny. When they get to the restroom and she settled down, she started to tell them what transpired, but Tommy interrupts her, and lifted the panties in the air. Then he explains, "I was sniffing her panties and she stepped in and caught me." The other girl laughs too, and she also turns red and gasps for air. Eddy is not accepting this laughing stuff, he defends his buddy Tommy and told them, "Hey you two, it's OK, that's not weird, it's normal. A bunch of guys like women's panties, and that's what they do with them, they sniff the crotch to see what the girl smells like and it turns them on!" The other girl trying to talk and laugh at the same time must break the dreadful news to the guys. "Hey, you stupit foo, dem panty yo dumm

ass be sniffin aint her panty, dem be her
grandmamma panty and she be like 180 pound, and
62-year olt (old)."

"No way, you are joking! Yukk!" Tommy could not
believe his ears, this was not really happening.
However, it works out the girl's loved Tommy's
humility and spent the rest of the night being sweet
and paying special attention to him. That is one
memorable time that neither one of these guys would
ever forget. Do you see why if you ever wanted to grab
a friend and leave for a road trip it's a must do? So, go
on a road trip!

THE GUYS GET A HOTEL

Comment [A]:

After the coon-ass episode, the guys are driving down the road enjoying every minute of this freedom, life is so perfect, no worries and nothing beats being alive. The usual day begins at a McDonald's, Burger King or some kind of fast food joint to do their early morning routine. Starts off with going in the restroom using the sink to wash off their bodies. How else were they going to stay clean, they had no home and what more creative way to get clean? On this particular day I'm getting ready to tell you about the guys did not do their normal early morning stop. They spent the day traveling and driving, no adventures were popping up and as the evening approached they talked about doing something different for a change. Eddy asks, "Instead of bedding down in the van why don't we stay in a Hotel, so we can get a regular shower and relax like we are at home for a change?" That's OK with Tommy and that's the plan. They passed a sign advertising bout the oldest historic hotel in the State. Tommy said "Hey Eddy, something about that strikes me. I think we should try that one." Continuing down the road they turn the direction the Hotel should be, but they can't find it. So, they stop at a store and ask the cashier where this Hotel is located. The cashier told them if you turn right then make another right it's on the right. Too easy, that's 3 rights, right? So, 2 rights later they pass one Hotel, "Is that the one the lady was talking about?"

"No, she said three rights." Still driving they find the third right then a little further down the road they are there. They walk in the lobby and the clerk greets them. He tells them that they were experiencing problems with the electricity but will compensate with a half-price deal if they want to stay. What luck, they are used to no electricity so who cares, and it's a half off special that includes water.

The guys get to the room. What a nasty smelling room, it has dust everywhere and the beds are half sunk in as if they were rotten through the middle. Now what? Tommy said, "Are you thinking what I am thinking?" Eddy replies, "If you are thinking it should have been 99 Percent off then yes!" Tommy said,

"Well since we are here let's make the best of it, what do you say?" Eddy's reply, "It's just another adventure so why not."

They did what they mainly wanted to do, and that was take a nice shower. Eddy went first and then Tommy took his turn. Tommy came out of the shower and said, "Man, you could have saved me some hot water." Eddy replied, "What do you mean, there wasn't any hot water when I took my shower."

"Oh, I guess the electricity problem explains it, no electricity, no hot water."

After they cleaned up they decided it would be nice to go for a walk to explore the area and exercise their legs. It's about to be dark outside and they take off walking down the street. They notice a Boy Scout campground. Tommy thinks this will be something worth looking into, so they walk down the path and find several different Boy Scout groups hanging around campfires. Tommy said, "Hey Eddy, this brings back memories, when I was young I went to boy scouts for about 6 months and loved every minute. The one thing I remember the most is the good grub these scout masters bring to feed the kids, so what I have in mind is let's do a dine and dash in a different way than we typically do." Eddy is curious of course, and asked, "What does your devious mind have in store this time?" Tommy orchestrates the plan, "You go over and get their attention, make like you are lost, those guys being boy scouts cannot resist helping you with navigating. When they get up to show you how to get back to the hotel I will sneak in, snatch the cooler, and run back to the edge of the hill where we will meet, and there we will find what our surprise dinner will be."

Eddy walked over and told one of the Boy Scout groups that he is lost and asked if anybody could tell him how to get back to the main road where the hotel is. The Scout leader proud to present a lesson to the young scouts stood up and challenged the boys to pitch in by using their compasses to help guide Eddy where he needs to be.

Eddy can see in the shadowy wooded area beside the campsite and saw Tommy zooming in like a Hawk swooping down on the cooler and disappears like a ghost into the darkness. Eddy went to meet him at the peak of the hill like planned and there is Tommy waiting with a big smile on his face. Eddy asked, "What did we get?" Tommy replied, "A bunch of good food but we have a problem, we need to find a way to cook it!" The cooler is full of bacon, ham, eggs, and potatoes. Well, nothing wrong with that, all they need to do now is persuade the boy scouts to let them use their fire and cooking utensils. As if that will happen. After that goofed up plan almost worked out they leave the cooler and walk back to the hotel. As they crest the hill by the hotel, they see what looks like the hotel clerk at their door. Tommy placing his hand on Eddy's shoulder with a tight squeeze stops him and said, "Stop!" Eddy is wondering what the big jolt was for. Tommy is giving a slight pressing down motion on his shoulder and said, "Get down!" Eddy is resisting, and Tommy just forced him to the ground and said:

"LOOK!" Eddy is looking and cannot believe what he is watching. The clerk is at the door with an Axe in his hand. "Tommy is trying to get a handle on what is happening there and at the same time sensing this was bad and told Eddy, "Let's make our way to the van and watch from there and see what this guy is doing." As they make their way over to the van, the clerk is putting his key into the door and gently opening it he walked into the room. Confused and a little scared of this very weird encounter, they wait it out. What seemed like 5 minutes was only about 40 seconds, the door opened, and the hotel clerk came out looking to the left and to the right and following him out of the room is this big gnarly monster of a man that was already in the room. The clerk said something to this big freak, and the freak went one way and the clerk another.

No need for discussion when the coast was clear they ran in and got their clothes then jumped in the van and took off. Finding their way down the hill they decided to take a quick turn to the campsite, so they could blend in with a group of people in case these weirdos were after them. Discussing this situation, what they really want to know is who the big freak was, where did he come from, why was he already in the room? That was too weird, enough that this kept them up all night. The next morning, they decided they should go to the police station and make a report of this. When they get there, the officer taking the report asked what the incident was about. They started by telling the story from the beginning when they got the room from the oldest historic Hotel in the state on top of the hill. The officer asked them, "Are you talking about the run-down office building at the top side of the campsite or the old two-story building at the curve by the hill?"

"Yes," they responded.

"Yes? Which one?"

"The old one on the top of the hill." The officer replied, "How can that be?"

They looked at him and Tommy responded, "What do you mean how can that be? We haven't told you what happened earlier." The officer replied, "That place has been closed down since I was a child." Looking at each other and realizing this wasn't going anywhere, they told him, "never mind," and left.

As they are leaving the police station they see the clerk sitting in a car in the parking lot. The guys make it to the van and ask themselves, should they approach this guy to see what the heck his problem is? Deciding to avoid a problem they got in the van and drove off.

Sure enough, the clerk is following them and maintaining close distance. After a short time of this, Tommy has had enough. He slammed on his brakes and stopped in the middle of the lane. He made that car stop and it turned sideways sliding about 10 feet behind the van. He jumped out and ran back to the clerk's car. Eddy not knowing what he should do figured he better get his buddies back and jumped out with him. Tommy wasted no time and pulled the door open on the clerk's car, yanked him out, and slammed him to the ground.

At the same time, the back door opens on the van and here appeared the big freak jumping out of it. Eddy was at the corner of the van and got startled by this big freak jumping out it. The big freak headed towards Tommy and the clerk. Out of instinct Eddy ran over and threw a body block on the big freak. Tommy didn't know this was happening, he is twisting the clerk into a pretzel and screaming at him to tell him what he wanted and why all the weird crap. He gets one fast answer, "You better check on your friend." Not sure what he is talking about sits up, and he can hear a skirmish going on behind the van. He looked over and there is Eddy being strung up by this big freak dude. Tommy jumped up like a gymnast ninja, swooped in and kicked the big freak in the middle of his spine, the big freak hit the ground and Eddy jumped out of the way. The next thing you saw was the hotel clerk spinning out in his car turning the other direction and leaving. Eddy told Tommy, "Good move boy! The clerk ran away, now what do we do with this ugly freak?" Tommy replied, "Nothing, he is in enough pain, let's just get out of here."

Down the road a while Eddy asked Tommy, "Would you have ever known that freak was in the van? I think it's obvious they were going to kill us." Tommy replied, "However it works out we are alive, and those guys are probably wishing they never met us." Eddy has only one thing to say about that, "One day I am going to write a book about this or make a movie about our lives."

A YEAR AFTER THE ROAD TRIP

Around a year later the guys are back in town all tamed down and readjusted to the calm small town living they left behind to go on their road trip. They

knew nothing happened until they came back home.
Their friend Doug had died one day after driving his
motorcycle to a biker convention. A bus pulled out in
front of the Satans Demons gang and took out 7
Demons including Doug. The guys were devastated
over his death and couldn't believe the awful news.
In a strange way, they felt a slight bit
responsible since they were the ones to introduced
Doug to this gang. I suppose it's a point when Tommy
and Eddy look at each other's friendship and have a
better appreciation for each other. One day Tommy Is
with Eddy walking into a restaurant, Tommy the
clown that he is walked in on his hands. They
approach the hostess stand and the hostess asked
them, "Can I help you." Eddy looking down at
Tommy, told her, "We want to eat, can we have an
upside-down table please." Laughing at Tommy's
outrageous appearance the hostess walks them to
their seats. Tommy is still walking on his hands to
their table. While passing through the dining
section he spots a fascinating young woman sitting at

a table with another woman. He thinks to himself 'If she looks that good upside-down she must be super fine looking.'

Tommy got the buffet, he walked up to the pizza section and took about ten pieces of pizza and went back to the dinner table. While passing the beautiful ladies table he tripped right beside them and basically dumped the whole plate on his chest. What a klutz, I guess that's what you get when you are walking and staring at someone and don't look where you are going. By being a klutz and making this mess he got the beauty to notice him. Making things worse for himself, when he got up he scraped the pizza off his chest then took all the cheese and toppings and stacked them back on the pieces of pizza.

Now that Tommy has established his presence in the room, the beautiful lady he spotted walking in has been smirking and staring at him. She keeps looking because she cannot believe what a dork he is. Tommy notices her looking and decides he will make the best of it. The first crazy thing he did was wink at her. She immediately felt embarrassed because she got caught looking. Now she surely has look at him again to see if he is still looking at her to see if she is still looking at him. This went on several times. She looked over at him again, and this time he blew her a kiss. Yikes, this dorky klutz is now flirting with her hard. The looks back and forth become how quickly can you get a look in without getting caught. Very fast she looked over again as though she is just glancing out the window near that direction. And, sure enough, this time he had a napkin held up facing her with writing on it. The napkin had a James Cagney's famous line written on it, 'Here's looking at you kid.'

Holy heck, she was busted, she got caught looking and now she is squirming with more embarrassment. A little time went by and she is still bugged about this. She was wondering if it was safe to look again, so she slowly turned her head to see, and, oh good! He is not at the table. So, she took a full hard look around the room and guess what? Now he is sitting at the table behind her. Oh boy, this guy is becoming too much.

Next, then Tommy decided it was time to walk over and introduce himself. He got there, looked at the older women across from the pretty girl he had been teasing and said this terrible little one-line poem,

"Hello, my name is Tommy, I sometimes trip, I sometimes fall, but I am sure this pretty lady here is a baby doll."

The older lady laughed and replied, "This is my daughter who I love, quite pretty compared to others that's why you could not help but to notice her, and she is as sweet as a Dove."

Tommy loves this, another living soul full of life. Tommy reached out his arm to shake her hand, they shake, then he turned to the pretty little lady and reached out to shake her hand. She reached out to shake his, then he grabbed her hand and held it firmly. And then he looked at the mother and started singing to her a song called 'Misses Brown you've got a lovely daughter.'

The original song was sung by Herman's Hermits, the words go like this; "Misses Brown you've got a lovely daughter... Walkin about even in a crowd, well you'll pick her out, makes a bloke feel proud" ...

This is about as much to take in as either Mom or Daughter have ever experienced. Tom asked the younger lady, "By the way pretty lady, I still have not heard your name, what is it?" She said "Wendy?" He immediately sang again.

This original song is from The Association- 1967- and he sang this to her,

"Who's bending down to give me a rainbow, everyone knows its Wendy, and Wendy has stormy eyes that flash at the sound of lies, and Wendy has wings to fly, Above the clouds, Above the clouds."

In the original song, the word is "Windy" not "Wendy" which is what Tommy was singing.

Without a doubt, this crazy stuff is about as big a hit with both women as you can imagine. Enough of a hit that the mother insisted Tommy and Eddy sit with them and finish their meal together. When they were done eating Tommy got Wendy's phone number then he and Eddy leave the restaurant. After meeting that hot sweet thing at the restaurant Tommy is stepping on clouds and exhilarated like he got hit by a lightning bolt. When they get to the parking lot He asked Eddy, "Instead of jumping in the van what do you say we do an old-time thing that we used to do and go hitchhiking?" Without a doubt Eddy cannot pass up a good time meeting new people, so they hit the road with their thumbs up. About 2 blocks away from the restaurant, Tommy being a practical joker thought to do what women did in the 1940's, which was to pick up their dress up to their knees to attract a ride and that was considered sexy back then. And he pulled the right side of his jeans up to his knee and is holding it up as though it was a skirt. Tommy has one arm holding up his pant leg and the other arm out with his thumb in the air, Eddy is holding 2 arms out with thumbs up and now they are hitchhiking.

Here comes a car passing by slow and looking hard at them, just as it was passing it came to a stop and guess who it was? Wendy and her mother. Wendy is on the passenger side and rolled the window down, she whistles at them and said, "Need a ride big boys?" Sure enough, they jumped in and this cemented the deal of Tommy and Wendy getting to know each other.

TOMMY STARTS THE COURTSHIP

A couple days passed, and Tommy couldn't stop thinking about Wendy. So, he took her number out of his wallet and contemplated calling her. He is stirring on the intention to call but he's a little bit nervous. With this nervousness going on he doesn't want to just call and be boring, he wants to come up with an idea to win her heart over. The only thing he can think to do now this prank call her, she will never know it's him till he has her laughing then he will tell her it's who it is. So, he hopes that will get her in a good and fun mood.

He called her number and she answered the phone, "Hello." He disguised his voice and pretends like he's a Chinese food delivery driver, and with a very clever distinct Chinese accent he said, "Hahro, (hello) I Chinese food dahrivery (delivery) man, I here to dahrivah (deliver) food, I find you cat in street." She replied, "how do you know it's my cat?" He replied, "it wear pink caurrah (collar) that say if rost (lost) to prease (please) car (call) Wendy at numbah." Wendy replied, "but I don't have a cat."

"OK, I take kitty home wiff me, sorry to bohrer (bother) you." And Wendy said, "don't you want to find the right person the cat belongs to?" Tommy answers, "no, I rooking for cat wiff a pink cahrrah, I want to give to Grandmurruh (grandmother) in old people home, thank a you, goo bye."

A couple hours later Tommy got the nerve up to call her one more time. This time he called her, and she answered the phone, "Hello." Tommy asked her if she needed her refrigerator worked on and she replied, "No, why would I need my refrigerator worked on?" He told her, "I'm with the appliance repair company. I am told your refrigerator is not running and you need it worked on." She replied, "No, our refrigerator is running." Tommy said, "If it's running you better go catch it before it gets away." And of course, she hung up on him again.

Another day went by and he is still thinking about Wendy, he wants to call her but he's still nervous. All he can think to do is to prank call her again, he is still hoping it wins her over, what a weird nervous tick this was for him. He picked up the phone again, dialed her number, and she answered the phone again, "Hello." Tommy asked her, "Is this the walls residence?" and she replied, "no, you have the wrong number sir."

"are you sure this is not the walls residence?" She replied again, "no there are no walls here."

"If there are no walls there, what's holding up your roof?" She hung up on him again. Couple hours went by, this time he wants to be serious, he dialed her number again, she picked up the phone, "Hello!" He did not have the nerve to follow through with a serious conversation, so he pranked her again. This time he told her, "I can't come into work today." She replied, "What are you talking about?"

"I can't come into work today because my cat is sick. I need to give him plenty of liquids and make sure he gets plenty of rest." She hung up the phone again and is now fed-up with all this junk.

Another day passed, Tommy is still thinking about Wendy. He tried one more time, he picked up the phone and called her again, she answered the phone, but this time she didn't say hello. She sat there waiting to see if she was getting pranked again. Tommy yelled out to her, "hello anybody there?" She recognized his voice and said, "Is that you Tommy?" He had nowhere to go with that, so he replied, "yes it's me, how are you?" This is when they finally got a chance to talk and they made plans for their first date.

Tommy went to Wendy's house to pick her up for their first date. They end up going to a French restaurant she chose, it's one she loves because it's elegant with a European atmosphere. The waiter introduced himself, "Good evening guests, my name is Jean Paul, "and asked them what they would like for dinner. Of course, Tommy wanted to have fun with this, he opened with what he thought was a funny line and asked the waiter, "Since you work in a restaurant, do you know where the first doughnut was fried?" The waiter replied, "No sir, I did no homework on that subject." Tommy told the waiter, "That's easy to figure, they were fried in Greece." Then Tommy asked the waiter, "You must know this one sir, which day of the week does an egg hate the most?" The waiter replied, "I see how this is going to be, so instead of making me guess why don't you tell me, sir?" Tommy replied, "That's too easy to figure also, it's Friday." Then he told the waiter this, "if you're thinking I talk too much, just tell me, and we'll talk about it." The waiter replied, "Hey buddy, there's this comedy club about a mile from here, you should take your comedy show there and go make the people down there throw up?"

OK, enough trying to joust the waiter. Tommy has never been to this place, most of the writing in French needless to say. So, the Suave Debonair fool that he is, figures he would pretend like he knew the menu. He told the waiter he would like some 'Tetines Langue de boeuf' and 'Escargots De Bourgogne.' Wendy has been taking French in school and is quite familiar with the menu. She is staring at him in amazement wondering if he really knew what he was talking about. Wendy ordered, and the waiter gladly left to go place their order with the chef.

After the waiter left, Tommy turned to Wendy and asked if he could tell her some knock-knock jokes and she said "okay."

He started off with,

"knock knock,"

"who's there?"

"cows say,"

"cows say who,"

"no, cows say moo."

Wendy said, "yes they do and remember that when you get your dinner."

"Knock knock,"

"who's there?"

"Kanga,"

"kanga who?"

"no, it's pronounced kangaroo." "Knock knock,"

"who's there?"

"Owlsay,"

"Owlsay who?" "Yes, they do say hoo and you finally got one right!"

~ 143 ~

They're having a nice casual conversation waiting for the food. Tommy the clown is constantly telling jokes and wants to keep the date on track in fun way, so he kept it rolling and poured on more funny stuff. He picked up a spoon and pressed it onto his eye, then took a drink from his glass of water, and told Wendy he has a drinking problem. She asked him, "What exactly is that?"

"I'm not sure what it's called, all I know is I went to the doctor and told him about my drinking problem. I told him that when I drink I always get a stinging sensation in my eye. He told me the simple fix would be to take the spoon out my eye when I am drinking, I have yet to stop doing that." Wendy said, "How about you take a minute and relax with me, talk to me and tell more about yourself."

Wendy □tried to be somewhat serious by asking him, "what are you going to do for a career?" He responded, "I'm thinking of going for a Ph.D." Impressed with that answer she asked him, "Oh, very nice, in which doctorate?"

"doctorate? I said P, H, D, that stands for Pizza Hut delivery."

"Oh boy Tommy, is there a human inside that comedic fun shell you live in?" OK, enough funny business for now. The meal arrived, and the waiter served the food on the dinner table. Tommy is staring at his plate with the darnedest look. He is trying to keep a straight face but it's just too complicated. Wendy is smirking with this kind of sideways smile but trying to hold back because she knew what he ordered, and he had no clue what he was looking at on his plate. This will be a test of Tommy's manhood suddenly. Tommy picked up a knife and started cutting into his food. When he went to put a bite into his mouth he stopped, he looked at Wendy and asked her if she wanted the first taste? Good move Tommy, if she eats it and likes it then it's OK to feed yourself. Wendy denied trying it and this forced Tommy to ask her if she had any idea what the heck he was about to put in his mouth. She looked at him and sure enough she bursts out laughing and couldn't answer him. She didn't mean to rub it in by laughing and kept cool for a while but then she snickered, and a snot bubble blew out the end of her nose. This caused a little embarrassment on her part and that made Tommy laugh, then she laughed at him laughing at her, then they were laughing at each other and that caused a laughing frenzy. She rolled sideways in her chair and tears were coming out of her eyes while this snot bubble kept popping in and out of her nose. Tommy laughed so hard he farted, the fart sounded as a loud as the horn on a car. This got the attention of almost everyone in the restaurant. You know how it is if you ever looked at someone laugh and then it made you laugh and then you both laughed so hard it made you cry. That's what happened here, they laughed so much that half the people in the restaurant laughed too. When the laughter turned into trying to breathe they settled down for a bit. She discreetly wiped her nose, looked at Tommy and said, "You are so cute! You have no idea what's sitting there on your plate, do you?" He replied, "Well, I gather those shells are some form of insect, more than likely snails since that's what they look like, but that long weird looking thing has me rather baffled." This is when she almost went back into a laughing fit and informed him, "Remember when you told the knock knock joke about the Cow going Moo? Remember when I told you to remember it when dinner came? What you're looking at is what cows use to go Moo, it's a Cow tongue." Tommy looked at her with total embarrassment and picked up the tongue. He wiped the side of his face with it and pointed at then said: "down boy, down!" Now that the cat is out of the bag, Tetines Langue de boeuf is Cow tongue and ESCARGOTS DE BOURGOGNE is a French delicacy known as snails. What a first date! Wendy is already in love with this guy, he is too much!!

Do you think this was the only odd date they had? Of course not! How about listening to what happened on a cold winter day when on a date later into their romance? Tommy is driving her out to eat at this really nice cabin type restaurant up on the mountainside to have some down-home cooking. On the way driving there, he told her that he needed to use the restroom. She told him that he needs to hold it in since they are about 10 miles away from the closest place with a toilet. About 5 minutes went by and he pulled to the side of the road. "Sorry, but I can't wait!" Wendy is wondering what he is going to do, the side of the road is covered with snow and he would have to do his business in front of people driving by him. So, he pulled off the road and stopped driving. He runs to the back of the van to do his business. Wendy is sitting and about 4 minutes go by and she realized what he stopped for, he is not peeing, it's the other. Being courteous she waits it out. About 4 more minutes go by and she yells out the window, "Do you need a magazine?" He yelled back, "No but I sure do need some help!" She cannot even imagine what type of joke this is going to be but since it's Tommy she can't wait. She reluctantly got out and walked to the back of the van. And there it is, Tommy's big butt is freeze glued to the bumper.

"What are you doing?" Embarrassed beyond anything imaginable Tommy replied, "Well this bumper was supposed to hold my butt up while I dumped that artwork on the ground. I never considered that this weather is at the freezing point where the moisture from my butt could cause it to freeze to the metal." Wendy laughs, "You mean like when you lick a frozen pole and your tongue sticks to it?" Tommy's only response is, "Not a good time to analyze what similar things are as retarded. Can you help me get off this without ripping my butt skin?" Wendy is standing there all whacked out by this, and all she can say is, "Forget about how we are going to get your ass off the bumper while all these cars are driving by, how are you going to wipe your crack?" Well, about a minute into this Wendy is brainstorming what to use to unfreeze his butt off the bumper, "Do I use the cigarette lighter?" No, this will take too many tries since it would apparently cool off before she got back to him. So here it comes, guess what she did? She did it nature's way, she takes her breath and huffed and puffed it around his butt till it came loose one part at a time. I guess you could say she huffed and puffed till she blew his butt away, or something like that. What now? She dug in his van and found an old newspaper and tossed it to him then got back inside. Tommy wiped, pulled his pants up, walked to the door and got in, he is about to drive off but before he does, he looks at Wendy and asked her, "Is this going to make you think I am weird?" Wendy looked at him and replied, "After some of the weird things I experienced with you already do you think this would make me think anything odd about you?" With an understanding look he smiled, and they drove off.

They get to the restaurant, Tommy went straight to the restroom and cleaned himself up the best he could. Back at the table they are in the middle of eating and Tommy reached over and kissed Wendy, then he told her, "Thank you for being a good sport."

About 2 minutes later Tommy's lips start swelling up. They are getting fat to the point he sounds like Fat Albert when he talked. Wendy is glancing at his lips

and asked him, "What the heck is wrong with you?"
Tommy said in muttered words, "Ibba Donbt Knowb,
why are youb askngmb." Wendy looked at her plate,
"Are you allergic to any kind of food? Your lips are
swelling up."

Tommy said, "It can't be the food we are eating." Then
it hits her, "Tommy, I think you are allergic to my
lipstick." Sure enough, she looks at his lips and there
are red marks where he kissed her. They took a
napkin and dipped it in the cold water in a drinking
glass and wiped the lipstick off. This worked to bring
the swelling down a little, so they put ice on his lips.

About 15 minutes later the swelling went down.
Tommy said, "I heard of Hot Lips on Mash, but you've
got spicy lips so why don't we call you pepper lips
from now on." (Hot Lips was the lady in the TV series
called M.A.S.H. from the 70's)

Later that week Wendy wanted to surprise Eddy with
a blind date. She told Tommy to ask him if he would

like to go out with her friend Angie. Tommy asked Eddy and the answer was yes, and she set the date up.

They go to meet at the movies. Tommy, Wendy, and Angie are waiting by the front at the ticket booth. Wendy looked over at this guy walking up to the front where they were standing and shook Tommy's shoulder and asks, "Is that Eddy?"

Eddy showed up at the movies with a cane painted red at the end and some great big sunglasses. The huge glasses must have been his mothers, with no question asked, they were women's sunglasses. Up comes Eddy walking and tapping this cane side to side, he purposely tripped over a trash can by the door where the others were waiting for him. His cane went flying up in the air, the glasses fly across the ground and he is upside down looking up into the air.

Tommy, Wendy and this blind date Angie walk over to him and Tommy asked Eddy, "Not sure what that was all about, but a beautiful entrance. What's up with the glasses and cane?" Eddy replied, "Well I wanted to be a funny guy like you and come to the blind date as a blind man, so we could say this is a real blind date."

Yes, Eddy is a cornball too! After all the ruckus is over everyone is seated in the theatre and Eddy is sharing the popcorn with his date. As it was nearing the bottom of the box he sneakily told her to let him hold the popcorn.

He is squirming and fidgeting, and Angie is wondering what his problem is. He told her that he would prefer she eats what's left of the popcorn because he considers it's more chivalrous to let her have the last bit of food. She put her hand in the box to get a bite and shrilled, she yelled, "EEK!" Eddy is holding back with a smug laugh, he asked her, "What's wrong?" Angie told him, "Something is in the popcorn." He replied with, "Of course, this popcorn is like Cracker Jacks."

"What do you mean like Cracker Jacks?" "Like Cracker Jacks, this has a surprise!" She wants to know what the heck he is talking about, "What's this surprise?" "Just reach in and pull it out." Angie is not sure what to make of this, she reached in and gripped the suspected surprise. She pulled on it, she gave a good hard tug, it wouldn't come out and she let it go. She asked him, "Why is that soft and stretchy, what is that?" Eddy told her, "That's the popcorn surprise, my wiener." "Eww!" At first, she had no idea what the heck to make of this. But, this got her attention, and now she is curious, and since she is a promiscuous sexual goddess she reached back in the box and had a great time with it. For the rest of this movie the surprise was a special treat for both and a treat Angie never forgot, her first Popcorn surprise! Its several months into Tommy and Wendy dating. The weather is nice out, so one-night Tommy picked her up and they took a short drive to this hill that has a spiral stairwell made of concrete. This hill is out in the countryside. When you get to the top there is this rounded concrete slab with an impression of the Universe in it. This hill belongs to an electricity company that uses it as a landmark for people to visit and see what the planets and the universe look like. The main idea is it's an advertisement for their company. In the middle of the universe, the Sun is lit up with an inscription around the Sun saying, 'With enough electricity to light up the Sun, Powered by Mountain Electricity company.' Mountain electricity is the name of the company sponsoring the hill.

It's dark, and this place is very romantic with its mysterious placement in the middle of nowhere. Since these two are becoming close, no matter what they do things are fun and now romantic. While they are sitting on the bench admiring this glowing Sun in the dark, out of nowhere, Tommy planted a kiss on her. So far, the early lovebirds have yet to be serious along the lines of touching or being sexual in any way.

They got real sloppy wet and sexy with their kissing. Tommy suddenly decided he wants to put his lips on her neck and kiss it, and he did. Then he was touching her breasts and guess what? She's liking this. Tommy is unbuttoning her shirt because now his testosterone is taking over and he's ready to get sexy. Wendy being a lady told him, "We can't do this up here." Tommy wants to be a gentleman and told her "That's fine, let's go ahead and leave." They walk down the hill to the parking lot, jump in the van and before he started it he looks over at her and she looks at him. Nothing was said, they grab each other and start kissing again. About 20 minutes into this both of their clothes come off. This has developed into a very intense moment, he is kissing all over her chest. He reached down and went to message her you know what and its soaking wet. Tommy is turned on like the movie Wayne's World, SHWING!

He knows this is it and by the way she is panting he knows she is ready also. This is when they do the first Dirty Deed. He gets her to the floor of the van, working himself in her he finds out how good this feels. Tommy is moving in and out of her, side to side, he is getting after it, his butt is all over the place. He stopped jack-hammering a minute and sucked her nipples, then he went down between her legs and licked and sucked her special spot, this allowed her a chance to breathe. Wendy is so overwhelmed by this machine named Tommy, the intense passion has made her incoherent.

40 minutes into the middle of this they hear a tapping on the glass. What The heck was that? It sounds like a rock is being smacked up against it. Tommy stops, and he looked at Wendy and he asked her, "Do you hear something?" Tap tap tap again. Wendy answered, "If you're asking about that tapping noise, the answer is yes." Tommy immediately wiped the window clean of the steam and he could the silhouette of a person outside the door. So, as fast as he could he handed Wendy her clothes and he quickly put his clothes on. As they're fumbling around getting dressed the tapping happened one more time. Tommy got his pants on then opened the door and there's a policeman standing outside the Van, then he shut the door. Tommy's heart was racing, and he was scared to death. He had no clue what was about to happen. He rolled the window down and asked the cop if anything was wrong. The cop asked him what he was doing,

Tommy told the cop that him in his girlfriend were having their first romantic kiss and listening to some music. The cop asked him "Is that all?" He told the policeman, "No, we are getting a bit touchy, but that's all sir." The policeman told him he had leave there because if he didn't he would have them arrested for public lewdness. Tommy responded, "Yes sir, no need to say anything else!" Then asked him, "Do you need anything else from us?" The cop told him no, but he would wait and watch them leave to make sure they left the parking lot. He turned the ignition switch on in the van, started it up and took off. Tommy apologized to Wendy. She said, "How embarrassing!" And Tommy agreed, he thought she was mad, and this might cause problems for him. "Again, I'm so sorry that I put you in a position like that." And Wendy said, "Honestly, you can put me in a position like that anytime you want from now on as long as it's someplace where we can be alone and not get caught!" This began what I would refer to as a Sexual Revolution.

Later in the week Tommy called Wendy and asked her
if she would like to go swimming, and excited about
that idea she said yes. They get to the swimming pool,
it's an Olympic size with lots of people there. This
makes a good place for them to hang out since they're
getting serious in their relationship. It's relaxing, they
can watch people swim and it's a cool place for them
to interact.

They're laying out in the Sun on the lounges. Tommy
is really eager to have fun and show-off, so he got up
and was doing back-flips into the pool. Then he
climbed the high dive and was doing flips off it. He
was spreading his legs when he jumped off and
making all kinds of faces to entertain Wendy while she
watched and sunbathed. When he was done showing
off it was time to take a 5-minute break, he sat with
Wendy on the lawn chair.

Wendy told Tommy she felt like she's catching a little
burn from the Sun. She asked him if he would rub
some sunscreen on her backside. For Tommy, that
was an opportunity to touch her hot body, maybe it

will make her feel good. It appeared this did make her feel good as she assured him with subtle sighs of approval. Massaging the sunscreen into her skin makes her feel good, but it also made him feel good in certain way. While he's rubbing her back with sunscreen he was singing to her this song by Foreigner called, 'Hot blooded.' The words, "You don't have to read my mind to know what I have in mind, now it's up to you, we can make a secret rendezvous, just me and you, I'll show you loving like you never knew, if it feels alright maybe you can stay all night. Should I leave you my key? But you got to give me a sign, come on girl some kind of sign, tell me, are you hot mamma?

You sure look that way to me, are you old enough will you be ready when I call your Bluff?

Is my timing right did you save your love for me tonight? Well I'm hot Blooded every night, Hot Blooded you look so tight, Hot Blooded now you're driving me wild, Hot Blooded I'm so hot for you child, Hot blooded I'm a little bit High, Hot blooded you're a little bit shy, Hot blooded you're making me sing, Hot blooded for your sweet, sweet thing.

Tommy is not only tantalizing her by stroking her very softly rubbing sunscreen lotion on her, he's Charming her by singing to her. He doesn't press hard when rubbing her and the sensation of her soft skin touching his fingers is exciting him, the softer he rubs the more it excites her. She had Goosebumps from the message and Tommy paid attention to that. Her bumpy reaction is exciting him in a way it aroused him. After he's done rubbing the lotion on her and becoming aroused, he suggested they get up, "I think we should go get a snack at the snack-bar, what do you think?" She replied, "That's a good idea."

They went over to the snack- bar, neither one said much because a passionate tension developed. They got to the snack-bar and gave their order. Tommy got a Coke, and she ordered a Popsicle. He sipped on his Coke staring at her and she was staring back. She peeled the plastic off the Popsicle and put it about 2 inches into her mouth. Then she slid it back out sucking the melting juice off it. In the meantime, they can't stop staring at each other. Wendy takes her tongue and slurps about five inches of the Popsicle with her long tongue.

Tommy is going crazy watching her eat the popsicle, her licking it is causing his imagination to think the Popsicle is him instead. She gathered that in her mind by the way he was watching her, so she put on a little show teasing him with it. A few special licks and a couple deeper than normal sucks on the Popsicle and that sparks a beast.

Tommy took her by the hand and walked her toward the end of the snack bar, he saw a secluded walkway leading to the backside. They walked back behind the snack bar and he put his arms around her, then he planted a big kiss on her lips. It's safe, nobody is looking because nobody can see them. The sweaty sunscreen from her skin is slippery, he pressed up against her chest. Her budding breasts are pressing against his chest, the next thing you know Tommy is ready and can't wait. He pulled his swimming suit down past his genitals and took her bikini bottom and slid it to the side while kissing her. He inserted himself into her right there standing up. She was leaning back against this rail and for at least 15 minutes they were going at it like two wild Animals.

When they stopped the sexual frenzy, they were sweating profusely. They looked like they just climbed out of the pool. They went back to the lawn chairs where they originally sat and laid down catching their breath. About five minutes later they glanced at each other, still panting a bit, still sweating and smiled at each other with deep satisfaction. You could tell that if this could happen again right there they would've done it, but good thing they were at the pool in front people, that's the only thing that stopped them. Tommy stood up, grabbed her by the hand, walked her to the pool and they dove in. That's the end of romance for them on their sexy day at the pool.

A HIKE AND A DAM SEXY ENCOUNTER

The next day they get together and decide this is a good day to have a new adventure. They head out for a hike up to the dam where Eddy and Tommy used to hang out listening to the water flow over the edge eating a picnic lunch, this relaxed them and brought them closer to nature. This is a vastly secluded get away that few people knew about. One day when Tommy and Eddy were on one of their adventures seeking a new discovery they found this place. This became the go to place to escape the city noise and get away from crowds of people. Tommy thought this will be a good way to find out if she has a country girl side to her. He wanted to see if she can match his love for nature at the same time enjoy it by indulging in its sounds and beauty.

They arrived and spent several hours roaming the wooded section around the dam watching the little creeks that feed it and listening to sounds of the woods come to life.

Birds chirp, and frogs ribbit, the wind that flows through the trees cools their bodies. The trees amaze them with their massive size from old age.

They hike back to the edge of the dam where they have a tasty picnic feast that Wendy threw together; it was her famous bologna and mayonnaise sandwiches. Little did she know this was Tommy's favorite lunch his other made him, he grew up eating these for lunch at school practically every day. Shortly after they eat they slow down. The next thing you know they have fallen asleep. That moment was like a love story, she is cuddling by his armpit and he embraced her like he would never let go.

Tommy woke first in the warmth of the Sun. He does not know why but feels the urge to sneak a kiss in before she wakes up. She is still sleeping but is responding nicely to his lips as though she is dreaming what he is doing to her. He unfastens her shirt and gently takes it off. Her shorts are next and then her underpants. She opens her eyes finding this happening. She wants to respond but makes like she is still sleeping so not to ruin the sneaky foreplay. The bra he left on, so she would not feel so naked. He put his face in her neck slightly licking the sides of her throat.

She must respond; the warmth from the sun breaking through threes and the breeze heightens the mood. Her hand touches his chest and slides around it with slow swirly motions. He lies still as a statue while her soft skin tantalizes his skin. Then she lightly rubs his nipples like she was the man and it was giving him enormous pleasure. She worked her hand down into his shorts, his penis is throbbing hard. She took it in her hand and explores it like it was part of this adventure they were looking for at the start of the day. Yes, a nice new adventure and not only with discovering new places that day but a new a relationship booster. She spent several minutes stroking the entire length of his hard-throbbing wand.

His skin is tantalizing and warm. In the next scene of this she is positioned on top of him, a position she assumes without instruction. It's half an hour of deep ecstasy before they stop meshing and grinding on top of this wall with water trickling over the edge. The inside of her thighs are soaking wet, and making Tommy a small version of the dam as her body pours itself on his.

"This is so nice! I can't believe you woke me up that way. How long will it take to make it again?" she asked him.

Tommy is pondering this question, processing what it meant, 'we just had sex so what does that mean?' He assumed she was talking about the lunch was asking about making sandwiches from the way she worded the question.

Guessing the answer, he said, "Just a guess, two or three minutes to put the meat on and spread the mayo, then a couple minutes to put the stuff up. Well, I'm not sure, you made it you should know."

"No!" she said. That is not what she meant.

She began to stroke his magic wand, that made it hard again. In a few minutes, he rolled her over, got on top of her and put it in her again. Intermission had ended and show time began. This time she got wild. The blanket is wadding up underneath her. Her breath becomes short with a heavy panting. Tommy had to brace his hands on the concrete. He hooked his knees outside her legs and drove himself deeper and stroking faster.

"Oh," she breathes out, "that's the way, don't stop!" When he cums, it ends him from any reserve energy. They whither to the end like a wilted flower. After a good 20-minute breath catching, he stood up at the edge of the wall, pushed his pelvis forward and peed over the wall as if it was a victory lap at the Daytona 500. She has not moved. She lies just where she was and deflated into a zombie.

Later that night they are on the porch swing in front of her house. Not much being said. Tommy looked at her and asked, "Is there any chance you feel the way I do?"

"Not sure? What are you feeling?" She responded. "What I mean is, we've been seeing each other practically every day and we have sex like we are the hottest porn show in town. Definitely, we are good friends and I want to take this to a higher level." Wendy is literally quivering with excitement! "I thought you would never ask me. So, if you are asking for an engagement and wish me to be your steady girl the answer is NO!"

"WHAT!?" Tommy replied.

"Just kidding, I love you like nothing I ever have known." Tommy sits back, smiled, and told her, "I feel so good with that answer I need to do a backflip." Next thing you know he stood up, turned backward and sure enough backflips once, twice, BOOM! He hits the porch window and lands on his face. That ends the 'A hike and a Dam sexy encounter,' and then making their commitment to each other.

Now that they have this commitment the mood changes a bit to a more mature manner. The normal Tommy is eager to tell a joke or do a stunt to make people laugh or do a something that shocks people. Instead, now he is Mack daddy in charge. Wendy's normal daily routine is patiently waiting for Tommy's phone call and Tommy is eager to make the call. Tommy began taking Wendy to more calm venues. He would rather take Wendy to the movies or places where it's quieter and more intimate. He found himself liking deeper and much more affectionate conversations.

Lately he just shows up to her house unexpected. One day he went there, knock knock knock, he taps on the door and rings the doorbell. Wendy's mother answered the door, "Hi Tommy, what are you up to?"

"I wanted to surprise Wendy and see if she would go to dinner with me." Mom is excited to talk to him,

"Oh, perfect idea, I heard you and Wendy chose to be more serious."

"You betcha, we decided that we liked each other enough to be a team and hang out together with no one else as an option. Personally, I am very excited about this." Mom has an intense look on her face, she asked him, "Well where's the ring?" Tommy turns a pale white and got a little clammy. "Rrring? Uhh, I wasn't quite ready for marriage." Mom trying to hold back from laughing keeps it cool told him, "When people go steady or get engaged you always get them a ring." Tommy wanting to find a way out of this discussion said, "Why would I buy a ring before marriage?"

"That's just it Tommy, it's an engagement, the ring is a pre-commitment for marriage. You are doing nothing more than telling her you are committed to only her with the intentions to marry her one day. So, you present it to her as a steady or promise ring, get it now?" Relief for Tommy as the blood was draining down his legs. Mom went to get Wendy and she peeked around the corner, "Tommy why didn't you call me?"

"I wanted to surprise you!"

Wendy is a mess, "Tommy you have to leave!" "But why, I want to take you out for dinner." She is hiding around the corner talking, while she is talking he is sneaking up the stairs and she still thinks he's downstairs. He leaped around the corner and yelled, "BOO!" She screamed and fell to the ground. Him, he blurts out EEK!" She screamed again then said, "What the heck are you eeking for?" "You look different! I almost didn't recognize you, I thought I had Boo'd the wrong person." She is embarrassed. "You can't see me this way!" "What, what way?"

She can barely look at him, "I am not wearing makeup, please leave!"

"Are you kidding, you are HOTT!" "Tommy please do not antagonize me!" "Antagonize? Do you think I am kidding? I can't believe how beautiful you are, why on God's green earth do you wear make-up? I never could say anything before because I thought it would upset you, but I don't like make-up!" "Tommy are you being honest with me?" "Wendy, look at me in the eyes, I am serious, and you are smoking HOTT! No need to talk any more about you wearing make-up. From this day forward, you need not wear any, I am serious, cross my heart and hope to die!" Good news to Wendy, "Wow Tommy, I can't believe you think I am pretty without make-up." "Wendy, look how clear and healthy your skin is, it's incredible. Think about this, make-up is what they put on dead people to make them look alive, it's what clowns put on to scare little kids! To answer your question, yes, you are so pretty, I can't believe how you look without make-up, you are way prettier than I expected!" Well, this is good news for Wendy, she hated wearing it and taking the time to put on her face.

TOMMY DROPS A BOMB ON WENDY

Tommy took her to the first fast-food Mexican restaurant that the town ever had. They went to Taco so Loco. It's a poor excuse to be a Mexican restaurant but works for people wanting a Mexican meal.

Tommy got the super spicy bean with red and green Chile burrito. Wendy got the regular beef taco. Tommy slurped this nasty concoction down and is waiting for his slow eating little beauty to finish. About seven minutes into this he is dealing with a little tummy churning. His belly is becoming tense while they are talking. Wendy notices he is squirming and shifting around in his seat. "What's wrong with you Tommy?"

"Not sure, my belly is kind of hurting." Tommy felt like he had to poop, he wasn't sure if he needed to. He leaned slightly to the left and barely pushing hoping to let out a little air. He is testing the back door to see what this might be, squeezing it and pushing out nice and slow, then he realized it's not a solid its gas. He pushes a little more with confidence, unfortunate for Tommy they are in a fiberglass booth, the seat he is sitting on is hard and hollow like a Bass drum. Why am I telling you this? Here's what happens next.

It's coming, just about the time he thought he had it sneaking out nice and quiet, BAVROOM! He farted, this thing came out amplified like an atomic bomb! It was so loud the entire restaurant became silent all at once. Everyone turned to see who made the enormous sound. It sounded like someone had erupted their entire meal out. Wendy is staring straight at Tommy not chewing, not moving her head any direction to see what she already knew was the entire restaurant staring. She could not breathe because she was so embarrassed. On the other hand, here is Tommy nice and cool. He looked every direction, to left people are staring, to the right people staring. A little boy laughed out loud, it was the only thing you could hear in the entire place. The kid followed through saying loud enough for the whole place to hear, "Hey mom, did you hear that? One of those people farted," pointing at them.

This is when you find out how cool Tommy is under pressure. He pointed at Wendy as he looks around the room and said, "Good one Wendy that was loud! I can't imagine how you managed to make that much noise from such a small body?" Oh boy! For Wendy, she felt pure fire hot anger, not only embarrassed but now blamed for the Atomic Fart! She got up from the table and walked fast as she could out of the restaurant, and never looked side to side just straight ahead like a Bull about to spear something. Tommy got up to follow her out of the restaurant. The place resumed back to normal and people went back to eating and talking to each other again.

He stopped to pay for the food, the cashier took his money and asked: "Was everything good today?" Tommy replied, "Food was OK, everything was fine until the Atomic bomb blew up." Cashier, "Yep, we heard all the back in the kitchen. I bet the people in the parking lot heard it too. Would you like to buy some Alka Seltzer, we sell it here?"

"Nah, my stomach feels better so it can't help much. I believe what I needed help with made its way out the escape hatch earlier." Tommy ran out the door and Wendy was sitting in the van. He opened the door and Wendy will not look at him because she is angry. "Come on Wendy, you don't know how hard that was for me, I tried to ease it out. It was about to pass through silently and the next thing you know I am the military taking out the whole booth and village with a bomb. Honestly, I had no clue that seat would boost the volume so much, I guess it did because its hollow."

Wendy doesn't know whether she should laugh at him or smack him, so she balls up her fist and punched his arm. "If you ever do that again I will get even with you, not sure how but I will." Tommy replied, "Let me make it up to you, I'll take you to the movies, you pick a movie and we'll go see it." That is what they did, went to the movies and changed the mood. They got a bag of popcorn, go into the theater and look for a seat. Tommy is in front walking down the aisle. He reached behind and grabs the backside of the crotch on his butt and pulled a wedgie out of his butt crack. They sit down, and Wendy thought she would be funny and said, "Why did you pull the gruff of your pants out of your butt? Did that explosion leave a little damage behind? Get it? Damaged behind, meaning a messy butt" Tommy smartly replied, "NO, we are at the movies, I was picking my seat, Get it?"

"Ha-ha, you are too funny."

The movie is about thirty minutes in, the popcorn is almost gone, and Tommy is firmly holding the bag. You hear Wendy murmur, "What the??" She pulled her hand out real fast, "Tommy, something is in the popcorn?" Tommy grabbed her hand and put it back in, "Shhh, try again." She took her time and continued to search around. Then looking at him, he is smiling, and she said, "Oh, I get it, Popcorn surprise? I forgot about that one" I guess Eddy taught him something. What a night, Atomic farts and popcorn surprises.

Weeks go by and these two are involved in a much more mature level. I guess because they are doing adult things like sex and sitting around in the evenings talking about the day as if they were married caused a change in them. Looks like they are full blown adults.

TOMMY HAS NEW MOVES FOR WENDY

Wendy is fine adjusting to Tommy's change of maturity, but something is wrong, it doesn't feel the same anymore. One-night Tommy is looking at Wendy and she seemed a little unresponsive to the conversation. "Hey girl, you're a little way down the road when I'm talking to you. Usually, you are a good talker and tonight you don't seem interested, what's going on with you?"

"Well Tommy, when I met you, you were very funny, always a jokester, I never knew what you were going to do next and you always kept my attention." This surprised Tommy because he felt being more mature is what she wanted, and he was fine with it himself. He knew she was serious, and he better respond with a good answer.

"So, what you are saying is I am boring? Because that can change real fast. Faster than a one-legged man in a butt-kicking competition, Faster than a fat kid chasing an ice cream truck, faster than a herd of cheetahs, faster than a speeding bullet racing a lightning bolt, fast enough you will get a speeding ticket, faster than..."

"STOP! I got the point!" Wendy was ready to get on with the conversation. "What do you have in mind?"

"Since we established you want a little action then I suggest you put on your boogie shoes!"

"Boogie shoes?" She replied.

"That's right, we've never been dancing, and its time Tommie boy puts the moves on you.

"Moves on me? OK, let's do this!" Later that night He showed up at Wendy's house. She opened the door and there stood Tommy with mirror finish aviator sunglasses and about four inches taller. She looked up at him and he is taller and dressed way different than she has ever seen him. First, she looks up, then she looked down and there it is, that's why he is so tall all the sudden, platform shoes. "What are those?" As she points down at his feet. The shoes he is wearing are four inches high.

"Those my lady be Disco shoes!"

"Disco shoes?? Do they play music? What the heck are disco shoes?!" Also, to add to the oddity he is wearing a giant collar long sleeve shirt made of silk with this flowery print like it was off the curtains from an old lady's house. The pants were corduroy and went all the way down around the shoes draping over the sides shaped like a bell, people called them bell bottoms.

This was not surprising to Wendy, the one thing that made this guy the highlight of her life was the crazy stuff he did, it drove the cog in her wheel and made this relationship a must have! They went to Star Castle, the local disco close to where they live. They walk in and all you hear is boom boom boom. Tommy is walking with a swagger like John Travolta did in the movie Saturday night fever which was popular at that time. If you have ever seen it, picture the scene where Travolta is walking down the street with the song in the background "Staying Alive." Now picture that scene but its Tommy walking with Wendy and that song is playing and he struts like a 1000-pound stud horse to these words, "Well, you can tell by the way I use my walk, I'm a woman's man, no time to talk." This was a time when Disco dancing is the trendy thing. If you were anybody, you went dancing to end your evening. It's about 10:30 and the place was packed full of people. Tommie a fairly popular guy is being bumped and poked by many people that

recognize him, they are getting his attention, so they
can say hi to him.

They're waiting for the right song to play; the place is
so loud they can't talk. Tommy is bouncing around
and bobbing his head, moving it forward and
backward like a chicken walking and is in rhythm to
the beat of the music. He's tapping his feet to the beat
of the music not once looking at Wendy. She is
quivering with anticipation and cannot wait to dance
with her Bo. Here it is, the big moment, the song he
was waiting on, the Bee Gees song "Staying Alive."
The first words of the song play, "Well, you can tell by
the way I use my walk, I'm a woman's man, no time to
talk." Tommy grabbed Wendy by the hand and walked
her to the dance floor. He made way for him and his
queen moving everyone out of the way with his large
220-pound body. Tommy gets in place and starts the
show. He positions his hips to the side, one arm
pointing up and the other down. He moved forward a
couple steps and wiggled his butt gracefully
simulating John Travolta's dance in the movie

Saturday night fever. Wendy is trying to keep up with him and with a couple swift moves he grabbed her and guides her into a spin. Continuing with another spin, then he waltzes her from side to side. The entire song Tommy has spun and guided her around. He was dancing with her as though he was the choreographer for the movie Saturday night fever. Wendy danced good also, no reason she shouldn't have, they were a perfect match.

That's how it was every time they danced that night. Halfway through the night, the disco has a dance contest. A dance King contest, a dance Queen contest, and a King and Queen contest. The king contest is a solo male dance, Queen Contest is a solo female and then the King and Queen are two people dancing together. Tommy asked Wendy to join him for the contest and she said, "No way! You dance well but I am not ready for anything like that, sorry." He looked at her and replied, "fair enough, I will enter the dance King contest, you can watch and cheer me on." So, he entered the contest. He is the last dancer and he picked the song 'Boogie Shoes' by KC and the Sunshine band. I wonder why he picked that song? I guess to make fun of his own shoes he wore that night, he did call them disco shoes. Here comes the song. He is dancing already and the words to the song are, "I want to do it 'til the sun comes up, uh huh, and I want to do it 'til I can't get enough, yeah, yeah

I want to put on my my my my my Boogie shoes, just to boogie with you, I want to put on my my my my my Boogie shoes, just to boogie with you.

The song is playing, Tommy is doing this move he learned from his friends Ronnie and Donnie, the Thompson twins. They were the disco Kings at this club for a never-ending time including that night.

He is weaving his hips side to side and he sways forward and backward. In the middle of several forward and backward movements, he threw his left foot around his right foot and does the ice skater kind of spin and twirls several spins. Then back to the hip-swinging, swaying, weaving and foot action. At the end of his dance he did two back flips then walked off the stage on his hands, the crowd went crazy.

A minute after that the announcer called out the winners. On the solo men's it was none other than Donnie Thompson. But when Donnie received the trophy he immediately grabbed the announcer and asked him to call Tommy up to the stage. The announcer called for Tommy to come up. Donnie grabbed the microphone from the announcer and said into the microphone, "To all the people here, I feel it's only fair that Tommy wins this because he was my personal favorite tonight. That exit with the back flip and walking off the stage on his hands was too cool and if you agree applaud." The crowd went crazy yelling whistling and applauding. Donnie handed the trophy to him. Tommy shook Donnie's hand and thanked him. Then he grabbed the microphone and said a quote from the movie 'Rocky' which was also very popular at that time, "Yo, Adrian, I did it." The crowd went even crazier but with laughter this time, and that trophy was the coolest thing Tommy ever got and Wendy was there to be a part of it.

The next song came on, "More than a woman by Bee Gees." Tommy grabbed Wendy and embraced her, he pulled her closer to his body and started dancing. He held her with pure power and he was proud, not only of his performance and a big win but with this vision of a lady that was his. The words of the song playing,

"Girl, I've known you very well, I've seen you growing every day,

I never really looked before, but now you take my breath away

Suddenly you're in my life

A part of everything I do

You got me workin' day and night Just tryin' to keep a hold on you Here in your arms I found my paradise My only chance for happiness and if I lose you now, I think I would die Say you'll always be my baby we can make it shine We can take forever just a minute at a time More than a woman

More than a woman to me

More than a woman, More than a woman to me."
They ended the night in the parking lot getting into
the van and the next thing you know is the windows
were dripping with steam. The only thing missing was
a sign outside the van that should have read, 'If you
see this Van a rockin don't bother knockin.'

EDDY'S TURN, ROCK THE DISCO

A couple days after Tommy's big win at the Disco he
bumped into Eddy. Tommy summarized the other
night's escapade at the Star Castle. Eddy has known
this trophy was past due since he had first row seating
to watch Tommy dance any time they went out. He
got to watch him breeze through the club and dance
the night away with all the fine-looking women. Eddy

asked him, "Hey man, you spend all your time with Wendy, why don't you and I go next Friday, it's supposed to be rock-n-roll night. "No challenge with that, Tommy is already there!

It's Friday night and they are off to the races! They jump in Tommy's van and Eddy is feeling the rock-and-roll mood like nobody's business. First thing Eddy did was light-up a joint and was puffing this thing like a dragon. He is being mean and ornery and kept blowing it at Tommy trying to get a rush out of him. Tommy is not affected by this and knew it was time to turn on the music. Eddy would wig out on the mixture of getting high and blasting his brains out to his favorite tune he listened to when he was high, a song called 'Frankenstein.' This is one of those songs you must go to YouTube or internet search and look it up to get the full picture of what these guys are listening to while getting cranked up driving to the Star Castle club.

Riding down the road not a word is spoken, no need to talk, the music is blasting, and these guys are just too cool! They get there, and the place is already booming with Aerosmith's 'Walk this way.' The words blasting, "Hey diddle diddle with your kitty in the middle of a swing like you just don't care... She told me to walk this way, talk this way..."

The guys are hanging out having the time of their lives. Girls are all over the place, music is very loud, and Eddy is smooching one girl after another. Tommy is entertaining the girls with walking on his hands and doing flips through the club. Around an hour and a half into the night Eddy came rushing up to Tommy, "Hey man, I was over here talking to this chic and the next thing I know out of nowhere this guy came up and pushed me. I tried being nice with him, but he wouldn't leave me alone and he told me he was getting ready to beat my ass. So, I told him no problem, get busy and make it happen chump! I went up to him and was ready, and the next thing I know there's around 5 other guys standing beside him. I told him I would be right back, and he said they would head me off at the door if I tried to run."

Tommy with absolutely no thought about this said, "Where is he I will help straighten this out!" They walk back over to where this confrontation started and when they get there this hot-headed jerk is jumping up and down bouncing and throwing air punches like he was in a boxing match. When they got to the trouble maker, he walked up to Eddy and pushed him. Tommy grabbed the guys arm and the trouble maker turned to him and said, "you want some of this punk?!?" Tommy said, "If you mess with him you mess with me!" Then around six guys surround Tommy, and one answered, "If you mess with him you mess with us!" Tommy is struggling to reason with them and when he looked around Eddy had left. Tommy was stunned and thought, 'what the heck? Eddy gets me into this and runs.' In the meantime, Tommy is being poked and prodded every which way by these guys and hoping for some relief. About 2 minutes into this uncomfortable moment which seemed like 30 minutes, here came Eddy and these two big thugs, and I mean big. The main guy in this part of the novel is this big Italian guy who looks like a millionaire GQ model getting out of his limousine. He was wearing satin clothing and looked like he was modeling it for an upscale clothing line like Gucci, but his face told a different story. His face was rough, you could tell he had been hit with some hard objects, I pity the fool that hit him.

I was lucky enough to witness a mafia transaction with a mob boss and one of his bill collectors. This guy I am telling you about looked like the mafia bill collector that beat people up for money owed to the mafia. This guy stepped in the crowd and asked Eddy, "who we are dealing with here?" Eddy pointed the direction of the group and said, "That guy there is my friend (pointing to Tommy) and that guy with those guys are the ones wanting to fight."

The big guy shoved the first two on his right and then the two on the left clearing them away making room for Tommy to get out of the way. The big guy took his finger and stabbed the big mouth trouble makers chest with his index finger, and in a manner his finger must have felt like a spear because it moved him back about two feet. He yelled out, "I found out somebody wants to fight, I like to fight! Are you the piss-ant wanting to fight? (Pointing to the guy he poked) I want to fight too, so come on give me a nice big punch in my face! Come on boy watcha waitin on? Come on!" He is getting really strong with his voice, then he turned to the five guys and pointed to all of them and said, "How about you guys? Come on, all of you, let's go, what the hell you are waiting for?" He got into a boxing stance and was moving his fists in a punching motion. And then he air boxed the face of one of the guys standing to the side, swinging his fists at a rate you couldn't even see his big long arms moving. Those guys were struggling trying to ask him to stop, stuttering their words, "P,Pl,Please sir, we don't wa,wa,want any t,tr,trouble." The guy who initiated the trouble to begin with was trying to talk, he was shaking, and his voice was squiggly too, he uttered, "I, I'm sa, sorry sir, I was just kidding." Then the brute said, "That's what I thought, you're a little piss ant pussy!" Then he told them to leave and in about 4 seconds they all quickly took off towards the door.

Eddy and Tommy were amazed at the outcome, and Tommy was really amazed since it was someone else coming to his rescue for a change. After it was all said and done Tommy told Eddy, "That was too frikken cool!! How did you end up with that brute?" Eddy answered, "I was desperate because I knew we couldn't take all those guys. I went trying to get the bouncer, but I saw that guy there who looked like he could whip the bouncer and that was a no brainer. I ran up to him begging for help hoping he was willing. I told him my friend is getting picked on by a gang of bullies and asked him if he could help. He looked at me and responded, "Where is he? I'll be glad to take care of it," and he didn't waste one second.

Later in life, many times Tommy would bump into this guy and became friendly acquaintances. He turned out to be one really nice guy and down-to-earth. Every time they bumped into each other they would spend quite a while talking and Tommy got to know this guy fairly well. Come to find out he was recently in a movie with Sylvester Stallone. The guy stands about 6'6" and is a professional fighter with titles under his belt. He now owns a successful boxing gym. We know now why this guy was ready to fight, he was a multi champion and would have wiped those guys out if a fight would've taken place, lucky for them.

TIME TO SHOW WENDY THE ROPES

Tommy has a zest for life, he always has. As time passed by, he was becoming a little bored with this romantic stuff for a minute, long enough to realize he still has some spunk left in him. He is going crazy and can't figure out what's making him squirm with anticipation.

Tommy has a date to meet Wendy at her house and went to get her. As he is driving and thinking, 'this dating stuff is good, but I need more action. Eddy is working a job that requires him stay there from Sun up till sundown. That meant things outside of romance that included hanging out with him and getting into mischief are now on hold.'

Tommy arrived at Wendy's house and he revealed to her this night wouldn't be the same as their regular date. "Hey girl, tonight I want to try something offbeat. I want to introduce you to an extraordinary type of fun. What we're going to do is go out and eat like we usually do, but we will initiate a little exercise-n-eat program."

"What do you mean exercise and eat?"

"We are doing something different tonight so jump in and do as I do and let me ask the questions! Now my question, what kind of food would you like to eat tonight?" She has a hankering for seafood so at this point they choose to go to Red Lobster.

Tommy explained to her the part that was exercise is to park at least a block away from the restaurant and walk the rest of the way. Wendy is game for this new program and happy to go along with it.

As they are in the restaurant he is fidgeting and slightly uneasy, and she can tell something is wrong. She asked him, "Tommy, tell me something, you're acting a little fidgety tonight and I'm sort of curious why?" He doesn't want to give up the surprise yet and didn't answer her. Curiosity is driving her mad, she is wondering if the fidgeting will result in another one of his 'blasting atomic-fart explosions.' She just came out and directly asked him, "Do you have gas by any chance? Is that why you're squirming?" Tommy laughs and then he answered her, "I am not squirming and I'm not nervous. But I am excited because tonight I'm going to break you in on a new style of eating, exercising, and getting a bargain meal all at the same time." The meal is eaten up, and it's time to pay the bill and leave. Tommy Put a $5 tip down on the table and started coaching Wendy. He told her to keep an eye on the waiter, and the manager who was wearing the red vest and black bow tie.

"Why do I need to watch him?" "It's a game we are playing, so play along and have fun with it girl." Wendy not knowing what he has in store for her went along with it. He told her "When the manager walks back into the kitchen I want you to go to the front door and wait outside." The time has come when she sees the manager go into the kitchen. "Ok, he went to the back." Tommy told her "It's time to go to the front door!" She went up to the front of the restaurant waited outside the door. About 20 seconds later Tommy briskly walked out and told her, "Now it's time for the big part of this, the exercise, get ready to jog right now!" She asked him, "Why are we going to jog for exercise right after dinner, I thought the walking was our exercise?" He answered her with, "It's time to run, see you later!" He took off running and without any thought she went running behind him. They get to the van, both panting and gasping for air from the 600-yard Sprint. Wendy demanded to know why this little game of eating and running is going down this particular night and this special way. This is when Tommy breaks the news to her that she is part of a very mild crime called Dine-and-Dash. "Jump in the Van now and I will explain but hurry!" "Dine-and-Dash! What the heck is that?" she asked him. "Dine-and-Dash is when you eat a good healthy meal, as much as you can eat. Then you run your butt off because you are not paying for it!" "What!? Are you kidding me? Are you serious?" Tommy gave her a stern look and said, "We just ate food and did not pay for it!" He is telling her that while his tires are peeling out on the street where they parked. Wendy is getting scared, "Tommy how can you do that?" Tommy answered, "It's unnecessary to know how I can do that. It's the fact that there's an adrenaline rush that goes along with it, and you are scared, aren't you? That scared feeling is your adrenaline. And as you feel that adrenaline it's a rush, isn't it!?" Since Wendy has never done this before she is getting the picture about this dine-and-dash stuff. She can tell this eating and not paying is something that Tommy is acquainted with. This wild nature he has in him is what she loves and if wild is what it takes to be a part of his world she's all for it.

WENDY TREATS TOMMY

A couple weeks went by and one-night Wendy decided to surprise Tommy. She called him and told him she would like to take him out for ice cream. Without a doubt Tommy is not going to turn down ice cream it's one of his favorite things. They get to the mall and Wendy suggested they park on the opposite side from where the ice cream store is located. Tommy told her, "I think that's a good idea you parked this far away, and we walk way over there. We'll need to walk off that sugar on the way back." She replied, "That's what I was thinking. I feel like doing something different today. I have a good idea, let's go jogging after we eat ice cream, what do you think?" And Tommy is thinking 'hey, that's something we haven't done, we've never jogged together.' So, he answered, "Sounds good, where do you want to go jogging?" "We'll figure that out after we eat." They go get ice cream and they are laughing and having the time of their life. Licking and slurping on the ice cream Tommy is detuned to everything going on around him. But, he is very tuned into this sweet sugary treat, and the ice cream too. Wendy is giving him a little show with the way she is licking the ice cream. This reminds Tommy of the day at the pool when she teased him with the Popsicle. They finish licking, slurping and teasing, it's time to leave. On the way-out Wendy said, "This is my treat so go ahead of me and meet me outside, I'll be right there."

Tommy's waiting at the front door of the ice cream shop in the main hallway of the Mall. No longer than a half of a minute of him standing there she came out and asked him, "how's your running shoes today?" He answered, "they seem to be okay."

"OK, I feel like jogging now, so follow me big boy if you can keep up!" Wendy took off.

"Hey, wait for me speedy!" She went through the Mall and through the parking lot, she jumped in the van and beat him there. Tommy caught up to her gasping for air and asked, "I thought we were going for a jog, not a full Sprint?" Wendy replied, "get in the van and get us out of this parking lot then I have a little surprise for you."

They get to the edge of the parking lot and as Tommy was turning right, she told him that her adrenaline is rushing and asked him how his was. Tommy looks over at her and asked, "Is that your surprise that your adrenaline is rushing? Why is your adrenaline rushing?" Wendy looked at him and said, "It was my turn to treat you to a dine-and-dash, and guess what? You just dined-and-dashed! BANG big boy!" Tommy is in shock and at the same time thrilled! How can this be? I have the most beautiful woman on earth and by far the coolest!" Good job Wendy, that won 2000 points.

TOMMY AND WENDY GET SPECIAL NEWS

One day, Wendy and Tommy are taking a walk. After talking about jogging they actually go do it. They walk over to the park that has a small jogging track. Tommy and Wendy are having the time of their life jogging along. Wendy is slowing down, and Tommy slowed with her, he turned to her and asked her, "What's going on with you?" She replied, "I'm not sure I got a small cramp in my belly." So, they continued walking a bit. After she walks off the cramp they get back into jogging. They get back home and the day has been wonderful, so far. After a while of hanging around the house Wendy was hungry and craving something gumpy. So, they went to grab a burger at Billie's Burgers. They got there and ordered the usual. Tommy got a triple Burger with triple cheese, extra onions, tomatoes and lettuce. Wendy likes to keep it simple, she got a regular hamburger with cheese, ketchup and mustard.

They are eating, and Wendy stopped to say she had a small pain in her abdomen again. Tommy jokingly told her "I know what's going on here, and listen, I don't care if you have to fart, if you gotta fart just push it out!" She snickered and thought that was cute then reassured him that she does not have gas. The rest of meal was about cracking little jokes and Wendy making fun of him for how much he ate and him teasing her about incubating a fart that was about to blow-out.

Days later they are eating breakfast together at the waffle shop. She keeps staring at him and he senses this. He blurted out, "I can't help but to notice you staring at me. I get the fact that I am gorgeous, but we've been dating a long time, and I can't believe you just now recognized how beautiful I am."

"Normally this would've got a giggle out of her but this time she didn't laugh. She kept staring at him. He looked into her eyes, he could see through them like there was a Hollow Forrest in the middle of her head. Then he realized something is bothering her. "Did I do something to make you mad?" She replied, "Not at all, I don't know how to feel about what's going on."

 "What happened? I'm uncertain what it could be because I'm not aware of anything wrong? Since we're on the subject tell me what you're feeling."

She sat there very reluctant to talk but did and got the courage up to inform him, "I'm late."

"Where were you supposed to be that you missed an appointment for?"

"I wasn't going anywhere Tommy."

"If you're not going anywhere how can you be late for anything?" She came out and told him how it was, "Tommy, I am late for my period." Tommy is typically ready to joke but has no funny words to say suddenly. He knew by her demeanor she was telling the truth. With a shaky voice he asked her, "Are you talking about the same thing I think you are? You might be pregnant?" She responded with, "Of course that's what I mean! How much sperm do you think you could inject into my vagina before it made its way to my ovaries? I assume you thought having sex 300 times a week was nothing more than team practice for the big game!" They spent more time talking about this. Wendy clarified that she does not believe in abortions.

Tommy has never dealt with this type of situation. He does not know what to say and told her, "Wendy, I'm not ready to be a daddy, are you actually ready to be a mother?" She replied with "If that's what it takes then yes, that's what I'm going to do. If you don't want anything to do with this then you don't have to hang around!" He told her he didn't think it was a good idea for them to start a family when they have no way to support one. She asked him, "Are you going to run from this, or are you going to help and spend time with me in the event I might be pregnant?"

Tommy usually able to say whatever is on his mind, this time he couldn't say anything more than, "I don't like this situation or this conversation." He got up, didn't say goodbye and walked out of the restaurant. Still sitting there, Wendy kept staring at him walking out the door in disbelief. Several days go by and she is sure that she is pregnant. Wendy called Tommy over and over. She left many messages and he wouldn't return her phone calls. She's beside herself and very sad, half the time she's been crying the other half trying to figure out what do.

The fourth day after Tommy came up to her doorstep. She opened the door; they looked at each other and no comments were exchanged. After they stare at each other for a minute, he handed her a small white bag. She looked inside, and it's a pregnancy test. She had nothing to say and turned her back to him then walked in the house. He followed her in the door, she walked through bathroom door then turned around, looked at him, and told him, "I'll be out in a minute." Tommy is standing outside the door, it felt like 30 minutes but 10 minutes later she walked out with a ghostly stare on her face. Tommy is standing there with his knees shaking and he asked her, "Well, the answer is?" She handed him the stick, he looked at it and had no clue what the answer was and asked her again, "What does it mean?" She replied, "Its red." He asked her one more time, "Don't keep me in suspense what does that mean?"

"Red means you are a daddy, now my question to you is am I doing this alone?"

Tommy told her, "I'm not ready to be a daddy but I'm ready to be a husband! I had several days to think about this and without a doubt I love you enough to get married. That might not be obvious to you but what is obvious to me is that I can't live without you! You've become the only person I care for. If keeping that baby is important to you, then I will be a man and stand with you every step of the way and take care of this little person!" Then he reached out for her hands, so he could pull her to him. He gave her a big hug and told her he loved her. She walked him towards the front door and they went outside on the front porch where they've spent many evenings together. She told him that they better have a serious talk and make some plans.

Tommy had been thinking about this and told her, "What it sounds like is we have about eight months to get our act together. Somewhere In the mix of this I must get a real job. This week I will hunker down and start applying for jobs that pay enough to get us a decent home to live in and raise our child." And that started what would be the beginning of a new life for them.

TOMMY GETS A JOB

Tommy woke up one morning knowing there is a demand for him to make a serious life change. At that time economy was not booming. A job paying enough money for a home, baby, car, gas etc. needs to pay more than the laborer job or a job at a gas station pumping gas for minimum wage. And yes, back then pumping gas is an ordinary every day job.

Tommy ran to the corner store, put a quarter in the Newsstand and picked up the Daily Journal. Flipping through the job section it's evident he is not qualified for much. He didn't have any training or job skills. The only experience he had was a construction laborer which wouldn't pay enough to furnish a home. Frustration sets in from going through the paper because what's available doesn't pay enough and will require a degree or technical school.

Then he figured it might be useful if someone who has capabilities to find a job would help him get a job. He ended up at the unemployment office where he filled out an application and waited in line to meet with a caseworker. When he met the caseworker, she asked him how he felt about washing dishes in a restaurant. Tommy answered, "Sounds easy, how much does it pay?" When she told him how much he asked her to hold on a minute. He was calculating, a minute later he asked her how much she thought it will cost to get an apartment. She responded, "Not sure, depends on how nice an apartment you prefer, how many bedrooms you want and so forth."

"Do you know if I can get a nice apartment for around $400 a month?"

"Not a chance. You might get a camper in a trailer park." "I probably won't be washing dishes then. I have a pregnant woman I need to marry soon, and we have to get a home. If I can't get an apartment for $400 a month, I can't work a job only paying $600 a month. What type of jobs pay $1,500 a month or more?" Her reply, "The ones you went to college for, at least two to six years and got a degree specifically to do that field of employment. Otherwise why would someone pay you very much money if what you know is nothing?" She recommended he go to the job board and look at the listings to see what was available. There he could get an idea what jobs he wanted to apply for. He stepped over to the job board and studied the various jobs. Passing over the laborer jobs knowing a laborer will not pay much better than a dishwasher he looks at the various jobs. He knew he didn't qualify to be a master plumber, electrician or any of the trade skills. He spotted the engineering section, "Wow, look at those jobs!" A newly established factory in town is hiring starting out at $2,500 a month. He stirs on this and can't stop thinking how much money that is. Keep in mind this was back in the late 1970's. $2,500 was a very substantial amount of money to be making at that time.

Tommy went home and spent the rest of the evening sulking. Thinking to himself, 'Boy, I wonder what it takes to go to school and learn how to be an engineer? There's no chance I can go to school and have a job at the same time and make enough money to cover the cost of school and the expenses of a home. I already know we can't stay with my mom or her parents.'

These things are running through his mind. 'Dear God, what have I done now? What have I gotten myself into? How am I going to take care of this?'

A couple days go by and he's not making any progress. The only thing he can think of is this engineering job. Tommy got a phone book from the local library for a city 150 miles away. Then he called another engineering company out of town and asked to speak to one of the engineers. He pretended he was a potential customer. Tommy asked the guy on the phone to give him several reasons why he would want to hire them to design the next building for the company he's representing. When the man heard him mention designing a building, he asked Tommy what the number of square footage's the building will be. Tommy told him 250,000 square feet, having no clue what the heck that meant. The man at the engineering firm took him seriously and told him that size quote required several days of calculating. He mentioned to Tommy how they have an award-winning architect heading up their firm named Cam

Worthington. And that Mr. Worthington is honored with having many awards for the outstanding Architecture on one of the tallest buildings in New York City.

To summarize what took place here the man spoke enough engineer talk to inform Tommy on several aspects of engineering. Tommy was trying to learn something from the conversation and memorizing what he could. The man sent him sample sketches and drafts of their work.

A few days later Tommy got the stuff in the mail and didn't understand what the heck he was reading. He went to the library and got a few books on engineering to cross-reference the samples and see if he could learn something from them. He ended up going to the librarian and asked her if they had such a thing as a crash course book on engineering. Humored by his question she walked him to the section with related subject matter. As they were looking through a couple the books she mentioned that the University was close by there and had a complete library for engineering.

With that suggestion he went there, ultimately, he used the University and it became valuable to him. Tommy made time to study as many of the terminologies as he could cram in his mind. Now you might ask yourself why is he doing this? Is he getting ready to sign up for college to learn drafting or engineering? The answer is no; it is out of desperation. Tommy is dreaming of working with these engineers at the factory. He knew if he could talk the talk he had a slight chance of at least being considered.

He awoke the next day and with all the courage and might he had stirring in his body he went to the factory where they are hiring. Tommy walked in and filled out an application. Back then you went in person to fill out an application, there wasn't any internet yet and most people wouldn't have a resume unless they had years of work experience. On the application, he claimed he had a degree from that University that had the big library of architecture and engineering he was going to. Cunningly he had used the man's name that had the honorable awards from the engineering company that sent material to him. The name he mentioned was Cam Worthington. He said he was Mr. Worthingtons protégé, and worked with him for nearly two years as an understudy until he graduated. A few days later Tommy got a phone call and the HR department requested he come in for an interview. The thought of getting called was overwhelming and he couldn't believe this. For the next 2 days was pure excitement and joy in Tommy's mind from the thought of ever being considered. I mean how could he have done this? Did he really fill this form out in a manner that they believed him?

2 Days Later it's the morning for this interview. When Tommy got there, he's greeted by the chief engineer with a big smile and a very pleasant disposition. The man is extending the utmost respect to him.

"Hello, I am Mr. Cunningham." Tommy was nervous and was ready to shake this man's hand, when he reached out and their hands connected Tommy squeaked out a tiny little nervous fart. The man pretended that he never heard a thing. The engineer went on to tell him, "What a thrill to meet you. I saw your application and the thing that struck me the most and why I had to call you in for an interview is because you worked under Cam Worthington. Likewise, I was an understudy for him and I don't even need to call your references to find out what your qualifications are. Mr. Worthington is the top in the nation in our field, he is recognized nationally for his brilliance. With that said I don't need to interview you. I willingly congratulate you for the new position here at our firm. The next matter we need to examine will be your salary."

Tommy is shaking in his boots and shocked to death because he didn't foresee this and now he must talk sensibly about salary. Tommy has 2000 things going through his mind, every other thought was, 'Is this real?' Tommy told the man he didn't know what the job offered but he will take whatever the starting salary was. Mr. Cunningham said, "I would never insult you with a commencing salary, we merely pay

$2,500 to our engineers. With you being a protégé of Mr. Worthington, I wouldn't think to start you for any less than $3,000 a month."

Tommy felt like he was going to have a heart attack. He is squeezing his butt tight, it's flexing because it's about to blow another fart, he is literally sweating. He could tell it was evident his physical appearance looked bad. To cover up for is nervousness he told Mr. Cunningham that he had a bad experience the night before and that he went to a Mexican restaurant where he ate some beans with jalapenos that upset his stomach and he wasn't feeling very well. The man asked him, "What restaurant did you eat at?" Tommy replied, "The Taco Loco." The man grinned and by mere coincidence told Tommy, "You won't believe this, but I ate there a couple months ago and had a very similar problem, so I understand what you're going through."

What an excellent response, this was relieving the pressure of Tommy's fear. "I expect you can start next week? Here's a packet I need you to go through. It has instructions from HR department on our policies. I need you to read over this, sign the necessary papers and fill out the W-2 form. The day you start work bring this completed paperwork back with you."

"Thank you!"

Tommy cannot leave there soon enough. He got to the parking lot where his van is, he sat down in the driver's seat. After about 3 minutes of trying to gather his composure he is pinching himself, literally smacking himself in the face and kept asking himself, 'Did this really happen? How could this happen? I called an engineering firm to learn some dialogue about engineering, I use the man's name for reference and coincidental as this is, that's why I got this job! Is this a coincidence or is God working in my life some way? If so, thank you God!'

Hours later he is still vibrating with excitement. Later that evening after the good news he called Wendy up and told her to meet him at the L&M Factory parking lot. She wanted to know what the reason is for meeting in that parking lot. He told her there was something special going on in the parking lot, "don't worry why we are meeting, it's a surprise, so just be there in 1 hour." Tommy ran home and grabbed a sheet from his bed, went to the fridge and grabbed a pack of Bologna to make sandwiches, and of course, if you remember the sexy dam story you remember that is one of their favorites. He made a couple sandwiches, grabbed a bottle of his mother's wine, two wine glasses, and cut the baloney sandwiches up into little squares. Packed everything up, put it in his van then drove down to L&M engineering and Manufacturing Factory. When he got there, he threw the sheet on the ground under a tree, got the wine and sandwiches and set everything up like a picnic. Then he jumped back in his van and waited in a parking space.

Wendy pulled up and Parked beside him. She got out of the car, walked up to his van window and asked him, "What's the big surprise?" He got out of the van and grabbed her hand and walks her around the building to where the picnic is. She did not say anything and looked at it with total confusion. Looking at him like he's crazy she had to ask him, "This looks like a picnic, and if it is a picnic, why was someone having a picnic outside of this Factory? And why are we looking at it?" He replied, "I set this up for us, let's go sit on the sheet and relax a minute."

They went to the sheet and sat down. Tommy took a corkscrew, opened the wine then poured each of them a glass of wine. There's a silence for about 2 minutes as they are sipping this wine. He is very mysterious and was not talking. She had nothing to say either, she's waiting for him to bring out why they are having this late picnic in this odd place. Tommy is looking at her with a smirk, "What do you think of this place?"

"What do I think of this place? My opinion, it looks like a good place to manufacture things and might help our local economy, but I don't find it romantic. So, my question to you is, have you lost your mind?" His reply, "Maybe I did, I think you are on the right track."

"Then the next question I have for you is what am I on track for? That this place is not romantic?"

Tommy chuckled and said, "Exactly!" She was very unimpressed, "I don't think you have to bring me here to describe to me what is not romantic, and I already know this place is not high on the list of most romantic places for a date."

"Again, you're on the right track but not about the romantic thing."

"You mean it's a good place to manufacture things?"

"I think it might be, I don't know yet, I've never worked here so I can't answer that. But I might know soon." She is still looking at him like he is crazy and asked him, "Out with it! How is that?"

"Because I will be working here next week, and I will come home every night and be able to tell you what it's like." She is staring at him, the silence is killing both of them, and she had to ask, "What kind of joke are you pulling on me? Are you being serious?" He replied, "I am so serious I could burst! You will never believe what happened. That is what the picnic is about, so let me tell you." He told her the story how he contacted the people at the other engineering firm to figure out information and dialogue to talk the game for an interview. And how he got the interview, and after the interview how the guy hired him because of saying he worked for Mr. Worthington. He said, "There must be a God. There's absolutely no other way something like this could happen. I don't know the first thing about manufacturing and nothing about engineering. I have no idea what I will do when I show up here and won't know how to do my job. But, if I can get one week's pay at least I can use that money for gas to find another job." She is ecstatic about him getting a job but confused about all this engineering talk. She asked him, "What is your job here?" He replied, "I got a job as an engineer. Can you believe they didn't even ask for my credentials?"

"An engineering job, how on God's green earth can you be an engineer? This is where you tell me you're joking and that you're starting off sweeping the floors, and you hired as an engineer is a joke, right?" "Wendy I am not joking! I really got a job as an engineer here. As far-fetched as this sounds it's literally taking place. Here, look at this, it's my information packet from HR." He took the cork back out from the wine bottle and added more wine to both glasses and he said, "cheers." When it sunk into Wendy at that moment he honestly got a job that he did not qualify for, she added, "I propose a toast. I toast this day that we will be successful and prosperous all the days of our lives going forward, and God will bless and guide us to our destiny." They tapped the glasses together and took a sip of the wine. Before they got done drinking the wine, their lips were all over each other kissing right there outside the factory. I guess it was good for them the place was closed, nobody would have ever known they got nasty kissing on the factory property.

THE FIRST WEEK AT WORK

Tommy woke up that morning and jumped in the shower to wake up and get his eyes functioning. Next stop the kitchen, he ran hot water into a cup, scooped 3 tablespoons of instant coffee into the water and drank it. Hurried out to his and van he took off to the new job. This part of the story is where he gets transformed from a fun-loving dork to a powerhouse of geeky amazement.

 When he got to the factory, his first stop was the HR office. He was ready to introduce himself to the orientation coordinator but then he thought, 'Am I committing what could be white-collar fraud?' His nerves were overpowering his body and he was sweating from fear. Before going in he paced the door outside of the HR office. From his walking, the HR manager could hear his pants scraping outside the door. She had to go see what the noise was. She peeked her head outside the door and there he was,

Tommy, the guy who had no fear and never backed down from a challenge. Now he is face to face with the first phase of 'operation, big fat liar pants on fire,' and no way can he pass-off this lie!!

The lady asked him, "Can I help you, sir?" Tommy wasn't expecting her to peek out at him and was a Deer in headlights. His eyes are bulging, and his face looked like it was about to pop. She was intimidated by this wide-eyed crazy man staring at her and not saying a word, the lady backed up a step.

Tommy was so nervous he stuttered when trying to answer her. "I'm, I'm, ha-here t t to...." Now the lady thought maybe he was a Down syndrome man or maybe he had something wrong with him that caused a speech impediment. His demeanor of appearing to be retarded helped her relax. She opened up to him and said, "Its OK son. We won't hurt you. Are you with any special groups? Are you selling anything or seeking donations?" Tommy was confused and didn't understand what she was thinking. Why was she asking those odd questions, it made him stare at her even more? He is perspiring, and his forehead is moist. She reached out and put her hand on his shoulder and said. "Why don't you sit down a minute, I can get you a glass of water. Tell me, do you need help for a certain cause, are you lost, and is there a group or anyone else with you?" He finally got the nerve to talk. As he is speaking his voice was shaking, and he did the one thing he was famous for doing. "Ma'am, (There is a background noise -pfooft, he farted) my name is Tommy, I didn't mean to make that nasty noise, please excuse me a minute. I will be right back." Tommy did an about-face and walked back outside of the building.

He was out there debating whether to leave and not follow through with this fiasco. Talking to himself he's reminded that he has no future planned, and no hope of taking care of Wendy and a baby. And with Wendy on his mind he dug deep into his bag of courage and created a new power and did another about-face. On the way back in the building he told himself, 'this is nothing more than another day of life, I can make an ass of myself many ways. Too many times in life I made an ass of myself. I will have this as a video in my mind forever to tell my children about, and what a good story! So, what do I have to lose?'

Now he has a different point of view. He walked in the door and down the hall to the HR department. When he walked in the HR, there was the entire department of HR employees. The lady he previously spoke to first walked up and greeted him again and said, "Do you have any flyers or papers for us to read, to see how we can help you?" He replied "My name is Tommy as you already know. I was feeling sick a minute ago and couldn't talk. I am here to start work today as an engineer. Mr. Cunningham instructed me to report here first and start orientation."

The lady greeting him was star struck when she saw him. She immediately warmed up to him. "Oh yes, I have been expecting you. Mr. Cunningham has prepared me for your initial visit. He instructed me to show you around and take you to your office to meet your understudy and your Secretary where they're waiting." Tommy replied, "Understudy? Secretary?"

Here comes that anxious feeling again, talking to himself, 'and what on God's green earth am I doing here?'

To answer him about this understudy and secretary thing, she said, "Yes sir, he is starting you out with the top-level position. That comes with an understudy for you to train, and he helps you with design and blueprints. The secretary will help file and plan your appointments to keep you on schedule."

 Well, there it is Mr. Tommy, you are a full-blown big-time professional actor. You managed to get this company to hire you with no education, to pay you top salary, to provide someone smarter than you to teach, and a secretary to organize your brainless scam, unquestionably a story for ages to come. After the introductions, Tommy is sitting at his desk reading the employee manual and signing his life away to what will be the shortest work history of any crazy job scammer.

Right before lunch break the secretary stepped into Tommy's office and told him he had an engineer's meeting at 2:30. 'WHAT?!?!? Way to go, first day on the job and I am about to meet the devil!'

Tommy went to lunch, he is going insane, he has every physical problem and psychological scare a person could experience in a 4-hour period. He spent most of his lunch in the restroom liquidating last night's supper, yesterday's lunch and any future food that could pass through his digestive system.

After lunch, he is using every minute preparing his nerves for this so-called engineers' meeting. Talking aloud to himself, "What if they ask me to speak, what the heck am I going to say?" This is the most trying time Tommy has ever encountered.

 Its 2:30 and Tommy walked in the door to the meeting, there is a room full of people, not as many as Tommy was predicting. The room has a table with perfectly organized snack trays. There are several catering employees serving the snacks and needless to say, that's the best thing Tommy could have seen to relax his nerves. Men were lined up at a portable bar with a bartender serving mixed drinks.

Mr. Cunningham spotted Tommy showing up in the place and dashed over and caught him instantly. With total excitement in his voice, "Tommy, welcome! Come in and make yourself comfortable." Mr. Cunningham took him to the bar and snack table and convinced Tommy to eat a snack and have a drink. "Tommy this is our monthly meeting. Here we unwind and talk about the specific events we have encountered, we update each other on all our projects, the progress we made with each one, and brush up on our socializing skills." Tommy cannot believe what he is looking at. This is what the heck he signed up to do. After Mr. Cunningham had walked around the room with him and introduced him to the other engineers, it was time for Mr. Cunningham to start the meeting. The first subject they focused on was introducing Mr. Tommy boy. "Before we start our meeting I want to introduce our newest addition, everybody this is Tommy whom I give high respect. He was an understudy of Mr. Worthington which most of us have heard of and know to be a pioneer to our industry. I am pleased to report Tommy will be here working in our Design area where he will accompany some of your projects and help with projects that are backlogged."

Tommy is ready to get up and take off in case he was requested to speak. Mr. Cunningham moved on with the meeting and the rest of the hour was a breeze, thank goodness he wasn't asked to talk. Tommy sat back and took notes on every single word spoke. This really impressed Mr. Cunningham because he received that as Tommy taking the bull by the horns to grasp what projects the team was working on. The truth is Tommy was taking notes, so he could research what he knew nothing about. He could show up the next day with at least some kind of intelligence that would allow him to talk the talk and get by to the next episode. After the meeting, Mr. Cunningham requested Tommy go back to his office with him for a brief meeting. They are walking past all the other engineers' offices. Mr. Cunningham was walking with pride because he was with his new hot-shot top-dog engineer. They went into his office and sat down. Tommy is asking himself, 'is this where he interrogates me about what I know? Is this where he informs me he feels I am full of crap?' Mr. Cunningham told Tommy, "This is what I expect from you and no less." Tommy thought he knew where this was leading to and not predicting a good outcome. "Tommy, I want you to be comfortable working here. During your first quarter working here, I need you to work with as many of our Engineers as you can. Help them review their work, make sure they have reached the benchmarks and achieve specifications accurately. Make sure the blueprints are formatted correctly and meeting all measures for manufacturing. I put considerable thought to what project you should begin working on. With your background, I believe you will be an asset to our team working in development and auditing new projects. I felt that would be better than putting you in final design." This was a mouth full for Tommy. He stood up and gave an army salute and said, "Yes sir, you have my word I will do what it takes to be the best I can be." This statement he heard on an army recruiting commercial. Mr. Cunningham found that amusing and chuckled, then he said "Tommy, go to your office now, and your secretary will organize your daily work schedule." This is not how Tommy thought this meeting was going to end, but thank you, world, thank you Mr. Worthington whoever in the giant world of engineers you are!!

The following day Tommy came into work and greeted his secretary. She advised him he will start working with the Sears project. Tommy went in his office dumbfounded wondering what to do next. Sure enough, he didn't have to think long, this understudy to be mentored by him is knocking at the door. He went to the door, and the understudy said, "Good morning sir, my name is Elfred Dexter, I am your understudy and ready to start work, sir."

"Elfred Dexter?" Tommy started to laugh but caught himself before he made it obvious he was blown away by his understudy's name. "Umm, I like nicknames, it makes business more personal. Do you mind if I call you Elroy?"

"Yes, you may sir." Ok, here is Tommy with the understudy, and Tommy has no earthly clue what to do next. Elroy asked Tommy, "What would you like to start with sir?"

"We're expected to start with the Sears project." Elroy jumped right in and told Tommy that he previously went to the company meeting. "I was privileged to attend the initial team meeting. They did an overview of the project and outlined the define phase. I have a SIPOC and a Value-stream map available to examine." Tommy lights up with relief.

"Did you say SICLOPSE? A stream map? I presume you can show me what you have. Can you give your opinion, where do you suggest is the best place to begin?"

 "I didn't say SICLOPSE, I said SICOP, S-I-C-O-P, which you know what it stands for, S=Suppliers, I=Inputs, P=Process, O=Outputs and C= Customers."

"I knew that. I was testing you to determine if you were paying attention. Sounds like you already have information ready for us to look at?"

"Yes sir, when they were meeting about it I was intrigued! I took extensive notes because I have a slight bit of knowledge in mechanics and quite experienced with tools." Wow, Tommy is loving the way this guy was talking. He can tell this guy forgot more about engineering than he will learn in the next 2 years. "Well, don't let me stand in your way!" Tommy said with excitement. "What do you think is the first thing that we should do to be on track with the project?" Tommy asked Elroy in a way he was hoping to sound like a leader with exceptional expertise. That was his way of trying to trick the young rookie into justifying his abilities. Hopefully that would make him do the hard stuff. With a little luck, Elroy might know enough to keep things rolling along till something either went wrong or passed to the next job.

After Tommy prompted him to give his theory where to open the Sears project, Elroy proposed that the first thing should be for Tommy to have the design engineer submit drawings of the prototypes. Next, the industrial engineer needed to set up the testing for manufacturing layout. And last, the quality engineer needed to be on standby for testing final model and evaluation. Wow! ZOOOOM, this went right over Tommy's head. That amazed him. This guy had a mouth full of words and sure sounded like he knew what he was saying. This was too good to be true.

 Tommy was struggling to get this whole job situation. He asked Elroy where he was attending school and how long he went there to get an idea what this guy knew. If he figured out that Elroy had enough education, and it was sufficient, he could use Elroy's brains to bluff his way through the job, long enough to collect some good paychecks. Elroy went on to tell Tommy he was enrolled at TCTI, Tri-City Technical Institute. He told him that TCTI had a Library where he studied from time to time for specific reference books and it's open to the public. As Elroy was talking a bubble popped in Tommy's brain and thought, 'that library has engineering books with material pertaining to work.' If he could go there to cross reference work questions and get some knowledge, then he could act like he knew what the heck he was doing.

Later that night Tommy met with Wendy. They ate supper together and Tommy was quiet. Wendy is not used to Mr. Tommy being so quiet. Double checking to rule out the obvious, she asked him, "Are we about to hear something?" Tommy was in a daze and awoke from her question. He glanced at her like he's lost in space. Then he nodded his head and shrugged his shoulders motioning to her he didn't know. She asked again, "Are you uncertain? Is it about to explode or not?" He still has a stupid look, he returned the question back to her, "Is it about to explode?" She said "Yes, only a few times have I seen you this quiet. It's always been right before you ripped an earth quaking giant blast gassing rooms full of people into a frenzy that only Hitler could be jealous of! The only thing different is you are not squirming"

"Oh, I got watcha mean girl." He smiled, that was what he needed. "Wendy I was thinking, we will have a Baby in about 8 months, I am lucky to get this unusual opportunity to make a living and support us. As bad as it is for me to scam these people into giving me a job I feel this is no mistake. I show up for work and I am treated like a king. I do not deserve that but love it. I want to succeed!"

She answered, "I like what you are expressing but what can I do to help?" He replied, "Be patient. I discovered that I can go to school basically for free. All I need to do is go to the Tech school library and read engineering books. I can take the work home with me and look up the information and see if I can make sense of it. I want to keep the job as long as possible, if not at least till I learn a little and make a few bucks in the meantime."

So far Wendy is on board from what she's heard.

"This means we won't be able to spend our evenings together as often as we have been." Wendy said, "When we get married we will have the rest of our lives together, then we can spend our evenings together and look back at this and appreciate where we came from."

TOMMY'S LIBRARY ROUTINE BEGINS

Time to go study at the library. When he got to the library the first order of business was getting the

Librarian to help him find books that introduce him to engineering. She showed him the section for first-year students.

While he was talking to her, she mentioned a specific book to him, "Not very long ago a student in his second semester told me about a book he used that aided him exceedingly. This book here, he found it easy to learn from because it summarizes in straightforward terms the ABC's of engineering. I recommend you give it your first read."

Tommy had no indication where to start, he grabbed it, opened it and got busy. With a sponge like mind he put it into gear and read all he could. About 8 pages in the book he read the best news ever from this publication. The book informed students this, in a work sampling study they found that 60 percent of design engineers use their time engaged in technical work. The other 40 percent is social work, taking time to interact with the Manufacturing engineer and the Quality engineer.

 Meaning he could further pick the brains of these other engineers at work for information. Finding this information will help him get answers to detail he knows nothing about on projects. And the more answers he gets, the more he gets done. The more he gets done the easier it is for him to continue bluffing his way through this blessing of a job.

 Tommy spent the entire weekend from opening hours to closing cramming as much information in his mind that he could. He took notes on everything that was quick to understand and memorized everything he thought would help him sound intelligent.

He overheard students in the library talking about a new computer program called Visicalc. They said Scientists, accountants, business analysts and several occupations have been using it and now engineers use it. They said It was fast, and when you input numbers in columns it computed varieties of numbers and yielded accurate statistical analysis. He was curious how this played a role in engineering and wondered if it could help him. He walked up to them, and he inquired if they would allow him to sit in on the conversation while he got the low down.

 If you don't know, engineers love talking about technical details. They gladly went on to inform Tommy it takes the mathematical equation out of research by finding averages and statistical values. It saves you time from having to hand write and calculate the columns of data. The best part is it will cross reference the data from diagrams and charts. It stores the work till you are ready to add or subtract more data. Oh boy! This is getting better by the minute, there is a software program that does this mathematical analysis stuff for you!

For several weeks Tommy has spent grueling hours studying at the library. He is gleaming like the sun at work because he is getting by with no problems. He has bluffed his way through every situation.

 In the book 'The ABC's of engineering', it explained how engineers spend about 40 percent of their time socializing with other engineers. Tommy had it in his mind he was going to spend time visiting other engineers and use that 40 percent to learn. Every day he is out in the factory aiming for 40 percent, but he ends up spending about 60 percent socializing with the other engineers. He's in other office's and departments seeking information and picking the brains of the engineers. Several weeks of reading and asking questions he gets to the point he sounded intelligent about engineering terms. He kept hearing such good things about this Mr. Worthington person who got him this job even though he will never know. One day Tommy got to work and decided he is calling Mr. Worthington. He had to know more about this guy and wanted to pick his brain.

So, he looks up the number and dialed the phone. He is passed through to Mr. Worthington after he was on hold for what seemed like 30 minutes but was only 8. "Hello, this is Cam Worthington, how can I assist you?" Tommy's heart starts beating hard, and he almost hung up when suddenly he found a little courage and spoke.

"Mr. Worthington, I am employed by one of your competitors who has a great deal of respect for you. They idolize you and I am calling to see if you would consider sharing with me what you consider the reason for your success is." Mr. Worthington replied, "I am honored to hear this. I don't feel like I deserve any special praise. But, as a pioneer in engineering I will be glad to tell you what I've used as a guideline for good work ethics. In the early years of manufacturing a product people made a sample piece then tested the item from there. It should be after the production line finishes many pieces that you do any testing. Delivering a refined and close to a perfect product is the most important aspect. If you deliver defective products, it sets the customer back and cost the manufacturer money, depending on the size of the order it could cost millions of dollars. For me, it starts with defining what will have the highest impact, the best results, eliminating any risk of failure. Set objectives, understand the customers' expectations. Make sure to include all the people that play a role in the development of a product and involve employees from the top management all the way down the assembly line worker that box's the product.

It's important to have a team instead of each department doing its own job not knowing what is involved in the other departments. The next thing is gathering data to digest, so you have information to process when there is a costly defect and establish baselines. Use the data to streamline the quality so at the end of your project you can determine if there has been an improvement. When there is a failure or defect make a list of potential causes and prioritize them. Collect data! Perform an analysis to find each contribution to the problem, include testing, plotting charts and histograms. You need to identify a solution to the problem, do an experiment, create something, test it and improve it.

I study until I have determined the root cause; it is much faster to use a statistical analysis software program.

Chart your progress and monitor it so it doesn't veer off course! Simply put, it's about engaging in disciplined data collection and analysis, so you can refine a method of satisfying your client's demands. If your analysis is accurate, you will minimize wasted resources and maximize profits. This is what I undertake that other engineers and manufacturing facilities don't. I take pride working with this attitude, it's not about the paycheck you receive but the legacy you leave behind."

WOW! That is more than a mouth full of significant information! Humbly Tommy replied, "Mr. Worthington, I didn't know you until today, but I have heard of you and now I understand why you are so well spoken of. You didn't have to take this much time talking to me, but you did, and I want you to know you didn't waste your time. I look forward to pursuing your footprints." Tommy took excellent notes which would ultimately help him become a superstar in what later he will master. He is brimming with confidence above and beyond his previous expectations because now he knows the secret weapon, yes, grass hopper snatched the rock out of the Masters hand!

Later in the month the boss gave Tommy this project that was in limbo for over 3 weeks. Taking the bull by the horns he attacked it in a hurry. He knew it was best to look like he was on top of it before people start asking questions whether he knew what he was looking at.

Late at night he is at the University library studying and cross-referencing terms. Using his calculator, he is computing equations from illustrations out of the textbooks. Every day he completes the workload and finishes with good results. Between Elroy's advanced knowledge helping and schooling himself on engineering this job has become doable.

Tommy keeps in mind that Mr. Worthington handed him the key elements to be a great engineer. Mr. Worthington made it perfectly clear that gathering data is critical. After observing the student's conversation from the University talking about how

Visicalc is skillful at computing and analyzing data he knew it was time to go get it. He went and got the software for him and Elroy to learn how to use so they could implement it.

In the meantime, Tommy is done with the Sears project, he was spot on perfect with his first completed assignment. After much anticipation, Mr. Cunningham sent a notification to him on how he did. The Sears project turned out .0012 defects in 220,000 pieces produced, the lowest defects in several years working on Sears tools. He was congratulated on his work because it had no irregularities and a higher quality finish in the final product. That project was generating a high profit while receiving excellent evaluations from the customer.

By this time Elroy has a sincere liking to Tommy and every day he looks forward to being a routine part of working with him. Elroy is uncertain why, but he knows Tommy is a unique individual and wants to be a part of his unit as long as he can. While Elroy is spending nights at school studying, he has no clue he is helping Tommy learn as well. Tommy had Elroy bring his homework to work with him, so he could check his papers, but really, he is using it to learn from. Easy to do since Elroy is an honorable A++ student! Tommy figured he could double up by studying Elroy's school work on company time and took the office work with him to the Library to aid his path through this extraordinary job. Tommy picked up the new program called Visicalc and has no inkling how to use it. He invites Elroy to meet with him at lunch and presented it to him. "Elroy, I heard this new software program can be used in our platform of engineering. It will equate many columns of numbers and terms and calculate the data, that's all I know so far. I need you to check it out and tell me what you think."

Elroy takes the bull by the horns and plunged into it. He studies it and followed the tutorial on how to use it. As he is navigating through it he doesn't know it, but the reality, Tommy is his student. Paying close attention to Elroy, he is amazed how he navigates around the software and found it was much simpler to use than he expected and understands it. Around 30 minutes into this he took over and plays with numbers, he thinks this is a blast and ready to put this thing to work! He sent a memorandum asking Mr. Cunningham to authorize him to go through the plant and down the assembly area so he could meet with all the different departments. Mr. Cunningham doesn't know what Tommy is doing but sure whatever he is up to will be worthwhile for the company. Tommy got the approval he requested and deployed this new agenda of gathering employees and digging up statistical data to use in the Visicalc software.

TOMMY STARTS HIS PATH TO STARDOME

Tommy constantly reviewed in his mind everything Mr. Worthington told him. He went to work the following week determined to find out how to gather data. Tommy made his first trip down the assembly area to meet the Production Manager.

"Good morning Mr. Soloman, my name is Tommy. I am employed as one of the Engineers here. Can I conduct a business interview with you, so I can better understand how the manufacturing for our company works from your angle? I need you to provide me a brief description on what you do, what makes your department tick and which operations could we chart and store statistical information from." Elroy was happy to help, "Sure Tommy, I will be happy to assist you with your research, and it's nice to meet you. The manufacturing or production manager of any organization supervises the production workers and the production facility. That's me of course. Most production managers' report to the executive manager who outlines the directives for managing a production process. To be on target as production manager, I seek help and feedback from my production line supervisors and production line employees on how effective we are with our strategy.

I report success and failures of the strategy to the executive manager. What I struggle with the most is not having direct access to other departments, which forces me to use only information distributed to me from the production line managers. Usually, information is delayed and causes us to put out fires which never is desirable."

Tommy not having a clue what putting out fires means asked, "Put out fires? What goes on when you have a fire? Do you call the fire department?"

"No, putting out a fire means you might have to shut-down production due to a failure in the assembly line. In real terms, 'fighting a fire, putting out the fire,' the fire is the problem you're dealing with on the production floor, it's a system failure. True manufacturing standards shouldn't need constant coddling, adjusting, sorting, etc., which we get caught up in sometimes. It's quite easy to fall into a trap of applying Band-Aids to these situations.

No research is devoted to the root cause of the problem or a solution to fix it because poor performance has been accepted as normalcy. In the worst case, the production run is completed without formal process engineering protocols followed and enforced." Tommy interrupts him again, "To understand you better, there could be a more streamlined assembly if the engineers had a better understanding how the production line is working? If up-line knew how the product assembles moving down the production line at various points, it would save mistakes and time, did I say that right?"

"Well, somewhat. The company's quest for continuous improvement is eagerly sought, but commitment to the theory can often fail. Production needs can sometimes make rushed systems sound logical. But most often rushing through the engineering phase into production leads to broken molds and poorly maintained presses cause scrap and defective parts which end up reaching the customer." Tommy interrupts, "So broken molds could cause time to repair, time can be calculated data, right? Scrap parts are pieces which can be counted thus making data, right?"

"Yes, everything that happens good or bad has numbers of things to be counted, measured and calculated." Tommy is trying to keep up with this long-winded sophisticate and replies, "Can you repeat everything you just told me, please? ... Just kidding!"

"Tommy, for me the most important thing to remember is approach each problem right away as it happens. Evaluate each process and resolve issues based on their level of priority. Locating the problem with a situation you are facing should give you data to collect each time. Also, there is data to collect when you complete any cycle or process." Tommy is thinking to himself this guy is a long-winded man. He decided to put an end to his technical jibber jabber! "Thank you, sir, this was very educational but is there any chance you could repeat that? Just kidding again! You gave me a couple good ideas. Thank you for your time and we will meet again." He is a slight bit confused but feeling sharper by the minute and is grasping this and taking mental notes and memorizing all that he can. Next on the list is the Production Line supervisor. Tommy heads over to his office and walked in like he owns the building. "Hello Mr. Archer, my name is Tommy and I am one of the Engineers here, I would like to learn a little more about what you do here. Please take a few minutes and let me ask you a couple questions."

"Sure Tommy, I am always glad to help." "Could your position here at L&M be smoother if you had more help from upstream management? And what areas can we collect information from that have failures, cycle times or things that are measurable or have numbers that we can log for data? I need it so later we can use it to help find defects in our company's manufacturing process?" He answered, "I feel things work smoothly for me and rarely need much to make my work more productive. Let me tell you what I do here. Production line supervisors are the liaison between the production workers and the Production manager. Although the Production manager handles the entire manufacturing facility, the Production line supervisor manages only the Production, or assembly line where he is stationed. A Production line supervisor may handle multiple assembly lines within a certain Production. It's essential for the production manager to explain the manufacturing strategy to us production line supervisors. The production worker is at the bottom of the manufacturing organizational chart, they report to me. However, the worker is one of the most important pieces to the manufacturing strategy. They need to be trained properly and given proper tools to perform at peak levels and they must be efficient. They can be the reason for success or failure of the manufacturing process. I could have them collect data from factors such as how many pieces came through not packaged correctly, to the time associated in transporting pieces to the defective pile, to how many pieces pass through each day, to…" Tommy doing his regular jokester routine interrupted him, "OH great, do you mind repeating that for me one more time?" A bit perturbed Mr. Archer replied, "Honestly, I have some work to catch up on and..." Tommy cut him short, "I am just teasing! I understand, and you gave me a bunch of good ideas. Excellent job explaining what you do, and I will put in a good word for you." Tommy said that as if he has pull with the main guys in the company.

The next day Tommy went to work and headed straight to the production line to ask some of the workers questions. He figured out after talking to the workers, a majority of them had no indication what the average amount mistakes were. And no one knew what the average pieces were with defects or how much time it took to do a specific task. He created a large list to work with from meeting them. His mind was awaking, picture the Tasmanian devil spinning with an idea light bulb burning over his head and the light bulb is about to become a laser beam, That's Tommy here at this moment!

A couple days went by and Tommy is plotting and brainstorming with a fury. He has ideas that seem to make sense but not sure if he is right. The following day at work Tommy heads straight to Mr. Cunningham's office. He walked in and approached Mr. Cunningham's Secretary, "I need to see Mr. Cunningham please." She told him, "He is busy right now Tommy, is he expecting you?"

"No, but I need to see him." Mr. Cunningham is looking through the glass in his office and notices Tommy outside and motions at him through the glass to come in. Tommy points at Mr. Cunningham to the Secretary and walked towards him, she went to stop him and looked at her boss, he nodded as to say yes, it's O.K., then she let him go.

"Good morning Sir, sorry to bother you unexpected but I have to talk to you about an idea."

"No problem ever with you Tommy! How can I help you today?"

"It's not what you can do for me sir but what I can do for you!"

"Sounds good so far, what is it that you have in mind?" "Sir, is there any one thing that you are manufacturing right now that seems to be a coming out as a loss in any way? I mean is there a problem in one of our products that are causing problems and you just cannot seem to get it right?"

"Of course, we always seem to have one thing or another that causes us grief. Right now, we have three different items that are breaking even or losing money." Tommy liking that answer wanted to know what item is the one that's the most important.

"Sir if you do not mind I would like to know which one the biggest problem is?"

"Well Tommy I am not sure, where is this leading up to?" "I believe I can help straighten out some problems using some ideas I got from Mr. Worthington." Mr. Cunningham perked up!

"Mr. Worthington? What does he do that you want to try?" "I know his secret and I want to try it out here!" "Well, if Mr. Worthington accomplished anything I need to try it! Where do we start?" Tommy feeling powerful now advised him, "Set a meeting with the production manager, the production line managers and anyone else that knows what is going on with your most problematic projects!" Mr. Cunningham had his secretary request all the department heads in for a meeting. They went to the conference room and then it started, the beginning of when Tommy finds out how gifted he was. There was his original executive brain-storming meeting. No longer is Tommy the class clown, the jokester, the go-to-guy for a good time. He now is the go-to-guy for uncovering ways to make things better.

TOMMY DEVELOPED A METHOD FOR IMPROVING MANUFACTURING

Everyone is here and ready for this experimental meeting. Not one person has a clue why they are there, some people are nervous hoping it's not a meeting of bad news. Mr. Cunningham opens the meeting saying, "Hello team, sorry for the unexpected meeting. I want to introduce one of our Engineers, some of you have met him already, everyone this is Tommy. He is a protégé of Mr. Worthington whom most of us know is a pioneer in our industry and one of the only Engineers achieving the Nobel Prize in Physics."

WHAT? Tommy was blown away! He thought to himself, you're telling me this guy I have been using as my escape goat to get me this job is not only a superhero in the engineering world but a Nobel Prize winner? I would have never put that together? No wonder I get so much respect, they think I am an expert engineer or renowned for being the apprentice of Mr. Wonderful Nobel Prize guy.

Tommy stood up and nodded his head forward as if he was bowing to the audience. He then put into effect the first stage of what later he perfects as the world's standard for all kinds of businesses. To name a few, Manufacturing, Trucking companies, Hospitals, the

Military, N.A.S.A., Chemical refineries and so many more business models. Tommy starts out with, "I understand that there are several items we build that are losing money or barely break even. You are here to help us brainstorm and determine which of those items has the most importance to this company. We will start with voting by a show of hands which one that is."

Tommy is guiding them to the methodology aspect of what he is developing. After they voted he went on talking, "Next we will Define the problem and where there is an opportunity for improvement. We will have goals and make sure we understand the customer requirements. After that we are going to Analyze the process to determine root causes of what is making the item defective. The way I want to uncover this is we will start logging data at every stage of the process which later I will visit all of you to determine where that information will come from. When we discover what that is we will research what corrects the problem and monitor our work to make sure it is winning!" Mr. Cunningham is amazed by this 'take the bull by the horns' attitude and admires every minute of it. After they voted and narrowed it down to 2 different items Tommy asked them, "Which one of these two have least extent of risk with the greatest return factor?"

Wow! Tommy has no idea where this is coming from, but it undeniably is working well and there seems to be a strong buzz from what he is undertaking. They decide which item has the biggest bang for the buck then Tommy informed everyone soon he will be going down the assembly line and working with them. He made it clear that all departments and employees will be responsible for collecting data for him to use for finding mistakes.

After this meeting Mr. Cunningham held Tommy back so they can have their own talk. He told Tommy, "I don't know where you are leading with this, but I like it! You are one of our engineers, but it doesn't feel like you are. I don't think we use you properly and need to apply your talents to the better of this enterprise. I am not certain what to call your new position." Tommy asked, "What new position?" "I can't have you wasting your talents in the engineering department, I need you to concentrate in this new program you are launching. So, I am establishing a new position for you, I don't know what to call it yet. Tommy, if your efforts produce success and everything turns out the way it's looking, the product will have a better quality from eliminating defects and it will make money. So, the end result means better quality. Then Quality will be the name of our new department!" Tommy replied, "If what I am doing here makes money, the product improves and results in happy customers then the quality is not only the final product, but quality is the total process, right?"

"Yes, that makes sense."

"Then we'll call my new position the Quality process manager!"

"Perfect!" Mr. C. said.

"This is my first Quality project." Tommy replied.

Tommy told Mr. C. the meeting they just put on will be called the meeting of the brains, later referred to as Brain storming. So here things change, all this time He was sweating and beating himself up to pass off being an engineer. His calling was to manage something. He had no idea this is what he was meant to achieve. But, he knew if he adopted Mr. Worthington's strategy and applied the rule of calculating data this ultimately leads to something great. If not, he could just go back to pretending he was an engineer.

Next day, Tommy the new Quality process manager took off to the assembly line. Before he went there, he asked Elroy to help him or organize a spreadsheet. He told Elroy to list all the specific things included in the manufacturing process of Project X, the new project they voted in. He went down to the assembly line and studied it from the start to the end and took notes about everyone engaged and what they did. Later he returned to see what Elroy came up with. He looked at the sheet and it had everything from what materials they use, to what temperatures the ovens and cooling tanks are and how long machines take to do their job etc... Tommy took the spreadsheets down to all the workers. He told them they had to log the requested information linked to their part of the manufacturing process and provide ample statistics, log all issues, mistakes and problems.

Several weeks passed by, Tommy went back and picked up all the sheets leaving new ones for them to fill out. He took the sheets of data to Elroy, then he and Elroy applied the data into the Visicalc program. Looking at what the spreadsheet computed they were amazed, they clearly found answers. The program analyzed the data and formed a chart. Reviewing all the information it hit Tommy like a swarm of bee stings!!

He could see on the chart that dots are not spaced uniformly along the horizontal axis, there were dots on the scale opposite the group going another direction. Elroy pinpointed the dots that were separating off the scale were aligned at the baking stage in the manufacturing. They ran down to the oven and watched the worker for several hours. They made several adjustments. After several adjustments and calculating measurements they figured out exactly what was causing the defects. A few more times through the software program they could see more problems down the assembly line. They found a problem with the punch operators' timing. It was a few minutes delayed before it passed on to the next step. Then they noticed a delay in packaging because of the slow time receiving the items before going through to shipping. Wow! Several things are found, and this looks like we are ready for action! Tommy could not wait, he headed straight up to see Mr. C.! He popped in the secretary's office and said, "I need to see Mr. Cunningham please." She never tried to stop him she just gestured him onward knowing the boss would not have an issue with him just showing up. Tommy opens the door and stood there with a big smile on his face waiting to talk to Mr. C.

Mr. C is on the phone and told the person he was talking to, "Hey John, I have an important call coming in, I must take right now!" Click, the phone hangs up, "What I can do for you?" Tommy said, "Not what you can do for me but what I can do for you!"

He set down the chart and continued to show him on the dot plot graph how several dots varied slightly off to the left. In the beginning of the assembly line there was a time lapse in the baking stage of F unit.

"The Bake Operator is baking the item too long, it baked three minutes longer than needed, that warps the edge almost one/one thousandth over specs. This changed the ability to maintain its shape causing a defect. The excess time warps it making it scrap. So, it needs less time in the oven and that will eliminate the defects. And we know eliminating defects ends waste, scrap, returned items and without a doubt a financial loss.

Down the line you can see a timing issue. The punch operator's time to move the item from assembly line B to line C. It's longer than line C can wait to finish it. If you move the punch operators' machine back I am guessing around 20 feet, this should speed up quantity and reduce the time to the packaging department. Thus, getting the product to shipping faster and then to the retailer faster. We found errors in all these departments with our software. Correcting these issues will save money on man hours of labor, increasing delivery time putting funds in the bank faster."

"Tommy, you are a genius!" Mr. Cunningham got a hold of Mr. Solomon the production Manager and handed this resolution to him and told him to deploy the changes immediately, and Mr. Solomon did.

Six weeks passed by and Tommy went to get the new data sheets. He took them to his office, Elroy and he got busy, familiar with how to do it they input the data. When it came back on the chart, there, it was! The big whammy! What he was waiting to see! The graph showed a consistent improvement with no variables off course. That could only mean one thing,

Project X was almost complete, but more than likely problem solved. He headed right up to see Mr. C.

The secretary just shewed him in and never looked back. "Mr. Cunningham, I have great news."

 "So do I! You first Tommy."

"Here, in a graph, look at this chart. A constant baseline so far, looks like we fixed the problem!! What we need to do now is monitor this for several weeks, if nothing changes we are a success! Now, what do you want to tell me, sir?" "We made our first profit on that product this month. We began manufacturing it seven months ago. Look here at this P/L statement, it's in black and white!" Tommy's heart is pounding with excitement, thinking to himself, 'God this is too good to be true!'

TOMMY HAS A SERIOUS TALK WITH WENDY

The week end has come. Tommy has spent no time with Wendy lately since he has been so overwhelmed with this job. He met with Wendy and things are grim. Wendy doesn't have much to say to Tommy, she is quiet, and her body language is stiff. "I notice you are being distant, is something bothering you Wendy?"

"NO!"

"NO!? Wow you just yelled at me, do you realize you did, you yelled NO!?"

"Tommy, I do not want to argue, you are someone I do not even know anymore!" Tommy is in disbelief. She is the true love of his life acting this way. She is shutting him down as if he is a criminal who committed a crime against her. "Wendy, please tell me what's going on."

"Tommy, you never call me, we have not seen each other but 6 times in the last few months. That tells me you don't want to be with me anymore, I do not understand why you are here now."

"Whoa! Wait a minute! This is all wrong! You have the wrong idea, I have not been avoiding you. I have been going crazy trying to make something of myself, not for my benefit but ours! I would rather sit at home resting, sleeping in, and taking hikes in the mountains and going to concerts and... Well, I hope you get the idea?"

"No, if you were preparing anything for us you would include me in what you are doing." Tommy is not the most eloquent negotiator in relationship conversation. He takes a deep breath, reached his arms out to Wendy and gave her a hug. Resisting at first, her hormones are raging because she is around five months pregnant now, finally she gave in and they hug in silence for a minute.

"Wendy listen to me. I need to tell you what's going on, I had no time to stop and include you. In the beginning I asked you to remain patient, and you said you would and responded like you understood. I suppose I should have remained more in contact, but I felt like I was in a race against time. I needed to prove myself at work, so I could afford to be a father and a husband. Let me tell you what has transpired up till now. You already know I have no education and landed this job that no way I qualified for, true?"

"Yes Tommy, and I should not have to mention it, but, I stay worried wondering what went on!"

"So here is the story from beginning till now Wendy. I get in there and have no clue what to do, they give me this helper kind of guy. He is in school about to graduate and it was a miracle because I delegated duties to him. That relieved me from knowing what to do, he handled the work I had no clue how to do. I have a secretary, she lines up my work and schedules meetings. Then I follow through by working with Elroy, my assistant." Wendy interrupted, "Elroy? Is that a person's name? Who names their child Elroy, is he from the future? Is his last name Jetson?" They both give a little laugh as things are finally easing up a little. Wendy is paying close attention since she is being filled in on what she's been missing.

"His real name is Elfred, when he first told me his name I almost laughed at him, I didn't want to embarrass him. So, I held back laughing and had to think swiftly. I couldn't see myself calling him Elfred"

Wendy has to interrupt one more time, "El Fred, Elf Red, L-Fred?? Who names their child Elfred, the parents of a butler??" They chuckle again, and things are relaxed and back to normal.

"So just as foolish a name as that is, it's in my favor to state his name a way I could without laughing. So, I came up with Elroy because I knew it would be easier to not laugh at. I asked if I could use Elroy as a nickname for him and he answered OK. Enough of all that about his name, I have too much to tell but need to compile it, so it doesn't take very long. Elroy is a blessing! Anyway, during the night I've been going to the Library reading and reading, memorizing, learning the basics of what engineers do. Somewhere in the mix of this I discovered that networking, or essentially, connecting with the other engineers is one of the best practices to manage your work. So, I reached out to other people in the company to understand from them, but they assumed I was simply curious about the projects they were working on. In the meantime, I had this hunch to call the guy who worked at the company I called when I was looking for a job. Before I worked here I contacted this engineering company to get an idea what language they used to talk engineering terms. In the conversation, I remembered the person I spoke to, I mentioned this man's name. I used his name as my ex-boss on my application and it turns out he was the key to my employment. His name had so much respect and clout with L&M and the chief engineer. So, I called him because I needed to pick his intellect to see what he knew and what it was about him that everyone had so much respect for. The man took his time and shared his secrets to success; he explained it so plainly and I understood everything he said. I took notes and learned so much in a 20-minute phone call. I took it to heart. The next week I went around the Factory and got a better knowledge of what the entire process is. I guess it's not something all the engineers do or involve themselves in because later I used that information to get to another level. I put together a proposal using Mr. Worthington's illustration, he's the name I used to get this job. I went to Mr. Cunningham and presented this concept to him and he let me have my way with it. Then I went to see the significant people in the factory and gathered a multitude of information. I took this software program that calculates lists of data, later had Elroy help me run it and between the both of us we came up with several noticeable flaws in their manufacturing. I actually understood it as if I had this programmed in my brain! Crazy! So, the end result, is we saved the company money. What we did improved their manufacturing process in the assembly line C of the Gillette project. Mr. Cunningham promoted me to my very own one of a kind position. I am the Quality Process manager."

Wendy is staring at him in total disbelief. "Typically, I wouldn't believe you. But, you seem like somebody I never met before, you seem so knowledgeable and so much smarter than you were months ago. Not that you are not smart, I always knew you were the go-to-guy, but you seem so well versed in your speech and sound like you really know all this!"

"I will take that as a compliment!" Tommy replied.

NEXT STAGE FOR TOMMY AND WENDY

Tommy had his first Saturday off work in many weeks. He began the day going to the bank depositing his paycheck. While he is signing the deposit slip, the banker approached him and asked if he would like to open a CD to earn some interest. Tommy didn't feel he was ready for anything big concerning Banks. He told the banker it might be better to save up money first before he investigated any banking matters. The banker said, "You only need a thousand dollars, and I noticed your account has enough to buy a ten-thousand-dollar CD with plenty left over." Tommy is dumbfounded, he asked the banker, "What are you talking about?"

"Your account has little activity and more than enough money in it, if you do not buy a CD at least put the money in an interest-bearing savings or checking account." Suddenly Tommy has woke up to something. Several months have gone by and he has been depositing his paychecks but hasn't been spending anything. He went up to the counter to make his deposit, he asked for a statement and waited. The teller hands him his receipt and a statement. He looks at the balance and it has $14,376.00 in it. What the heck??? He is ecstatic! "I did not realize I had that much money."

What to do now? Tommy calculated what he had to work with and figured out the time has come, it's time to get married. He concocted a plan to propose marriage to Wendy. He got ahold of Eddy and they came up with a good plan to propose.

On the day he wants to propose he picked Wendy up and talked her into going for a walk in the park. They get to the park and Wendy told Tommy, "It's so nice to be with you." Well, Tommy took that as an opportunity to sing to her, you already know he is big on this stuff, so he sings a song by a group called Gallery. The song, 'It's so nice to be with you.' And here he sings, "Oh Wendy it's so nice to be with you too, I love all the things you say and do, and it's so nice to hear you say you're going to please me in every way, I got something that's real, I know it's going to last a lifetime..." By the time the singing was over they had walked several hundred yards. They came across a puppy tied to a tree. Wendy said, "Look! It's a puppy tied to a tree with a ribbon around it and there aren't any people around. Do you think it's abandoned?" Tommy replied, "Let's go investigate." They walk over to it and the puppy is wagging his tail hard and jumping up trying to get attention. "Look Tommy he wants us to pet him." Tommy replied, "Why don't you take that ribbon off of him, it looks uncomfortable." Wendy took the ribbon off and as it came off a piece of paper fell out that was wrapped up inside. Wendy picked it up and opened it, and a ring fell out. The paper had a small message on it and it read, I am a little slow to get this going and sorry for taking so long, but I am ready if you are, Wendy will you marry me? Wendy staring at it is undergoing a dizzy spell and almost fainted. As she wavers up and gets her thoughts together Tommy snatched the ring out of her hand, got on his knee and Proposed, "Please Wendy, will you marry me?"

"Oh God, yes, yes my crazy sweet guy, Yes." They kissed and kissed and the next thing you know Wendy pushed him away and asked, "How long did that poor dog have to be here by himself?" Tommy told her how before they left he gave the ring to Eddy, and while they were in route to the park he picked up the puppy. Eddy then put the note and the ring in the puppy's collar and watched hiding in the wooded area till they got there. Eddy then tied the dog to the tree on the trail he and Tommy previously picked out.

Then out of nowhere Eddy enters the trail with a boom box playing 'with this ring by the platters.'

 "With this ring I promise I'll always love you, always love you, with this ring I promise I'll always love you, always love you, they used to call me the wanderer, who never wanted to settle down... Yeah

But I'll tell you, baby,

I wander no more, got to stay around cause, with this ring I promise I'll always love you, always love you. With this ring I promise I'll always love you, always love you,

Got nothing but this old heart of mine Baby, please, believe in me, Girl, you know, sweet heart, I'll always try to keep you satisfied, cause, With this ring I promise I'll always love you, always love you, Baby, I never thought so much love, could fit in a little band of gold, But I'm telling you, darling I feel it in my heart, got it in my soul." Tommy and Wendy are slow dancing right there on the trail in the park. Wendy's face pressed up against his chest, tears streaming out dripping down his chest soaking his shirt. The couple melted into one becoming more connected and truly a momentous occasion.

BACK TO WORK

After the big proposal Tommy gets back to work. When he returns to work his secretary informed him Mr. Cunningham left a message for him to go to his office. At the appointed time Tommy went over to his office. He doesn't know what to expect, Mr. Cunningham is sitting at the other side of his desk with a complacent look on his face. Tommy is trying to figure out what's going on and he's wondering if Mr. Cunningham learned he is really not an engineer. Sitting there long enough he said, "Hello Mr. Cunningham, I got your message and I'm here to see what you need." Mr. Cunningham still sitting there not doing anything, he throws his index finger up telling him to hold on a minute. He keeps pondering in deep thought. The guilt of lying about being an engineer is constantly haunting him. Tommy is not prepared for this, he is assuming the worst. And as you know by now he has trouble with pressure when he gets nervous. What's going on is Tommy's butt wants to play music, and by that, I mean gas escaping through the lower canal sounding like a trumpet when air passes through it. He's holding back, the pressure is building up, his forehead becomes moist and sure enough his butt blasts, out came the sound of an explosion. Tommy is looking at Mr. Cunningham who was staring straight back, and harder now that the sudden unexpected distraction happened that is not proper for an office meeting. Tommy was trying to keep a straight face. He told Mr. Cunningham, "I'm sorry sir, I did not mean to do that. I apologize, but as a part of this apology it's necessary that I leave the room for around 10 minutes, if you don't mind can we reschedule this for 10 minutes from now, sir?"

Mr. Cunningham is trying not to laugh. He is holding back from any facial emotions and told Tommy "Please, feel free to come back in 10 minutes." Tommy gets up, runs straight to the bathroom. Apparently, part of the air that came out had some liquid as well. This is better known as a shart. He sharted, for anyone who doesn't know what that is, sharted is the word Sh_ _ (poop) and farted mixed together. Sorry if that's too descriptive.

Tommy cleaned himself up then went back to the office. Mr. Cunningham has a flush red tone on his face because when Tommy left he was laughing uncontrollably. What happened, when Tommy had this little sharting accident, Mr. Cunningham's secretary turned and looked when she heard the blast and could see Mr. Cunningham through the door. She was turning red from suppressing her laughter. When Mr. C saw her holding back her laughter, it gave him the bug to laugh. He waited till Tommy left so he could bust out laughing and between him and the secretary they laughed so hard they had tears coming out of their eyes.

I guess that shows Mr. Cunningham has a human side to him.

Mr. Cunningham eventually calmed down and Tommy came back in and sat down, and Mr. C. was able to talk. "Tommy, I don't think we should use you as an engineer here." Tommy is sick to his stomach. He already sees this conversation going towards him being fired. He replied to Mr. Cunningham and said, "I'm very sorry sir, I actually anticipated this and knew this day was coming."

Mr. Cunningham told Tommy, "I'm sure you saw this coming since your talent extends above and beyond what we expected from you. That's the reason we would like you to head up a department specifically designed for managing Quality instead being a Quality process manager. Your new job will be to oversee the entire Factory and you will have an assistant who becomes the Quality process manager. In the short time you've been here you found and eliminated defects that we've never uncovered before. The way you did this was brilliant. So, with this said, Tommy I hope you accept this position and it will come with a pay raise. Now Tommy, the rest is up to you, tell me what you want to do." Tommy can't believe this! He's about to have another sharting attack, holding back confused and baffled over this mysterious moment. Tommy looked at Mr. Cunningham and told him, "Sir, I wasn't expecting this and it's actually opposite what I thought you would say to me. Either way, I feel very honored that you would even consider me as the person you would rely on to manage this company at that level. I hope I can achieve whatever goals you have set aside for me. One thing I insist upon, I have to have Elfred be the Quality process manager!"

"Not a problem Tommy, you are the boss in that department, hire Elfred as your assistant."

The following day Tommy was in the office and slightly disorientated. He's not sure how to put this ball in motion or where to start this new high paying job he doesn't qualify for. So, he called Elroy in. They sit down and have a business talk. Tommy explained to Elroy that he's moving to a new department and as part of the move he wanted Elroy to follow with him. He let Elroy know he has a lot to do with the amount of success he had up to this point. Little did Elroy or anyone else in the company know that Elroy is the power force behind Tommy's development. After Tommy explained to Elroy what they would be doing Elroy was glistening with excitement. From everything Tommy could gather he has the authority to give Elroy a raise and proposed this to him. The raise sweetened the deal and got the ball rolling. This began the partnership of two guys implementing the first strategical process improvements for the world of business, Manufacturing, in corporations and many businesses.

TOMMY FURTHERS HIS EDUCATION

Tommy went back to the manufacturing area and questioned the people in management positions further. When he was finished, he felt confident he understood what the manufacturing process is. But, something rang a bell in his mind, he needs to make another phone call to the master who gave him the job opportunity at this big company in the first place. He is in his office with the door locked calling his good old buddy Mr. Worthington. When Mr. Worthington answered the phone, Tommy introduced himself as the gentleman who recently talked to him about his achievement in Engineering and work strategy.

"I took notes during our conversation. What little you told me I took to heart, and I adopted your approach." He then he acknowledged Mr. Worthington because the talk helped him with a promotion, from a Quality process manager to the executive of Quality over all. Tommy asked Mr. Worthington if he could champion him further with more success secrets. If so, any suggestions for helping a manufacturing company increase profitability and how to have an efficient management strategy as the head of Quality.

Mr. Worthington gladly enlightened him again. Tommy was taking notes like he was chiseling commandments etched into stone.

 "Tommy, it's so nice for the opportunity to help sharpen the wits of a fellow professional seeking higher standards. Let's open with the correct terminology of what you will be doing. What I call it is continuous improvement. Your goal is constantly improving products and processes without ceasing. Continuous improvement, referred to by the Japanese term kaizen is the most significant rule in manufacturing. It should establish the principle of your operation. Without continuous improvement your progress will fail. As the name suggests, continuous improvement promotes constant development toward accomplishment of a needed resolution. The transformations can be big or small but must lend itself toward improvement, often many small changes are involved to achieve the objective. The process is continuous because there is always room for improvement. Continuous Improvement should be a mind-set throughout your whole organization. Do not get caught up in only seeking to find the big ideas. Small ideas will often lead to big improvements. Manage toward perfection so that the number of steps, the amount of time and information needed to serve the customer continuously decline." Mr. Worthington had a feeling about this guy on the other end of the phone. He knew Tommy made these phone calls because he would be the one carry on his legendary creation. Mr. Worthington made time to educate Tommy with complete understanding how to make this happen. He gave many examples how and where to find data. He outlined where to start defining what projects to tackle and how to do experiments to make sure the correction would result in continuous improvements. Every time he gave Tommy the next step to do in each phase, he asked Tommy to repeat back what was said to assure he got it.

After this final conquest to pick the brain and learn Mr. Worthington's success was done, Tommy took off and never looked back. This is the breaking point to what the final part of this story is about. Tommy is ready to uncap the depth of his brain. He spent his whole life being the class clown, the jokester, a butterball of love and a spark of energy full of all life has to offer. The truth is, Tommy's almost a genius, his development was delayed because the life he was living and from the type of people he co-existed with that hindered him from using his intellect. He never asserted himself to focus at a higher rate. When Elroy used the software to digest the numbers, it demonstrated another dimension in Tommy's brain, and awoke a beast inside his mind.

TIME TO FIND A NEST

Wendy is about 6 months pregnant. Time is coming soon when they will tie the big knot. Tommy is consumed with his work career and getting ready to make a life with his true love. They need to get things in order before the wedding.

The couple went out looking for potential nest homes to start their new endeavor of a family. They are driving around where they think they prefer to live. They called on a house with a sign in the yard that looked perfect. The Agent picked up and answered,

"Greene Realtors, my name is Cleetus how may I help you?" Wendy has a slight chuckle when she hears his name. She told him she is calling on the house for sale and believes it will be a good starter home and wanted to see it. They make an appointment and show up. After they make their introductions with the Realtor they go look inside. When they were done viewing the property, they went to the agent's office to discuss what the details are for buying the house. Being a new buyer Tommy wanted to know if there was anything else they should know about the property. Cleetus was the original listing agent and had all the information about the seller. He told them, "Well, there is one thing, the man who owned the house died in the master bedroom."

"Oh, hopefully in his sleep?"

"No, his wife murdered him. But don't worry, she is institutionalized, and you shouldn't worry about her coming back to start any trouble." No need to say it but that was a bit too yucky to go any further.

A couple days later Cleetus called Wendy, and maybe it was an attempt to redeem himself. He drove by a house for sale, the sign said open house. He thought it looked to be a good fit for them and said they should drive by and check it out.

So, they did. They arrive, and the open house is jam-packed with people. The couple admires the house's architecture, loves the layout and upgrades and they are getting excited about this house. They never been to an open house before, there was a decadent catering company on site and a group of elegantly dressed buyers. They give Cleetus a round of praise, "Good job! This might be the one!" As they are piling caviar onto their plates and sipping champagne, a woman who they presumably figure is the listing agent was roaming the house shaking everyone's hand. She made her way over and introduced herself to them. They tell her, "This is a lovely home. Please tell the seller we are very impressed," to which she responds, "Um, who are you?"

"We're here for the open house," replied Tommy. "This is an open house indeed.... for my friends and family. I am the new owner if you look at the for sale sign it has a sold tag on it." Embarrassed beyond belief, they put down their plates. Tommy asked the lady, "We stand here embarrassed because we thought this was a house for sale that our Agent told us about, needless to say, we should leave, do you mind if we finish eating what we piled on these plates?" The lady just stood there staring and had no reply, He told her, "Enough said." And the two just slithered out.

Wendy has taken over shopping, looking in the paper, back then there was no internet or cell phone apps to shop with. She called on an advertisement that read– House for sale for only $2,000.00

She figured this was a misleading ad but curious she called on it. When the person answered Wendy said, "I see your ad for the house and I am sure there is a misprint but it's in an area where we've been shopping. Is that a down payment or is this a misprint missing a bunch of zeros or...?" The lady on the other end replied, "To be quite honest last week my husband of 15 years informed me he was divorcing me and leaving to go on a trip with his secretary whom he left me to go be with. He told me I could have all the Real estate we owned except the house we live in that's for sale as long as I help him sell it, and I thought that was fair enough."

Wendy asked, "How is he able to price it so cheap?" She replied, "Well after we discussed the terms he asked me to list the house and sell it while he was out of town. He never said what to price it for but to spite his cheating I am burning his butt on this deal. I doubt what I am doing is legal and it might cause me problems later, but I will make him pay one way or another!" Wendy told the lady she wasn't looking for any trouble and good luck with the outcome then hung up. She found another house and called to see if it would be a workable home. The Agent answered, "Hello this is Bob, I am happy to assist you in the sale or purchase of your home, which one are you doing today?" Wow, what a mouth full Wendy thought. She told him, "I found a house in the Evening Post and wanted to know where it is, 2737 Luther Pine Street, is that far from Hwy 225 and loop 66?" No ma'am, it's about a 6-minute drive." Wendy thinking about the area and not sure if it's a bad neighborhood asked him, "Is that a bad place for crime or trouble?"

"Absolutely not, you will be OK there." Wendy informed him she would like to see it now and wouldn't be able to get there for about 20 minutes because she would have to walk there since she was without a car. The Realtor spoke out, "No! You shouldn't walk down there by yourself, you're a lady, that street is no place a lady should be by herself!"

"Uh, never mind, I think we better forget this, thank you, good bye Bob."

Another day goes by and Cleetus their first realtor called Wendy to tell her he found a house that he's sure she will like. Later that night Tommy picked her up, and they met him at the address.

It is dark outside, Cleetus told them to follow him in the door, they walk in and obviously it's dark inside. They are all feeling their way around, Cleetis assures them he has this and will get the lights on. He spends about a full minute looking around and finally felt his way into the living room and found the light switch. Lights come on, the place is nice but looked old. The walls were a deep tan, and the floors were solid oak wood. Back then wood floors were out of style and shag carpet was in style if you were keeping up with the Jones. Wendy feels right at home and Tommy just doesn't care. She looks in the Master bedroom and is innocent to what she seen. There is a set of 10-foot-long mirrors on the ceiling. "Why would people put mirrors on the ceiling?" Cleetus was in Real estate for a while and knew the answer. He told her, "I believe most people would use that to view themselves while in the process of creating what you are carrying in your belly?" Wendy stared at the mirrors with a puzzled look, yet an "oh yah, I get it" look. She turned to Tommy, he is smiling ear to ear because he got it right away. He said, "We will take this house!" The mirrors weren't the clinching reason to the sale because Wendy really wanted the house. This was the house they ended buying. Cleetis redeemed himself after a couple of not so good experiences.

FIRST COMES MARRIAGE

Fast forward, and here we go folks, now it's wedding bells and chapel time. As expected for Tommy and now including Wendy there will be the basic interesting things going on with their wedding. Marriage day comes around and Tommy is nervous. He gets to Wendy's mother's house where they decided to have the wedding because she has a very large backyard with a beautiful pool. Tommy stood outside and wouldn't come in.

Eddy greets him in the front yard and tried to get
him to come inside where most of the people are
already waiting. Tommy is so nervous he can't walk
in yet, he is about to turn around and leave then
Eddy grabbed him. He is so strong he is pulling
away telling Eddy he needs to go somewhere and
get a drink. Eddy is trying to reason with him,
"What the heck are you doing? Your future wife and
everyone else are in there waiting for you and it's
time to go in!" Tommy usually never afraid of
anything turned and walked towards his Van. Eddy
grabbed him and began wrestling him like a scene
out of a movie, some way they locked up and both
guys flip up in the air and land on their backs.
Laying on the ground both guys are looking straight
up at the sky. Eddy laughs and reminded Tommy of
the time when they used to wrestle after school.
One day they were both trying to win this one
match, and they were rolling around all over the
ground then smelled something nasty. They
realized they had dog poop all over them, but they

kept wrestling till the smell got so bad they called it off and a tie match.

Tommy finally lightened up and gave a little chuckle as he re-lived the dog poop match that forced them to run home and wash the smell off. This eased Tommy's mind a little, they got up off the ground, brushed off the dust and went inside. Everyone greets Tommy and now that he relaxed he is mingling. Here comes Wendy's cousin, he's the preacher. He indicated it was time for everyone to go outside and get a seat. The backyard was decorated very nice and looked like it was decorated professionally for some giant movie star. The preacher directed the bridesmaid and Tommy to go to the platform and stand where the best man is waiting. All of them are at the platform, Tommy and Eddy stood to the left and the bride's maids to the right of the preacher.

The platform was built 3 feet above and overlooked the swimming pool. People were talking, and it was intense. The music started playing and suddenly everyone stopped chatting. Wendy rounds the corner and you can see the front of her coming out of the house. She walked down through the middle of the seating with her Father bracing her arm. Father and daughter get to the front where Tommy, Eddy and the bridesmaids are standing with the preacher. The music stopped, and the preacher asked, "Who gives this woman to be wed?" Wendy's father said, "I do."

Then Wendy walked up the platform and stood opposite Tommy. She is staring at him with tears in her eyes. This made Tommy become nervous again, his legs wobbled and everyone in the seating section could see it. Wendy could hear something, and she looked down at Tommy's legs and seen his legs wobble. She sternly looked him in the eyes, and some way or another to him it felt as if she was scalding him. The look in her eyes told him she was displeased. It was more like she knew he was not sure about wanting to follow through with getting married and he knew it was time to stop the nervous wobbling.

He stiffened up his legs as strong as he could. The pressure from tensing up was so tight it made him do his famous nervous reaction, he blasted a huge rumbling fart and then complete silence!

Wendy lost it! She laughed and as she was laughing she did her famous embarrassing stunt. Her nose was wet with snot from the tears that she made a minute ago, then she blew a snot bubble out of her nose about 5 inches round, then Tommy laughed at the snot bubble. Eddy standing behind Tommy got a gasping whiff of the fart and started gasping for air, he began laughing then it was the entire group of wedding guests laughing, this went on several minutes. After the laughter settled down the preacher started talking. Thankfully for the couple the way the preacher orchestrated the wedding vows it was in a way they did not have to memorize a bunch of words. When the preacher got to the final wording he said, "Wendy, repeat after me, I Wendy take you Tommy to be my lawful wedded husband," Wendy was sure she's about to be done with this and said, "I Wendy take you Tommy to be my awful wedded husband…"

The guests laughed again and Wendy not sure why they were laughing realized what she said and was embarrassed. Tommy at that point was relaxed and finally having fun with this. When it was his turn to repeat the vows, he also said awful wedded wife to keep everything enjoyable.

Now the big ending. Preacher asked for the ring. Eddy on the lower step grabbed the ring out of his pocket, took a step up to hand the ring to Tommy and trips forward into Tommy who was not so stable footed on the platform. Eddy knocked Tommy into the preacher, the preacher grabs Wendy as he is falling backward and all three fell into the pool. Splash! What a mess! After they make their way back out of the pool they walk out to the front of the guests seating area and finished the wedding on the ground.

 Later that night they have the reception inside the big house where Wendy grew up. Tommy got loosened up and a bit tipsy, he decided he would stir up a little action. Grabbing Eddy, he sneaks back into Wendy's mother's room and convinces Eddy they should liven up the party. Next thing you know Tommy and Eddy come out and both are wearing dresses that they nabbed out of Wendy's mothers' closet. There they are, everyone speechless, what the heck is this? They started slow dancing together, and this was more like a bromance kind of thing, like a last dance of freedom because they would no longer have each other to go and raise hell whenever they wanted, and they sure wouldn't be hanging around any more like the good old days.

Here is where Wendy throws the bouquet, the only single women in the room was Tommy's Grandmother and the bridesmaid. Wendy is standing there looking at the old lady and the younger lady. She is a bit confused what to do; she knows Grandma won't need it and doesn't want to insult her by not asking her to stand up and try for a catch. Quizzing Tommy to see what he thinks is the right thing to do, "Tommy, do I ask your Grandma to join in? And should I try to throw this to your grandmother or Linda?"

"Why do you ask? Just throw it!" Grandma walked up and included herself before Wendy could ask. Wendy feels like this will be odd, she turns her back and gets ready to throw the bouquet. Before this awkward instance happens Tommy's Grandmother whispers into Linda's ear, "You know I am too old to get married, so when she throws it. You just reach out and catch it."

Wendy thinking it would be nice to give the old woman a thrill aims and throws the bouquet toward grandma and sure enough on target to the other side of her, in order to catch the flowers Linda has to jump a little past the other side of Grandma in her high heels, she slipped, it looked like a cartoon were the feet of the character spins and they don't move. Trying to avoid the Grandma, she is taking steps going nowhere then finally falls forward and lands on her face. No one caught the bouquet, and the reception continued to be full of crazy excitement. That concludes the wedding day.

THEN COMES BABY

Work continues and as time goes by Tommy is superb at his job, he's becoming well known for the quality improvements program he designed for the L&M company and what he is doing to help the manufacturing company increase profits with fewer defects and waste.

And for the home life the newlywed couple has the house fixed up very nice and comfortable. They have the baby's room ready and everything is good. The weekend rolls up and Tommy is just as content as he can be, his job is good, his wife is great, and their house is perfect not to mention his bedroom has mirrors on the ceiling. After supper Wendy complains her belly is aching, she thinks it must be gas because she feels like she must do number 2 and can't seem to get anything to happen. She's feeling backed up and constipated and made several trips to the restroom and a few attempts on the toilet to get rid of the bloating. She knows something is about to happen. After a few attempts she gives up, kicks back with Tommy watching his favorite movie called Saturday Night Fever with John Travolta.

Tommy gets up and starts dancing at the part when John Travolta is dancing across the stage in the movie. Travolta is dancing to Disco Inferno and the music is playing loud from the TV. He figured this will lighten up her mood and make her laugh a little. So, he's doing his version of John Travolta dancing wearing his tighty-whitey underwear. He is spinning around in the front of the TV and knows every move since he has it memorized from watching the movie so much. Making faces with his eyes crossed, he has his un-serious joker face while shaking his head wildly. Wendy's laughing and having a good time. After Tommy gets done dancing, she makes one more attempt towards the restroom and this time when she comes out of the restroom she walks over to Tommy and is breathing heavy and panting from nervousness and tells Tommy, "I just broke water over the toilet." Tommy thinking she's trying to tell a joke replied, "You mean wind?"

"No!"

Still trying to make a joke of what he thought was Wendy making a joke, he added, "You broke water, so I guess that made it easy to flush and you didn't have to use the handle." Wendy with a light red face is looking at him and giving him that stern look. One more time she told him, "I broke water, the water our baby was in!"

No, Tommy didn't get a smile from her, so he knew she was serious. Wendy said, "Pretty sure that means we need to go to the hospital." Tommy is no way near ready for this, respectively since he's in his tighty whities. He turned to her and asked, "Are you ready to go now?" And she responded, "Ready or not we need to go." Then Tommy answered, "Let me get dressed and I'll go get the car started." Tommy gets dressed, went outside, started the car, came back in and Wendy suggested, "you need to pack me a bag, I need underwear and socks and a comfortable shirt."

Tommy wasted no time, packed an overnight bag for Wendy, ran to the van, put the overnight bag in the trunk, jumped in and drives off. He gets several blocks from the freeway and as he's approaching the freeway, he realizes he is a in the van and there's no Wendy. He busted a U-turn in the street, went back, pulled up in the driveway and there's Wendy standing right there at the front door with her arms folded, her face even redder because now she's mad. Tommy runs up, grabs her by the arm, gently walks her over to the van and never said a word. Wendy never said a word either, obviously the stupidity of driving off without her was enough said.

Tommy drives off again, he's trying to talk to Wendy and keep her calm, and he has the music playing in the car, the music you hear on an elevator. Wendy is getting upset and yelled at him to shut off the retarded elevator music, she told him it felt like the music was burning her ears. Then Tommy is getting the fact she's cranky and quit talking. Steadily driving they finally approach the hospital and the first thing they saw when coming down the driveway at the Hospital is the emergency room, thank goodness it's the first place available when you pull in. Tommy runs to the passenger door, opens it, and Wendy can't get out of the car her belly was hurting too bad, so he tried to pick her up and carry her. Unmistakably, this would not happen, he couldn't lift her, it was too awkward, and she wasn't having anything to do with it.

Tommy ran up to the emergency room doors, nobody is standing there and no one's around that he could ask for help. There's an old man sitting in a wheelchair, Tommy yelled at him, "Hey, get up the old man," he's all frantic, "Mister, mister, I need you to stand up for a minute."

"What is it young man? Why do you want me to stand up?" Tommy yells at the old man again, "my baby is having a wife, hurry my babies having a wife." And the old man is baffled with Tommy's demeanor, but he gathered that Tommy is with a woman who is giving birth to a baby. Respectfully the old man stood up. Tommy grabs his wheelchair runs down to the van, and gently works her into the wheelchair and pushed her into the waiting area of the emergency room. They go straight up to the check in and he tells them the same thing he told the old man, "my baby's having a wife, she needs a doctor." They get to the delivery room and Tommy is becoming more nervous and Wendy became angrier the more nervous Tommy was, and this made her meaner and madder. The Doctor comes in and talks to them, he asked Wendy, "How far apart are your contractions?" Wendy replied, "I'm not sure but before we left the house it felt like it was every 20 minutes because I thought I had to poop and every time I went to the toilet nothing happened and then I broke water so I figured what I thought was poop coming was gas or the gas was contractions or something, but needless to say I broke water so I'm here." Then she gets on a stretcher and into the operating room. They gave her an IV then she relaxed.

The contractions are now 5 minutes apart and the doctor enters the room to wait it out with them. Contractions were down to the final wire and the doctor said it's time to push. Wendy starts pushing and nothing's happening. The Doctor told her this wasn't a problem. "When I tell you to push again give it all you have." Tom is standing right on the opposite side of the doctor watching all this and this time when the doctor said push Tommy said, "NO, don't," and the doctor said, "Yes, push, it's okay push!" Tommy said, "No you have to stop!" The doctor kept insisting, "No do not stop, it's okay!" Tommy more insistent, "No, Wendy you're pushing the wrong hole!" The doctor said, "No she's not, that happens sometimes!" Wendy is getting mad at Tommy because he's saying no, she screams at him "Why in the heck are you telling me to stop when the doctors trying to get me to deliver our baby?" Tommy tells her, "you're pushing on the wrong hole and what's going on is your starting to poop!" Wendy is embarrassed and doesn't know what to do but the doctor told her, "Don't stop pushing! It doesn't matter if that comes out we have a baby to deliver!"

So, number 2 comes out before number one, which number one is the baby, the nurse took the dookie elsewhere and suddenly the baby's head was crowning. Close to 15 minutes thereafter here comes precious little Athena. The doctor gave little Athena to Tommy first while they wiped the baby off. All Tommy could do is stare at her delicate little face. The first thing he recognized is that she has the prettiest baby lips and they look just like mommies. Less than 5 minutes into this you hear this little squeak from the baby. Tommy is proud with emotion and announced, "She has your lovely lips and my outrageous gas."

Tommy has a new problem. He drove up there in a van and now he needs a second-row seat. He must leave immediately because Wendy will be leaving tomorrow, and they need a place for the baby. Tommy took off and went car shopping. He didn't want to spend much time on this, so he went to the first car lot he found. He got out and was looking at the four door cars. He noticed this beauty, it's a green Ford LTD wagon. He went to look at it and this salesman walked up and asked, "Are you ready to take home a nice car today?" Tommy replied, "More than ready, I need it now!" The salesman asked, "Is that the car you like?" He said, Yes, it's roomy and has a nice color." The salesman said, "If you like that one then let me show a nicer one with an even better color."

"OK, where is it?"

"Follow me, it's at our lot across the street." They walk over there, and he showed Tommy this red Cadillac. "Here you go, this baby is more elegant, a better color and will have better resale value!" Tommy is flabbergasted. "WOW, that is nice. Can you make it ready right now, so I can drive it home?"

"No problem, you might want to go get your van and bring it over here while we get the Caddy ready." Off Tommy went across the street and got the van. He came back and did his paperwork and finalized the purchase of his new car. When he was leaving he noticed the sign across the street had a different name on it. The name on his bill of sale said 'Country Bob's Used Cars'. The sign across the street said 'Bestway Motors'. Tommy looked back as he was leaving and noticed those were two different car lots. The guy from Country Bob's snuck across the street and took Tommy off their lot and sold him a car. Damn car salesman, they need to get a job!

NEXT PHASE IS GETTING A BETTER JOB

Sometime has passed by and Tommy loves being a parent. He had no indication that having a child would make his heart so complete. He admits to himself over and over how in the beginning he didn't want this baby but realized he had to take care of her. Now that thought is trash and he felt bad for not knowing the tiny life he holds in his arms would be this great.

The first couple months the baby cry's and wakes up all night and the commotion that comes with the baby was more than he could stand. He was bitter for a short time. One night when Athena was about four months old she was screaming because she had somewhat of a stomach issue. Tommy was nerve wrecked from the screaming, he picked Athena up, shook her and yelled at her. Athena stopped crying instantly, then she glared at him with her little watery eyes full of tears. For some odd reason that little baby stared him straight in the eyes, and with her itty bitty little quivering lip puckered under she kept peering at him. Tommy couldn't figure out why she did this and to this day doesn't understand it, but about 10 seconds into this stare the baby broke out the biggest smile then reached out her arms to pull herself to him as if she needed to hug him. It confused Tommy how this little baby could smile at him after he was so terrible and yelled at her. Whatever it was it melted his heart, he realized how unjust he was for yelling at her; it wasn't her fault that she was sick. The fact that the little baby was forgiving and loving towards him after he was mean to her told him she adored him. From that day forward, they became inseparable. When he came home from work, the first thing he did was give her a hug and spend time together, she was the pride of his heart and the joy of his life.

So far as work is concerned Tommy is outstanding at eliminating problems and improving the process in the manufacturing for the company he works at. The progress the factory made is big news to other businesses. They see how the manufacturing company turned itself around from getting by into thriving. L and M is performing remarkably well to the extent they have become the number one manufacturing company in the region.

A CEO for an electronics company called Molorota Electronics got Tommy's office phone number where he worked and called him. The man left several messages for him asking Tommy to meet him for lunch. Tommy didn't know why this guy is seeking to meet with him, eventually he responded and made the lunch date, this is when the biggest change of events developed in his career and later in his life. The day of the meeting for this lunch date Tommy went to meet the man at the restaurant for lunch as agreed. Tommy went into the restaurant and has no idea who he is searching for. The hostess greeted Tommy, and he told her, "I am here to see Gavin Bobs." The hostess escorts him to the dinner table with the reservation that was made by Mr. Bobs.

Mr. Bob's wasn't there yet. Tommy is peering around this restaurant and realized he has never been in a restaurant this fancy. He's looking at the napkins, the way they were folded on the table looks like artwork or origami to him. Tommy notices the fish tank and he's watching the fish swim around the tank, it's mesmerizing him. He's checking out the waiters, they're very demure and formal like butlers for the Queen of England. Finding them humorous all he can think of is, it's time for English tea and that makes him to chuckle because they seem so tight, walking with their butts clinched together.

Finally, appearing from behind him he heard, "Hello, I am Gavin." Tommy stood up and shook his hand. After the introduction they sit down and have a lot of surface conversation. Finally, the waiter asked them what they would like to drink. Tommy was deciding to be modest and asked for water. Mr. Bobs said, "Tommy I prefer you order anything you want off this menu, I have an account set up here that I take care of once a month, anything on this menu is on me today, so please, order the finest meal and enjoy." Tommy said, "That's fine sir, thank you very much, then I'll have a tall glass of orange juice." As Tommy is sitting there looking across the table at this gentleman, he can't figure out what the reason for this is, so he broke out and asked the man, "Why are you taking me to lunch? I don't know you, what is it you want from me?" Mr. Bobs told him who he is, "I am the CEO of one the largest electronics companies in the world and news gets around in our community when something is going good for other manufacturing facilities. You are the news today. It's out that you are considered the main reason for the achievement in the factory you're employed with right now.

I know we use a very similar process in our electronics company like what you do for launching projects and eliminating waste. But what we don't know is how you've taken it to a different level. I know you developed a streamline process for continuous improvements and I know its superior to anything any business strategist or process analyst has developed to date. So, with that said we would like you to come work with us." Whew, Tommy is puzzled by this and he asked the man, "What do you know about me?" Gavin told Tommy, "like I said, in the manufacturing world it's a tight community and information travels around when another factory is performing well. It's not my role to steal secrets or the elite level employees from other companies but it is my place to make certain my company prosper. With that said, at this point I wish to offer you a position with my company and a generous offer to make sure that you think earnestly. I am ready to propose what I'm speaking about." He reached in and snatched a pen out of his shirt and he scribbled on a scrap of paper. He turned the paper and slid it across the dinner table and he said, "Tommy, this is what one month would pay you working with me, do we have a deal?" Tommy looked at it and then he looked Gavin back in the eyes and said, "Hey, this is obviously a joke and I'm not sure why you're carrying on with this, but I'm truly not amused."

Mr. Bob's grabbed the paper, put a plus symbol on it and adds an amount to it and said, "Does this appeal to you?" Tommy glanced at it and answered, "Listen mister I'm doing wonderful, I don't believe you because this is at least six months' worth of my salary that I earn now, why would you be interested in paying me that much money?" Mr. Bob's told him, "We put out a volume over 1000 times greater production than that of the company you're with now, we are a billion-dollar company, this is nothing more

than chicken feed to us and with the surplus money
we would produce from your Quality improvements
that would be invisible money for us! Again, my
intention is to grow the business and never quit till we
are the greatest manufacturer in the world. With your
guidance we can do this. I'll give you a few days to
think it over, in the meantime let's have a marvelous
dinner and get to know each other better." I will cut
through a bunch of jibber jabber talk and take you to
the point where Tommy's at home and spoke to his
wife about this, they've considered it, now Tommy
must decide. It's time to call Gavin bobs to find out
more details, the luncheon was nothing more than an
introductory conversation to get the ball rolling.

Tommy calls Mr. Bob's up and the number he called
was a Chicago number. Tommy doesn't think to put
two and two together that he's calling an out of state
number until he starts the phone call. He rings
through, gets ahold of Mr. Bobs and he spoke to him
about the position and what he required and other
specifics. This is when Tommy realized the company

is based out of Chicago Illinois. Tommy told Mr. Bobs right then that his family is stationary where he lives and he's not in the frame of mind to move out of state. Then he told him he was sorry, but he must decline the job and was very disappointed, respectively since he liked the notion of making a substantial salary.

The following day Mr. Bob's called Tommy, and he answers the phone somewhat inquisitive to hear Mr. Bob's is calling him back. Gavin told Tommy, "Listen to this, I found a way that we can do this, and you don't have to leave your home if you're willing to fly over here one day a week. I assume you'll be able to collect enough data to do your work and not have to be here all week and then you will stay home with your family as you prefer. I believe this will be a way for you to work with us."

WOW! Tommy is thinking, 'I cannot believe how much effort this man is putting into getting me to work with him, this must be a very serious gig here'. Tommy runs and tells Wendy, "You will not believe it, this man has found a way for me to work with him

and we don't have to move or uproot our home."
Wendy asked, "How's that possible?" Tommy replied,
"There's one catch, I have to fly there once a week and
that should not be a big deal if it's merely one day so
what do you think? Wendy, should I do this? This is
big money for us baby!"

Wendy replied, "I see no reason on Earth why you
shouldn't do this, it will put us into a position where
we can put Athena in a private school and continue to
build our household." The next day Tommy called Mr.
Bob's back and told him, "I'm on board, I can't wait to
get there and tackle important issues for you, my only
concern is I want to give my supervisor a one-month
notice since he has been more than helpful to me and
it's possible that might cause slight distress for him. It
will be somewhat tough also since we have become
very close over my time of employment there and I
have a great deal of respect for him. I expect you will
allow me at least 30 days to gather my composure and
bring this together." Mr. Bob's told Tommy, "That's
absolutely splendid, we'll have you set up here in

advance so when you do get here you will not have to struggle to uncover material for our projects. And by the way, I know you are such an excellent choice, when you informed me you wished to hand over a 30-day notification to your company that tells me you have integrity and will work out nicely here."

The following Monday morning Tommy got to work and carried out his first stop to Mr. Cunningham's office. He informed him the news of him withdrawing his employment status. They had a lengthy conversation and Mr. Cunningham is distraught. Tommy created a newness to this company, and they became fantastic friends over the short course of time Tommy was employed there. Mr. Cunningham told Tommy, "There comes a time in every individual's career when they move up to a higher degree, I wish we could have the same opportunity here that they have for you and I respect you making that choice."

Tommy gets to his office and he let his secretary know the same news and again the same situation with her, she is unhappy to see him go, they've become close with good work principles and a great work relation. Then Tommy calls Elroy in to inform him that he will be taking off. Elroy is not having anything to do with this, he cannot accept it, "Why are you leaving? I've watched you come in here and get this place to an extraordinary status and I feel like I have something to do with that. I sincerely feel you and I were a team!" Tommy could see how sincere he is and was feeling a bit sad, and by his reaction he admitted to Elroy that he certainly was one of the keys to his achievement there. And without a second thought Tommy looks at Elroy and challenged him, "How content are you with working here?" Elroy came back, "I love my work and I certainly loved it since you and I have been working together. Also, because we are successful with analyzing data, that made this a challenge every day, and it's been fun and educational. But, if you leave, I won't appreciate my job and it won't be fun working here anymore. I can barely imagine how it will be, back to the same grind it was before you showed up here and back to boring." Then

Tommy asked him, "What if I could get you a job where I'm going with a considerably larger salary increase, is that something you'd be interested in?" Elroy replied, "Without a doubt! I'm a single guy, I have nothing else going on in my life except for climbing the company ladder and building my career."

They resumed their workday, at lunchtime Tommy's first order of business is to make a phone call to Gavin Bobs. When Mr. Bobs answered the phone Tommy greeted him with, "Hello, boss, this is your new process improvement leader." He is happy to hear from Tommy and eager to know what the purpose of the phone call was. "Gavin, I have a minor problem, I hope you give me a chance to explain. My assistant from the company I'm working with now is the person I consider essentially responsible for my success here. He is the guy who has helped awaken the beast inside of me that strengthens my abilities and empowered my accomplishments. I don't feel I can achieve much without him. He's my colleague, and he's remarkably sharp, together he and I are a dynamite package. I am prepared to give up a percentage of my salary if you'd be willing to hire him." Mr. Bob's replied, "Allow me a day to ponder on this while I consult my upper administration. I will get back to you after I determine what we can work out."

The following day at work after lunch he receives a phone call from Mr. Bobs. Tommy is excited to hear from him and can't wait to find out what his answer is going to be. Mr. Bobs told Tommy, "You have a giant green light followed by a little yellow light. What I need to convey to you is, the green light is we will accept your proposition to bring in your associate here, but the yellow light condition is we have to look at good numbers within the initial 6 months to support this."

Tommy was more than thrilled to find out this out, he expressed to Mr. Bobs, "For whatever reason I know this is meant to be, there's no chance you'll regret this, and you won't be disappointed. See you in a few weeks."

At the end of the workday Tommy called for Elroy to drop in his office. Elroy wanders in his normal character, a particularly calm natured guy and he said, "Hey Tommy, what's up?" Tommy came back with, "Take a minute and sit down. Elroy, let me ask you something, how do you feel about giving your notice of leaving here to go to another job?" Elroy looks at him with a bewildered expression and asked him, "Are you saying you got me a job with you at that other company you're moving to?" Tommy's reply, "Done deal!" That ends the L&M job and sets up the course for these guys to build new and better business processes that pave the path to industry standards.

TOMMY TAKES THE WORLD BY STORM

Tommy and Elroy show up to the big company, the magnificent Molorota. They are greeted by the management team as if they were celebrities. They go in their office and it does not look like a real office because everything they see makes this place look like a plush palace or a prop in a movie. The office walls are an elegant solid Bearlwood. It includes a refrigerator stocked with soft drinks and snacks. It also has an espresso bar and a restroom with Brass fixtures. The first day is orientation. Starting with learning the company policies, taking a tour of the facility and viewing the company's manufacturing facility. First, they meet the primary people they will correspond with and then the management staff. They stay another day to get paperwork squared away, receive files and then to brainstorm with the management team. They familiarize themselves with the engineer's projects and what obstacles the company needs to overcome.

After they finish identifying the priority projects, they go back home and devote the rest of the week to researching and understanding the information they acquired. They spend endless hours each day working

over the projects. The following week they go back to
Molorota and have a powerful first-time meeting with
the team leaders. They go back and forth asking
questions and getting details. In the meantime, they
find out that Molorota is adopting a different
analytical software program. It's a more powerful
scientific software version of what Tommy and Elroy
learned with. This one will analyze with greater
accuracy and equates deviations to .0001 parts per
million where the other program they used
couldn't produce a result that precise.

Tommy and Elroy are accustomed to using analytical
software, but that one they were using was no way
near as complicated, the new program is a myriad
greater in complexity. The program they were using
digests data and creates graphs but involves a
different foundation. So, this will be challenging to
learn but these guys are pumped and ready!

They get the software and learn its functions. With a
6.4 defects per million goal they use their sharp-
witted intelligence and ability to analyze data and they

jump right in finding defects to make improvements! They stay busy working on the problems. After several months between these two geniuses they've mastered the software and figured out something new, if they went three more deviations in the bell curve the graphs displayed a higher level of accuracy and an almost flawless equation every time. By going an extra step from 3 deviations to 6 deviations they discovered a more consistent P value and the Sigma level increased while the defects decreased.

In the beginning, using data and analytical programs to find defects was called Sigma, meaning standard deviations. When Sigma started the standard number for finding deviations was 3.4. After Tommy mastered the software he changed the 3.4 to 6 deviations. Because they changed it to 6, they coined the phrase 'Six Sigma' which later became the standard terminology for using Sigma in Quality and Process improvements.

The 32-bit microprocessor that Molorota manufactured became so reliable from using six sigma that it had zero defects. All the big enterprises such as Atari, Hewlett-Packard, Apple and many more are now using specifically and only Molorota microprocessors. During this time the Molorota pagers are developing into the phenomenon for communication. You would be dining in a restaurant hearing these things beeping or your kid would be at school and you could send a code with specific digits meaning something that only you two knew what it meant. For all the younger people who never seen or heard of a pager, a pager was about 4"by 4" in the shape a square. People would send a signal with their return phone number, it beeped several times, displayed the number sending the signal then the recipient owning the pager knew they had to call you back. People are using these for business, personal use, drug dealings.... The lousy thing with the pager was you never knew who was calling you unless it was a number you already recognized. I am only describing this because I recognized some people reading this may not have ever seen one.

Tommy learned that the company had a prototype on hold for a handheld mobile phone and he wondered why they weren't producing these. At one of the meetings he proposed the idea of including this as a modern standard for communication alongside of the pagers they were manufacturing. They ultimately went with the idea and within a couple years they developed it. They made the first commercial Digital radio system that could bind paging data and Cellular Communications with voice dispatch in a single radio network and handset, meaning, the introduction to Cellular phones.

When Tommy and Elroy first went to work at Molorota, Molorota was working on microprocessors and doing well. But, after they came up with the Six Sigma method Molorota became exponentially profitable. When they documented the impact on the results of using 6 Sigma they became the top sought-after company to learn from in manufacturing improvements and Quality control. No need to say it but Tommy and Elroy are also the top improvement problem solvers other companies seek. Working at Molorota put Tommy on the map. He was becoming rather prominent in the manufacturing improvements world because there was always an analyzing step to finding problems, but he and Elroy perfected the way to analyze the data and a step by step method to refine it. The word went around to any type of industry that could use Tommy's program. Many companies are adapting this method but have yet to understand it in detail. Tommy's big claim to fame was he came up with a procedure that before any project was considered there would be a gathering of many people in the company to have a meeting that could add important problems to solve, now referred to as Brainstorming. It varied from the assembly line worker, up to the managers thus covering every area to find problems. He instructed everyone to record data in these meetings. All the departments would start the week with a brainstorming meeting which he referred to as defining a project to work on. Tommy outlined in his handbook of rules a method, he called it a top-down solution by number. In this exact order is what he came up with first.

1. Adjusting the procedure for critical Recovery efforts, 2. Organize teams to attack high-impact projects and using accurate data to decrease variations in the manufacturing processes.

3. Speed up the corrected manufacture results and manage their resolutions till corrected results are continued. Ultimately, this developed into what's called the D.M.A.I.C. methodology which stood for Define, Measure, Analyze, Improve, and Control, a 5-step method. Molorota manufactured so many things, Laser Printers, games, computers, integrated circuit boards and had a factory in Japan manufacturing TVs. The 6-sigma was instituted in every aspect of their manufacturing to the pointless than 5% of all the manufactured products had any defects. They were

the world's most watched and envied manufacturer at that time because they were continuously winning awards for outstanding quality. Essentially, most of the other manufacturers in the world were watching to see what their next big quality achievement would be. The corporate office had to request Tommy's expertise at their Branch in Japan that was undergoing issues, and Tommy went on the mission optimistically. He leaves the family behind and flies over to Japan. When he gets there, he is moved by the welcoming and amount of respect they have for him. In the meantime, during the short time of him working with this company he gets daily compliments and constant praise with high respect. He is being treated as if he's a royal king, his head has been exploding with pride. Tommy has become focused in a way he's not a normal person anymore he's like this machine! He's became highly technical with every new thing he learned about manufacturing and engineering. Being around these engineers has made him technical and geeky. Tommy, the guy that used to

walk in the restaurant on his hands to get a laugh out
of people is now the guy that you can hardly have a
conversation with. His mind doesn't focus on
conversation that is normal because the background
noise in his mind focuses on what's going on at work
and how to learn new technical things about this, that,
and so on. Tommy, the loving dad to his daughter and
the man in love with Wendy that would do anything
for his wife has carelessly abandoned them the point
he won't answer the phone to Wendy and he won't
return her phone calls.

This trip to Japan was a challenge above and beyond
all his previous efforts and he would not stop till he
got to the top and nobody knows where that is yet at
this point in his life. After he settled in at the TV
Factory, and he saw that they are at a 9% defects
level, he didn't quite understand why they need any
help but sure enough he started the whole process
lining up all the workers, the managers and engineers
then he structured the first meeting. He spends his
time watching people work, and he is impressed

with what he sees, these are great people with much work discipline, not like the Americans who jibber jabber and gossip all day as they're working. They take great care of how they're handling things throughout the entire plant. Several weeks have gone by, he is learning and observing and after the third week he computes the collected data. Immediately he has a plan to correct an undetected problem. Two months of him working there and already they are at a three percent higher efficiency rate which is practically unheard of in this time frame. While he's in Japan working, the CEO for one of the large car manufacturing companies learned about him and pulled a Gavin Bob's, he invited Tommy to lunch. Tommy accepted his offer. This is a different type of meeting then it was with Gavin Bobs. When he got to Mr. Toyolas office, it's as big as some people's homes. In his office he had what looked like a dining room and they held the luncheon in Mr. Toyolas office. It's a surprisingly different thing for Tommy to eat with these people, the tables are only a foot-and-a-half tall;

you take your shoes off before you enter the room then you sit on a pillow on the floor to eat. This is something that Tommy in his wildest day never thought he would do during a luncheon with the CEO of a major corporation. They took their time eating and getting to know each other and it was an exquisite meal. Afterwards they resort back to the desk area where they had a long talk. Mister Toyola told Tommy that the word of mouth was what they heard about Molorota and how it was taking the Electronics industry by storm. He went on to tell Tommy one of the inside people of his car company talked to one of the inside people of Molorota and found out Tommy is the key element driving the Quality improvement process there.

Mr. Toyola told Tommy he would like to hire him to do the same thing for his car manufacturing company. Tommy told Mr. Toyola, "I love the fact that you respect me enough to oversee the Six Sigma Quality concept at your company but right now I'm a committed employee for Molorota and I want to finish what I started there." Mr. Toyola respected this, he thanked Tommy and left it as the offer has no expiration and will be waiting to hear from him to negotiate the cost to employ him.

A few more months went by and Tommy has completed his mission for the Molorota Factory in Japan. Later when he gets back to the United States it's time to reunite with the family. Tommy is soaring across air as though he has no feet to walk on. He's floating with so much confidence and pride from all his remarkable achievements that he can't hardly talk to Wendy with her meaningless conversation. His daughter is normally the first thing he would tend to, he would kiss her and hug her, but he doesn't even acknowledge her. The first thing he did when he got home this time was go to his computer to calculate new data and stay working. Several weeks of Tommy being home Wendy has noticed that he isn't the man she married, and he's become so distant that they don't eat dinner together, and most nights they don't sleep together because he falls asleep at his computer.

Wendy walked in the bedroom one night when Tommy is getting out of the shower and ready to call it an evening. She asked, "Guess what? Your daughter starts school tomorrow, did you know?"

"No, did you need something from me?"

"I think it would be nice if you would attend her first day of school." Tommy turned her and said, "How can I, we have a very important meeting in the morning to head up a new project we're working on, it's for a satellite unit that will go into space. I'm sure you can understand that making progress in technology is important. I feel like that plays a much higher priority than me missing a day of school with Athena." Boom! That was a lightning bolt striking her straight in the heart. It's been few months of living with this new person who Wendy doesn't know anymore. Now she's attending a church and making some new friends there, in the meantime, this is helping her to cope with the change in the structure of their marriage. She goes to church a couple days a week in the evenings with a group of women to do an aerobics class which the big trend in exercising. She's spending a lot of time with these church people who are caring. They send a lot of time doing Bible studies to the point that Wendy has become a bonified good faith Christian. Athena is going to church with Mommy and loves it, she's making friends herself and becoming involved with all the kid's activities the church offers. Somewhere In the mix of all this, one of the men Sunday school teachers takes a liking to Wendy, and she finds him quite the guy as well. The Sunday school teacher spends a lot of time with her after Bible study and these two are becoming a little too close.

When she goes home from church one night, she told Tommy she felt like the church people have more interest in her than he does. Tommy's not even paying attention to her talking. She tells him that she and Craig the Sunday school teacher have been spending a lot of time together and that she's finding him quite attractive. Tommy replies with a question that's very shocking to her. He asked her, "What do you want me to do? You want me to put a mask of his face on me, so you can kiss it?" What kind of question is this to ask somebody who is presenting something that's not supposed to happen in a marriage? In her eyes this was a dagger in her heart and made a huge statement that he did not care about her. She asked him, "What could you possibly be thinking? I just told you I found a man at church interesting and attractive and I think he finds me attractive as well. What am I missing? You should be angry and unhappy with me saying something like that!" Tommy told her that he was better than that and all this crap was stressing him out and he didn't need her and all her church goo to be slugging up his thoughts.

3 more months go by and by now the home life is terrible, nobody can get along in the house. Every time someone says something to Tommy he becomes very short and always sarcastic. One night when Wendy made dinner for Tommy he sat down and ate the food, he could taste that the salt was a bit more than normal. He asked Wendy, "How many teaspoons of salt did you put in this tonight?" She replied, "I

don't know I've cooked this meal so many times I don't measure anymore." Tommy scolded her as if she was a bad dog then he told her, "I know you didn't measure the precise amount, you know I dislike my soup with over 2.5 teaspoons of salt per gallon. This must be at least 4 teaspoons! Next time I sit down to eat a meal like this and it has over the amount specified I'm dumping it on the floor."

Then Tommy got up and went to their bedroom. At this point Wendy had all she can stand and stormed in the bedroom. She told Tommy, "There needs to be a change, or I will not be here anymore when you get home!" Tommy is still irritated because he cannot believe she put more salt in the soup than she should have. He answered her, "If you're too stupid to cook a bowl of soup maybe you shouldn't be here in the first place." Wendy cannot believe what she's hearing. "You know what, I've been eating lunch with Craig, the Sunday school teacher, and he treats me like a lady. I should spend more time with him than just a lunch, maybe it's time to take his friendship to another level!" She packs up her stuff and ran to her mother's house and spent the whole night crying.

Wendy became depressed. The next day she went to talk to the preacher at church and he advised her that spending time with Craig was very wrong and Craig was about to have a real big talking to about sin! He told her it would be a good idea to come in with Tommy and do some counseling, this enlightened Wendy's heart. She thought 'great idea! I'll present this to Tommy when he gets home tonight.' Later that night she went home to talk, in a very soft-spoken way she presented the idea to Tommy. And what do you think Tommy had to say about that? He told her, "Why don't you go to counseling and see if you can't get yourself fixed so that you can have a different marriage."

This went nowhere fast, Wendy made another attempt and went to talk to the preacher again. The preacher told Wendy this time it would be better to separate for a little while till they get to where they can communicate better. The next day Wendy packed up all her and Athena's clothes and took Athena to her mom's house.

Several days went by and Tommy didn't even notice she was not there. One night when he got there he realized supper was not sitting on the table. He looked around the house and noticed Wendy and his daughter are not home. Okay, no big deal, she must be over her mom's house or a friend's house. Thinking to himself, 'I'll call her mother and see if she's over there.' He called his Mother-in-laws house, Mom answered the phone and Tommy asked her, "Is Wendy over there?" She replied, "Yes I'll get her for you." When Wendy answered Tommy asked her why she was over there and why supper wasn't on the table? Wendy told him that she left three days ago and there would be no more suppers on the table till he attended Church counseling with her. Tommy asked her, "What are you talking about, you left 3 days ago?"

"Yes! I left 3 days ago, are you just now figuring this out?" Dumbfounded, Tommy replied, "Are you serious you haven't been here for 3 days? What have you been doing?"

"I am staying at my mother's house, I left home because you and I aren't getting along, and I think separating for a while will be good for us to get our heads on tight, so when we get back together we can be nicer to each other and work on improving our marriage." Tommy told her that was absurd and if she had to leave to get her mind together, she wasn't strong enough to be with him and to stay gone.

Tommy Met with Elroy a couple days later. Elroy began asking Tommy necessary questions about a certain project. Tommy turned to answer him, he looked him square in the eyes as if he was getting ready to punch him and he asked, "What's your problem?" Elroy looked back at him with a confused look but figured he must be joking and replied to him, "My problem is that I'm missing some data here and I can't seem to figure out if it's my mistake or if possibly you might know anything about it?" Tommy hatefully replied to him and said, "You're the one who started this whole data calculating routine with me, how in the heck do you not know where your stupid data is? Do I have to babysit you!?”

Elroy asked him, “Hey buddy is everything okay?”

“Yeah everything’s okay with me but everyone else is so damn stupid and I’m sick of stupid people?”

“Hey Tommy, I’m not sure where this is coming from or where this is going but maybe you need to take a day or two off. I can hold the fort down for a while and you can get your thoughts together. When you come back, maybe we can revamp this thing.” In a very ugly way he replied, “Quit calling me Tommy I’m not a damn child and I’m not a baby. I do not want to be called Tommy anymore! If you want to call me anything call me Tom.” Then Tommy turned towards the door walking, and then he stopped by the door, and he looked at Elroy saying, “You know what, I am leaving for a few days, as a matter fact, I’m leaving for a bunch of days, I’m not coming back, I’m sick of working for people and with people. I want to work

for myself for change so keep the job, good riddance
to you, and I hope you make it work, bye!" So that day
he quit his good high-paying job and parted ways with
his old friend. Elroy was his accomplice in creating
how to make problems better in Manufacturing and
never understood what came over Tommy, but he was
very upset over the friendship ending and missed him.
He would always remember him for the success they
achieved together. Tommy has alienated the best
people in his life, what's next for this class clown
turned geeky A-hole?

TOMMY HELPS A WORLD GIANT

After he gave up working for the company that put
him over the top and where he created the new
industry standard, and after chasing people out of his

life, Tommy stayed home for a while and took about two weeks off. The house is empty and it's driving him crazy, all he can think of is what he will accomplish next with his work career, this is the only subject he revolves around. Then in his conclusion he went back to the lunch with mister Toyola and his proposition to go to work at Toyola Car Corporation. He passes through the channels to contact Mr. Toyola to ask if he was still contemplating him moving there to structure a Quality improvement division. Mr. Toyola gladly accepted Tommy's phone call and made an appointment for them to meet. Tommy flew to Japan and met with Mr. him. When they get together they make a minute for the normal introductions and surface talk. Tommy wasted no time getting to the point, "Mr. Toyola, let me cut through the chase, I'm not interested working for you as an employee, I am my own company and I will work with you as your consultant. If you want me to come to work for you this is what it will cost you," Then Tommy boldly threw a figure out that was above and beyond a couple years of his last salary. "This much, and I expect within 6 months I will be finished with the first stage of launching a program. If I am performing at your expectations, then after the six months it'll cost you that much again Plus a bonus of 13% over how much money I saved you the first 6 months." Mister Toyola is an executive in business not a negotiator in a manner he makes financial decisions the first time he meets, so he told Tommy, "I need to submit this to my board of directors and officers of the company, and we'll go over this to find out if this is within our budget." Eight days passed by and Tommy was looking at other companies to call because he was giving up on the Japan venture when finally, he picked up a phone call at home, it's Mr. Toyola. He informed Tommy, "I will accept your proposal providing the first 3 months the financials show profitable results, if you agree to that we're on board and ready to bring you here to execute your expertise." The deal is done, Tommy is now a Six sigma consultant thus initiating the first to consult Six sigma.

Tommy made his way to Japan and is directly engaged with top priority issues. He organized a team and aligned a strategy to gather statistics. He worked 12 hours seven days a week and wasn't considering any type of failure! Within three very grueling months, as he agreed to do, Tommy finished working with his team completing the improvements of the initial production line of cars with urgent issues. His skills and efforts saved the company over the million dollars mark the very first time. This came from reducing defective door hinges, door handles, and fixing Equipment that was failing in that production due to non-maintenance. Without a doubt his bonus was going to bust more than $130,000.00 Back in the 1980's that would be like a Half million today and you can add to that the older this book gets.

Tommy went in the Car factory and dissected the entire place like a madman. He brought in specific employees from inside the factory and trained them the procedure he developed to record data and use software to analyze it. Starting with the Brainstorming meeting, they defined priority problems, then collecting data for those projects. He structured the way these people ranked in their positions and made one person in charge of the DMAIC methodology and the rest were team members by level. Since they were in Japan, he came up with something interesting that he believed these people would show respect to relating to Karate. He structured it from the top tier team member in charge; he called this person the Master Black belt. Then next down the list would be the Black belt, the Greenbelt and last the yellow belt. This standardized the level of knowledge, importance, and experience that each employee has. If you were a Six Sigma Greenbelt, you are one of the lower-level employees, maybe on the factory assembly line or maybe you're in shipping. If you are a Black Belt, maybe you were in the engineering department or a department manager. If you are the Master Black belt, you are well versed in the method, you completely understood statistics and could use software to analyze the statistical data and determine the output of defects. The Master Black belt had to delegate the structure of the project, oversee the Black belts and the entire project and sometimes oversee all the factory projects. Black belts had to teach the yellow and green belts, oversee them and update the Master Black belt on daily progress. The employees were surprisingly receptive to this. When Tommy first got there, he had to sort through what Toyola was already doing. They had in place a system for improvements called 'Lean'. Instead of explaining in detail and boring you with how Lean worked, I will summarize it in one sentence. In the Lean method they stressed more on waste seen through the eyes where Six sigma is waste through data. So, why am I telling you this? Tommy eventually learned the Lean method and came to find out how valuable it was for eliminating waste. He found a way to use this with in his method analyzing data. When he combined the two it made an absolute flawless process. So, he initiated what was

Lean, Six sigma. Now we proceed forward about 4 years into this, the corporation is world-renowned for excellence and earning top Quality Awards around the world over all the new car manufacturers. Example, the capability of their manufacturing became so precise that one in one thousand transmissions had .0323 thousands of an inch in tolerance outside its baseline which was virtually impossible in automotive manufacturing. This structured innovation of the Lean Six Sigma method became the National Standard for problem solving and Quality improvements.

Tommy carried out the greatest achievement for Toyola. His abilities made him famous around the world in the manufacturing society. After that it was time for him to move on to new projects and bigger challenges, so he ends his work with Toyola as a full-time consultant and worked with them on an annual basis. He put the word out that he is available as a consultant for anyone in the Industry needing to solve problems with a process that needed to improve its performance. Tommy had many companies reach out to him and went to work for several companies that applied his DMAIC method making all of them more successful. He realized that what he's created was not limited to Manufacturing and that by analyzing data it could improve anything with a process while increasing productivity. It served many industries including hospitals, pharmaceutical, insurance, transportation, energy government, military...

Before you know it almost every industry or organization is using Six Sigma to refine, streamline and improve their business processes. Tommy couldn't keep up with the entire world and couldn't control the fact they used his method to fix problems because he had no patent on this, you can't patent a method. But, he was vane and enjoyed seeing his method save hundreds of companies. Also, he could help regulate its purpose in the industry and he came up with an idea. He started the first organization dedicated to Quality improvements. He called it QAW,

Quality Association of the World. There he invited every factory, company, college and organization to join so they could have annual conferences and meetings to discuss and help understand the Lean six sigma method. Within QAW he allowed companies to educate and certify people as different level belts.

One day after many years of not talking or seeing each other Tommy bumps into Eddy. They get up to speed with what each other have done with their lives. Tommy was very proud and boasted about his income from his success of teaching businesses how to solve problems in their processes with his methodology creation.

Eddy at this point in his life wasn't really rolling in any money and he was the basic everyday guy. But one thing was different about Eddy, he was a Christian involved in church. During his course of getting involved in church he had bumped into Wendy many times over the course of the last few years. He was aware that Tommy and Wendy were divorced and heard of how Tommy changed his demeanor. Within this time Wendy had already been granted a divorce from the court system. Tommy would visit Athena from time to time and he was content with Wendy being the sole parent to raise her. Eddy was trying to get Tommy to sit down and talk with him about God and Jesus. He tried telling him about his dealings with Christianity and the ministry he's involved with. Eddy had an experience that he wanted to share with Tommy. He knew it would make Tommy want to hear more about this Jesus guy that he knew was the real deal. Tommy wanted nothing to do with this, as a matter of fact his old buddy seemed like an idiot to him, he's somebody who is just uninformed and brainwashed, a big dummy not going anywhere in life. The more Eddy told him how he felt good about finding this Jesus person the more it aggravated him. Eddy was very understanding of Tommy's irritation and he tried explaining to him, "You know I've had an experience that I know I couldn't' have endured if it wouldn't have been for a higher power. I believe this Jesus character did what the Bible said he did, and I would like to share this with you. I know his existence is real and here is what happened that made me discover this"

Tommy told Eddie "Before you go blabbing religious crap to me I want you to understand this is nonsense! Do not waste your time telling me these fairy tales." Eddy insisted he know what happened, "Tommy listen to me! I got in trouble and was about to go to jail, I went to this Library to pay back my community service and discovered how to know the Bible is true, listen to what happened. I had the privilege to touch an 1800-year-old book with dates logged in the cover to prove its age. I figured after seeing this in person I know the Bible has withstood it's history in time and is accurate."

Tommy interrupted, "If you do your homework you'll find out that we came from a microorganism, it evolved into human life and evolution is real, you big dummy. You need to understand that energy existed, and the chaos of this energy exploded causing the universe. There is no such thing as God, and this

Jesus who you think is real, he's nothing more than a fictional character used by people to enslave each other with hope of an afterlife! Just like your bible, it's a book of fake stories, a fable book full of fairy tales." He told Eddy the way things really work!

Before Eddie and Tommy parted ways that day the last thing Eddie told Tommy is, "I'm sorry you can't see what I see, you have a very grim look towards life. Your soul is not made from cellular mass, it's like electricity, you know it's there, but you can't see it. I will pray for you to have an experience that will bring you closer to Jesus, and hopefully you'll get to experience something like I did. Maybe that will help you open your mind and learn Gods way of life. It will be exciting to see you find true life. I claim victory in Jesus death for you receiving this! I can't wait to see you again, so I can hear your testimony."

Tommy has heard enough of this babbling religious garbage! "You sound like you were brainwashed by some cult, you better get wise and look around you, this is reality, not a bunch of floating spirits and angels!" Tommy managed to exterminate another close person out of his life.

He has become such a phenomenon that even NASA scientists at the Space Center had to call him when they got stuck with determining which data to use from samples that were collected from an experiment. One project they were working on was so precise, when they were measuring the surface, it kept coming with up such a fine measurement they couldn't get it to measure properly. The measurement was so small they couldn't see it with the human eye. The only way they could measure it was by sliding a stylus over it and measuring sound vibrations that came from it. To cut through the story, on this particular project it took him seven days to find the correct area to collect data from. He then calculated the data and determined the correct value to pursue from there.

His work on the NASA project was a record in his history book for the absolute most extreme difficulty to find out where the problem was. But, he also did this in a record amount of time compared to what was normal for him.

At this time Tommy felt like a God. He has the attitude of a Rock Star and this is better known as a God complex. He's just a mean gnarly person, very arrogant but the best at what he does. After much success with this DMAIC method helping business' he is the top consultant and trainer in the industry and now he is opening six sigma colleges.

During his teaching and consulting he discovered how people down the line of command are having trouble finding the correct way to collect data and do experiments and using this scientific software that is difficult to understand.

He can't believe how stupid people are, he battles with himself to understand why people do not get this stuff, it is so easy. Tommy thinks to himself, 'I need to find a way to have this where people can do it without being treated like babies that need to be baby sat while doing it.' What could he do? He is not able to be everywhere at once like God and be explaining this to everyone. He can't make a reader's manual because it's a method and no two projects are the same. And, according to Tommy people are mindless idiots and can't follow directions, right? After brain storming with himself, and finding ideas and following his own DMAIC plan, he came up with it! 'What if I had a software program that all they had to do is input the data then hit a go button and it helped them run projects and understand better? After that idea rang a bell in his brain the next question was who can make the software? He spent several days calling people and putting the word out that he needed someone to design a software system for him. Tommy spent several days seeking software developers. Eventually he found someone who had the ability to build a system based on the criteria he required. He met with them at the designer's office. Tommy showed them what operations he wanted it to perform and the developers made a temporary bid based on the information he gave them. The design estimator came in with his offer and told him, "That will cost you in the range of $13,000.00."

"What? Are you joking? Why the heck does it cost so much to make this?"

"That is very affordable for time involved in configuring the source code. This is an extraordinary level configuration, it will take almost 5 months to develop, test and fine tune this to your specs." Tommy cannot believe the price they bid! "What specifically do you need to prepare this, a team of NASA Scientists?" Surprised by Tommy's statement they replied, "We use a CAD/CAE software system." Tommy heard all he that he could stand to hear, "I will get back to you on that, mister." Tommy was in disbelief! He is wealthy but too frugal.

O.K., how hard can it be to make software if you are using software to design it with on a computer? Tommy does his research and found this CAD/CAE software they were using for $1,200.00. That's what he wanted to hear, "I can spend $1,200.00 and save over eleven thousand dollars, my first problem solved for my problem-solving software!"

The software was ordered, a week later it came in then Tommy got busy. The first week was certainly difficult navigating through it till he figured out the basics. After two weeks he was zipping through with ease, he self-taught himself how to use this. He spent every night with grueling hours of designing and developing it and a couple months later he finished it. It was brilliant, it combined all the key people working on a project in a click of a button to reference each other's activity. This eliminated having to meet every day in person, it allowed them to input data, and then it processed the data with an explanation of what to and how to do it next. This did so much more it would take another novel to illustrate everything it does. He would hand this out to all the companies he trained in Six Sigma, so they could use it. After the software helped Lean Six sigma employees and companies execute their projects, he figured he could sell it, and then he did, colleges and businesses alike bought it, used it, had success, and it made him money.

At this stage in business Six Sigma was a prerequisite in virtually all industries and business alike. Tommy is making so much money he doesn't even know how much he has but compared to other prosperous people he is in the upper tier of wealth.

THE BEGINNING OF THE END

Fast-forward about 15 years. Tommy's barely seen Athena, she has already graduated high school and in College. Tommy hasn't seen Wendy in years and doesn't care either. He is doing well according to his standards with more time on his hands and he spends most of it keeping an eye on who's who in the world of business that wins Quality awards.

Tommy read an article on the awards the Japanese motorcycles companies were getting. He's amazed at the performance of their sport bikes. They are lighter, faster, and more aerodynamic than any other brand of motorcycles. They have the 4 fastest production motorcycles in the world. You can partly credit this to how Tommy developed the method for solving problems and eliminating defects with Lean Six Sigma, and how the Japanese companies implemented it to keep quality at the highest standards.

One day Tommy got a wild hair up his backside and decided to go see the motorcycle dealer and look at these fast machines. No time to lose, in the car and Tommy takes off.

You can see him in the showroom standing there staring, he is in love with the way they look, he loves the technology and already has his facts down about the statistics of these machines.

A salesman walked up to Tommy and asks him, "How would you like to take it home today." Tommy replied "Not interested in buying one. I feel like these are amazing and I wanted to see one in person." The salesman tried to tell Tommy how that motorcycle performed and how fast it would be on top end, etc... Tommy looked at the guy and asked him, "Do you think I'm stupid or something, why do you think I of all people need to know that crap?" The salesman replied, "I'm sorry sir I was just doing my job, I thought maybe you'd be interested in knowing some of that information in case you didn't know. Maybe you'd like to take a quick drive on one, let me go grab the keys." Tommy turned to him and said, "Oh no, I'm not interested don't worry about it."

He's squatting down looking at the tires and the fairings imagining the wind passing by and how much the coefficient drag would be, meaning how streamline the surface is. The salesman came back and put the key in ignition and started it up. Tommy jumped back and very intently listened to it. He said, "Wow! That sounds frikken powerful man!" This verbiage was how the young Tommy would've talked, it immediately brought out an inner beast from Tommy's spirit.

The salesman said, "You have to try it, that doesn't commit you to buying it. I bet you will have a better view of how it performs if you take it for a spin." He tossed the keys to him, "let me know what you think of it." Smart salesman, the urge to drive it was killing Tommy. The rumble from the motor is more than he could stand. It was around 27 years since he was on a motorcycle back in the day when he and Doug raced their dirt bikes. He said, "Maybe, it would be interesting to see what one of these things can do, so OK! Out of my way!" The salesman got him a helmet and off Tommy left. He gets out on the road, opens it up full throttle and he almost pooped his pants. This is not what he expected and had way more power than he could handle at first. Tommy had no experiences with motorcycles that have this much power and speed. He got back to the dealership that sells the motorcycles and parked it outside by the door. His heart is pounding, his hands are clenched tight, and he's shaking when he gets off the motorcycle. The salesman walked up and told Tommy, "I can have this ready to go within 1 hour." Tommy's is heart pounding, his butt cheeks are clenched, he looked at the salesman and said: "I' need this, please hurry!" Tommy has his own office now where he does Six Sigma training for his new clients and occasionally has people fly in from out of town. Its summer now, and mornings are nice and cool which motivates Tommy to ride his speed demon to the office! This formed into an obsession and became an everyday situation. He fabricated a way to put headphones into his helmet for listening to music. Using his Walkman radio, he plays his special riding song that inspires his ride on the speed machine, the group is called Iron Butterfly, the song, "In-A-Gadda-Da-Vida" it's about a 10-minute-long song. Pure rock!

While he's driving, he's learning the leaning ratios for cornering. For quite some time he's been fantastic at hammering corners really fast and leaning the motorcycle way over around curves. He has a large curve that he must go around every day on his way to the office. He's been approaching the curve in the high 60's MPH and wants to reach 70 miles per hour.

Because Tommy is the Guru of designing a program for collecting data and analyzing it, he began using this idea to improve his speed times around the tight curve he must drive on to get to work. He's been using different places in the curve and different depths into it to see if it changes his time and records the information. Then he sampled the pavement particles to see if there were size differences at the inner part versus the outer part to see if they affected the gripping on the tires and recorded that data. Next, he is timing how long it takes to go from one point to the next by where he started into the curve opposed to where he ended up in the curve and recorded that information. Last he measured the edge of his tires to see how far up the tire the pavement had worn a pattern into the sidewall to see if it leaned further each time, and he added this to his data. He kept calculating day after day. After a certain period, he gets to the point where he takes the corner at the highest speed possible without wiping out and makes 71 miles per hour.

This gives him a thrill beyond his wildest imagination. Sometime later Tommy is on his way to work cruising on his sport bike. Not a care in the world, he's listening to In-A-Gadda-Da-Vida, it's blasting his brains out. He is thinking about the last few recordings he got from the big curve he challenges when on the sport bike, he's not satisfied with the last numbers he got when he made his goal of 70 miles per hour because he thought there was room to beat it. He knew beyond a shadow of a doubt he could beat his all-time record so this particular day Tommy tries something different; he went down one gear and pulled the throttle back a little 1/10 of a turn further giving it more gas, and as he's leaning into the corner he must have hit a pebble in the road because the front wheel skipped a step sideways and lost traction causing his motorcycle to lie on its side, and before he knew it, the thing had flipped. It went up in the air then came down, after sliding what seemed like ¼ of a mile he ended up flat on his back. He did not have his helmet on tight enough, the impact of the helmet hitting the pavement and having a loose gap caused his head to slam harder inside the helmet knocking him out.

There's total darkness from being knocked out. About 4 minutes later Tommy resumes consciousness and nothing was going on anywhere around him. No cars are driving by, no noises, it was as if time stopped. It's complete silence, he looks around and he can see his motorcycle approximately 60 feet away from him. As he looks over at it the back and front wheels are still spinning from wiping out. While Tommy gathers his composure, he realizes he wiped out. Now we see Tommy find out what life is all about.

TOMMY HAS AN INCREDIBLE JOURNEY

For whatever reason as hard as he landed he felt no pain. There are scratches and scuffs all over his body, he's a little weak, sore, and bloody but he stood up and shook off the impact. Still looking around he noticed there's not a car on the road, he doesn't know what's going on, but he knew something's different in a strange way. Then he walked towards his motorcycle and felt a slight

cool breeze blowing through an opening in the wooded area alongside the highway. For whatever reason, the wind from the wooded area is mesmerizing him and inviting him to it. He looked over and noticed the wind was coming from this formation of the trees that looked different than it normally did when he passed by every day. It has a V shape and it opened itself up as though it was a funnel drafting him through it to visit. Tommy thinking to himself that something about those trees are enticing and mysterious enough that he must go check it out.

Tommy walked over to the opening, the breeze becomes a little softer as it slows down and became a cooler. He noticed this change; it entices him even more. He entered the opening, as he's going through the it he can see a pathway, and it has the most elegant bright green grass around it as though it was manicured specifically for a pro golfing tournament, about like the grass on a Golf Course green but neon-like and way more brilliant. The center of the path looks like it's red granite with sparkles, it has a glowing reddish-orange tint, nothing he's ever seen before, it's sparkly and hard, but it's a form of dirt and it's beautiful! The trees are not like the regular trees he has seen all his life. They are sweeping and calming; they provide this cool shade that he can taste in his mouth with a minty flavor. Strange! The tree trunks are triple the width of regular trees. These trees are like the huge California redwoods with smooth bark and the bark is almost like it was alive with living skin. And the branches relaxed outward with subtle soft looking leaves that seemed to flow whether the wind blew or not. Any noise is utter calming, but the flowing breeze is the only sound he can hear, its gentle and tranquil. Tommy is determined to find out what this is; he wants to know what brings him to this cool Forest with vibrant colors. He looks to the left at the weird skin-bark on the trees and when he turned back to look down the path there was a man standing there. He is fuzzy-headed about what this was and figured he needed to see this man. He heads towards the man and as soon as he started walking the man took off walking also. He kept walking at a distance behind then he decided he needs to catch him; he walked faster till he caught up with him. He touched the man's shoulder from behind and gives him a little nudge. The man stopped but did not turn around. Tommy asked him, "Where are you going?" What exactly is this place? Why do I feel so different?" The man turned and looked at him, Tommy could see deep into his eyes, they were clear like water with a hint of blue coloring, not your typical color for eyes. When Tommy looked in his eyes it seemed like he could see for miles like there wasn't anything inside of his head.

The man never moved his lips, but some way Tommy can hear his words, "You are on the right path. This path is a journey, an experience for learning, gaining knowledge, to develop understanding, pass through judgment and become wise to many things." Tommy could taste the words as if they were going into his mouth instead of through his ears. Tommy blurts out, "Judgement? Understanding, how did you transmit that to my head without talking?" It was not a typical verbal conversation and more like the words are vibrations penetrating his chest flowing up to his mind. When the words went through his body, it was relaxing yet so vibrant and he could understand clearly, it was scary and more than he could handle. The man continued walking away. The air around this path was taking his breath away and it felt like he did not need to inhale, the air didn't flow through his lungs like oxygen but more like water streaming through gills.

 Tommy continued following this man as if this was what something supposed him to do, he noticed a cloudiness in his vision. The man became harder to see so Tommy sped up his pace to catch this guy again and when he got up to his back he tugged on the man's shoulder again, causing him to turn toward him. Suddenly there was a darkness around the path. They locked eyes, he could see the man's clear eyes becoming a vibrant neon blue. The man was overpowering him with his stare, and while he was locking his eyes with Tommy's, he became a completely different man. Then there was a light shining directly around this man. The man smiled and said, "Hi Tommy, I am about to have a little talk with you and I want you to listen intently. "Tommy's vision became clearer; the man was easier to see. This man's appearance changed, at first, he looked like a scavenger from a harry potter movie then he evolved into this elegant masterpiece of a male model. He had a face like Robert Pattinson the movie actor in Twilight, glowing long blonde hair like Brad pit and his voice was smooth like Leonardo DiCaprio. In other words, this man was drop-dead gorgeous, and Tommy who is not even gay was intimidated and overpowered by this man's swagger and how stunning he was.

The man was speaking while they continued to walk down this path. "I once had the second highest seat in existence, I was second in the matter of the dominant order." Tommy is overtaken by his speech and shut up listening intently. "Allow me to introduce myself. Some call me Apollyon, those that refer to me as that say I am the destroyer. Many people call me Beelzebul or Beelzebub, and those that refer to me as that believe I am the lord of an evil army. Others call me the Angel of light, those people who refer to me as that know about my masterful ability of imitation and counterfeit proposals given to individuals. I have many names all of which describe the many terrible things acquainted with my evil. I am cunning like a wolf in sheep's clothing, disguising evil in a good-looking package. When you look at me do you see a figment of your imagination?" Tommy nodded his head no. "But people see me as a little-horned character with a pitchfork to jab people in their ass, like a figment of their imagination.

An example of my work. I like to break up families; it creates a weakness for the members as they move on through life. I start with temptation in the union of marriage. When I come to destroy a marriage, I attack the wife like I did Adams wife Eve, ha-ha can you believe I talked her into looking under the lid of that box! Women are my favorite, much easier to work with because a lot of them work from an emotional concept and can be led astray faster. Thank you, Eve! Those whom I am speaking of can be more promiscuous, deceptive and sneaky and because they are sexy, seductive and able to lure a weak man quickly with temptation, they work better for me. Most men believe their wives would never fool around on them, but normally it starts with married women and seduction, again temptation!

Look at me, do you think I look like the overweight plumber with a hairy butt crack? I am what women refer to as hot! When I approach a woman, I am irresistible and charming, pure sex! I tear up the marriage by fooling the wife into believing she is hot and sexy; I make her feel good about herself giving her a false sense of self-esteem and blind her eyes to her husband being any kind of good man. I block her ears from hearing his words as loving; I lure her to my body then make her believe she is having the sex she never had before then she dislikes being with her husband. She becomes addicted to my sex, she will do anything to get me, sneak off at lunch and meet me in the middle of the day while her husband breaks his back at work. She can't stop thinking about me and breaking up the marriage to be with me. She will leave home and her children with her suffering husband. Eventually, the husband moves on and finds a better wife. Then I slam dunk her and leave her all alone wishing she never met me, she wants her husband back but too late! He found another woman, (laughing loud) Ha-ha, that feels so good! When I break up marriage from the other standpoint by luring the husband away I use hot women. I cause them to be sexy, heavenly demons, seductive deceitful angels feeling sexy by dressing inappropriately so it seduces men. They show their big lusty cleavage and go braless or wear skin tight pants and lower their pants to show their butt crack or wear too short a skirt flashing way too much junk, men are visual, so they lose control of their thoughts. Temptation, the lust becomes tantalizing, and even the best of men are seduced into cheating, and they blow all their money chasing something that's not real and the next thing you know they are homeless and the wife and children are suffering from a broken home. I have caused marriage to simulate dating, people now feel it's not a forever commitment but more like dating, if you get sick of your spouse or find someone you like better you quit and move on. Not the way it was intended!

The children in the family are deeply affected by all this too. It causes them confusion, weakness, insecurity, and lack of success in their future. So yes, I am beautiful to women while I am ruining them, and women are beautiful to men while they trample their hearts, and the reason I use seduction, lust and sexual misconduct will always destroy families! Another way I attack people is clouding a person's mind, I open the door to wealth. Nothing beats a vain person who can only focus on what worldly things they have outside their heart instead of what they have inside themselves. It really takes away their need for a higher power to help with life, and it distracts their desire to go to heaven. When people take pride in their things and themselves I am winning the battle to rob them of an eternal life, their heaven is on earth. So why would they need a God?

Tommy, do you know anyone who takes pride in themselves or their money? By the way, how was your marriage to Wendy? Do you remember anything about yourself while you were at the peak of your marriage with her? Ha-ha, I was there the whole time, I got both of you good!"

While this conversation is going on Tommy can see a shadow over the shoulder of this man. It's another person eavesdropping. The person is getting closer, and the closer this person got to them the easier the person was to see, and Tommy's hearing became isolated. That man was chaffed with a steamy yet smoky burnt skin, he was in agony and his face was ridden with pure torment. His face seemed so familiar, maybe this was a close friend or maybe a distant relative since it seemed to be someone that he knew so well. It consumes Tommy with this suffering eavesdropping person, he would not stop looking at him until he saw the reason for feeling this close familiarity. The eyes gave it away, when that person looked straight into his eyes it told him all he needed to know. It's Tommy looking at Tommy. In the mix of this conversation and being distracted by the smoky stranger, he had a vision. He saw himself by a Volcano that was erupting and as the lava was running down the side he was running from it, but the lava surrounded him and all he could think of was drinking water. Shocked by the vision and his spirit looking at him he felt his heart vaporizing into a dryness like the blood left his body. Tommy blinked and when he opened his eyes, the shadow of himself was gone, then his hearing returned and on continued the conversation with this man.

"You had the most beautiful woman, but when you were ignoring her you opened the door for her to be attacked by me. I was deceptive in who I was, I took her to lunch, walked with her in the park telling her incredible love stories to fulfill her mind, and resembled a handsome Sunday school teacher named Craig. When I attacked you, it was to chase your wealth and personal desires, you left Wendy to be devoured by wolves, me. I quit talking sexy love things and romancing her at the same time you two separated, and now she suffers much loss. In the meantime, you lost more than a good woman, you lost other things that have an eternal effect in more ways than one. I love you Tommy, you are a good find! You are a proud selfish fool and a giant sucker! I won you and now you get to spend a lot of time in total darkness with my family of demonic angels. Maybe, you with your geeky big brain can gather up some data and analyze what's going on here. You don't believe there is a creator, a God, and it's too late to become a Christian but don't worry, God is too nice to send you to hell, Not! Ha-ha!" What an ugly laugh from such a handsome man, it has an annoying echo! Tommy does not understand the reality of what's going on here and is trying to force his mind to catch what this man is about. Thinking about it, he asks himself, how does he know Wendy and why does he know so much about me? Maybe this is a dream, he asks himself, 'If I can wake up then maybe I can end this and go on with my day.'

Without moving his lips, the man transmitted words to Tommy's mind saying, "You are on a journey and you can't alter your path. While you are here, you cannot control your thoughts, you can only hear things and remember the things you heard. Keep walking and pay attention to everything around you and any person you meet and be sure to remember me! I will see you again, and make sure you bring your sunscreen next time, possibly it will protect you from the burns you will get when you stay with me." Laughing at Tommy with an echoing sound, the man went on to tell Tommy if he wanted to end the conversation to start walking and do not turn back because if he did the path only ended right back to him and the next time they met was going to be bad. Tommy is feeling very sleepy, he is nodding off like he is about to fall asleep then his body jerks several times like he was being shocked by electricity, and then he snaps out of it and is wide awake. He can't see that man anymore. 'What the damn hell was all that about?' he asked himself. That was a weird dream, I think!?

Looking forward down the path he walked on. Making good time, it draws him down the sparkly path like there is a tide pulling him onward. He hears a very soft sweet voice call out to him, "Yoo-hoo." He looks around and the voice is repeating, "Yoo-hoo"

"Who is Yoo Hooing?" Maybe he's hearing things. Again, "Yoo-hoo!" He looks around again and here pops out of the wooded area this pretty woman, it's her saying Yoo-Hoo. That's is her saying hi in her own weird way. 'How sweet looking is she' he thinks to himself as he is walking towards her. They are about to cross paths, "Hi there, what a nice day. You sure are pretty! What are you doing here all alone?" he said to her.

"I wander off from home time to time and come over here to enlighten people with my laughter."

"Laughter? What's the laughter about?" "Well, Tommy, my name is Sarah. God has made laughter for me, everyone who hears will laugh with me." "O.K." Tommy said, "And how is it you know my name, I never said who I am?" Sarah replied with "Knock Knock!" Already knowing what to say Tommy replied, "Who is there?" "Meeno."

"Meeno who?"

"Me know you!"

That's a good one and a good opening line to break any tension, Tommy laughs after she lightened up the mood. "See, People laugh with me! I want you to know there is more to life than strict focus on yourself and possessions. You were a nice guy once, you were full of humor and good fun, I know you took a turn to a completely different direction, and for no good reason, you could have kept your sense of humor while you came to fame and blessed many people."

Tommy taken in awe of this lady has not much to say and is intently listening waiting for more of her good-natured speech.

"Tommy, what do you know about seating arrangements?" He shrugged his shoulders motioning, I don't know? "Do you know where will you be seated in eternity? Smoking or non-smoking? Ha-ha-ha, get it?"

"How about this Tommy?

These two preachers were sitting in a boat duck hunting on a lake, 1rst preacher is positive, he brags about his dog and how he is the best retriever ever! Preacher two is negative and denies this is true devaluing the dog as just another dumb dog. Preacher two shoots a duck, preacher one yells to the dog, "Go get it!"

The dog jumps off the boat and he never entered the water; he ran over the top of the water like Jesus did when he walked on the water; the dog grabs the duck, runs back, jumps in the boat and drops the duck in preacher two's hands.

Preacher one said, "Now you see what I mean? My dog is incredible!

Preacher two said, "It's like I said, I knew he wasn't all that, he can't even swim."

Tommy laughs, "That was definitely funny." Sarah was laughing, "You see, people do laugh with me!"

"Hey Tommy, one day Adam woke up to Eve poking his ribs. He looks over at her and asked, "Woman, what is it you are doing to my side?" Eve replied, "I am counting your ribs to make sure you are not seeing another woman!" "Cute!" Tommy said.

"Hey Tommy, how about this, an atheist was walking through the woods, talking to himself,

"How beautiful the animals are!" "How majestic the trees are!"

"How powerful the rivers are!" As he walked along the river, he heard a rustling in the bushes behind him. He turned and saw an 8-foot grizzly bear charging towards him. He ran along the path as fast as he could, but when he looked over his shoulder, he saw that the bear was closing in on him.

He kept running, he looked over his shoulder again, and the bear was even closer. Then he tripped and fell to the ground. The bear was right on top of him with his right paw raised to strike him. At that instant, the atheist cried, "God help me!"

Time Stopped. The bear froze. The forest was silent. A bright light glazed upon the man and a voice from the sky said, "You've denied my existence for all these years and have taught others that I don't exist. You've even credited creation to a cosmic accident. Why would you expect me to help you out of this predicament? Are you now a believer?"

The atheist looked into the light and said, "Well, I would be a hypocrite to suddenly become a Christian, and ask you to treat me as a Christian now by answering my requests, but could you, maybe, you could make the Bear a Christian?"

"Very well, I will do this just this once," said the voice.

The light went out.

The sounds of the forest resumed. The bear lowered his right paw and brought both paws together to pray. He bowed his head, and said, "Lord, thank you for this meal, bless this food which I am about to receive into my body, in the name of Christ our Lord, Amen."

Tommy is laughing, "How cool it is you make humor with religion." Sarah said, "Yes Tommy that was God's gift to me to experience laughter and share it.

In that story about the bear, does that remind you of anyone? The part about denying God and crediting existence to a cosmic explosion? Jesus did say that if you deny him in your earthly body before other men that he would surely deny you entering the final kingdom of heaven before God.

Well, I hope you are not denied at the pearly gates for denying God while you were alive. I had fun talking to you and hope you remember a day when you too were fun to be around. My day here is done Tommy. I hope if I ever see you again it won't be looking down from a higher place watching you suffering from any grave mistakes you have made, may your journey be a blessed one, Bye-bye now!" She turned and walked away, and he just sat and watched as she became smaller and harder to see. He is thinking, 'wow that was one crazy and cute little lady, she sure did make me feel good and laugh a bit, I am glad I met her because I really needed that.

Tommy is walking again; the path is dreamy and nice to look at. The scenery is peaceful and so heavenly. He is walking along, and it comes to his mind, 'what am I doing here? Where exactly am I going? This is strange! I am walking like a hot wheel's toy car on a track only going the way the track makes it go.' Talking out loud, "Who is behind this? What do you want from me? When does this end?"

Sure enough, Tommy sees a man resting under a tree. "Hey, you! Where am I, where does this path go? Who are you?" This man is calm and very noble like, and he answered, "Someone told you what is going on, are you not on a journey?" Tommy stops and recalls, "Um, yeah I guess so."

"Then do like you have been doing and take a good listen to me about who I am. I am Paul, once known as Saul. I considered Christianity to be a false religion; a religion that was in direct conflict with the Jewish tradition I so devoutly followed. I was zealous for Judaism, and against this new religion Christianity that I actively persecuted and murdered Christians to the death over, I was binding them and delivering them to prison, both men and women.

Along the road to Damascus, I also was on a journey, the resurrected Jesus appeared to me and questioned me why I was persecuting Him. It is interesting to note that Jesus equated persecution of His followers to be the same as persecuting Him personally. I responded by asking Jesus who He was. When Jesus answered that He was the leader, the founder of this new religion I was attacking, I immediately responded, "What shall I do, Lord?" The resurrected Jesus told me that I would be a witness for Him. I could not disbelieve what I had seen with my own eyes, I was of sound mind and very clear in my thinking. Jesus was very clear how he appeared to me, he was in a fleshly body I could touch. I said, "Lord, they themselves that you ask me to witness to, they know that I am in one synagogue after another hunting Christians, I imprisoned and beat those who believed in you. And when the blood of Stephen your witness was being shed, I myself was standing by approving and watching over the garments of those who killed him." Jesus then walked down a path with me as he explained so much.

He enlightened me as he told me, "You are on the right path with me. This path is a short journey today, an experience for learning, gaining knowledge, develop understanding, and pass through judgment." Tommy, have you ever heard those words before? I was truly a good guy in my heart but went against the law with murder including that I was acting immorally thinking I was right with God. But whatever gain I had, I now count as a loss for the sake of Christ and knowing he is the truth. Indeed, I count everything I did thinking it was a good loss because of the surpassing worth of knowing Christ Jesus as my Lord. For his sake, I have gladly taken the loss of all my personal things and count them as rubbish in order that I may gain Christ and be found in him, gaining eternal life. Not having a righteousness of my own that comes from the law, but that which comes through faith in Christ who is real, documented in history and not a methodical character. The righteousness from God that depends on faith that I may know him and the power of his resurrection, and may share his sufferings, becoming like him in his death, that by any means possible I may attain the same resurrection from the dead. I consider myself a bond slave of Jesus Christ. I am so committed to Jesus that everything I was, my body, my thoughts, my very life, is no longer my own, I belong to Jesus.

After walking along this path, I knew that I had not reached the end of the road; rather, I was just getting started. God had big plans for me and I was completely surrendered to Him. This change of heart from a murdering monster to speaking on behalf of Jesus death for all of us attests to the power of the Holy Spirit to bring about change in anyone who submits fully to the will of God. I had been a man totally committed to wipe Christianity off the face of the earth. However, the love and power of God took hold of my heart and changed me into His holy servant. Moreover, the world was changed by my obedience. However, I knew that my life of true faith had just begun, and I bore the responsibility of keeping my eyes on Jesus, the Source of salvation.

What could turn around a man who was so dedicated to his beliefs and so intent on squashing the beliefs of others? Only the loving power of Jesus Christ which was embedded in me by the meeting with him and the small journey he took with me to help me understand what all this is truthfully about. As many people experience today, Jesus is still the same as he was in my day. As Christians around the world, I also can attest, Jesus can take a hard heart and make it live again. All it takes is for one to respond to Jesus' call as I did, I asked Jesus, "What shall I do, Lord?"

"Tommy, do you have a hard heart? I hope to see you again one day my friend. Respectfully, with love and truth always. Goodbye." This character reached his arms out to Tommy and went on to give him a hug, after that he said nothing and turned the opposite direction walking off leaving Tommy bewildered yet thinking deeply. Again, Tommy was seeing off another interesting encounter. He has something to think about. Is this real? Does this have any meaning?

Steady walking, Tommy is approached by a very strange little creature. This creature is a weird chicken looking thing without legs, instead of legs the bottom half of its body is like a snake but has a pointy type of arrow looking thing for a tail. "What the heck are you? Get away!" No, this little guy slithering up to him is not leaving but gives him an eye to eye stare and nodded its head as if it's asking him to follow the direction he was already walking. No fear here, just get in line and follow the little creature, so Tommy just kept on moving and follows along. This is a funny little creature to Tommy, he finds it amusing to watch because it wobbles and shakes to move since it does not have legs. Tommy imagines the song by Sir-mixalot called baby got back is playing and this creature is wobbling to the beat of the music. As the creature is wobbling along Tommy is singing in his mind, "I like big butts and I cannot lie! You other brothers can't deny, that when a girl walks in with an itty-bitty waist and a round thing in your face, you get sprung, want to pull up tough, Cause you notice that butt was stuffed, Deep in the jeans she's wearing, I'm hooked and I can't stop staring!"

Going further down the path, it dawns on Tommy that he hasn't had any other thoughts since meeting this little guy but imagining its wiggly wobble to the beat of, I like big butts. "So where are we going little creature?" No reply, of course, it turns to acknowledge him with a quick little one-eyed wink. Tommy thinks he is cute now. The little creature stops and waits for Tommy to stop. "Good idea little guy, we need a rest. Well, do you have a name?" No reply. The creature moves forward one more time but this time it fluffed its wings up and sped forward, and out of nowhere here came this other creature, it charged towards them. This creature looked like an alligator with the head of a hyena. As this other creature was charging them, it looked like it was about to attack and eat the little chicken headed creature, and its size was way bigger, so Tommy assumed this chicken creature was about to die. In a flash, the little chicken creature raised up with a flap of its wings over the top of this alligator thing and with a swift whip of its barbed arrow tail, it struck the creature like a swinging axe and chopped the head off with one swift hit. The beheaded creature slid forward about 10 feet from Tommy. The chicken headed creature knew that other creature with the hyena head wanted to kill Tommy and it saved Tommy's life. "WOW! What a badass Bird creature you are! I owe you, man! You are frikkin awesome, I knew we were both dead the way that thing was coming after us, but you put that thing out of its misery."

The little chicken creature looked up at Tommy as though it had deep respect for him, it gave him a one-eyed wink again then turned and continued down the path, and without hesitation Tommy fell right in and followed. The creature reached a spot on the path where it stopped, it turned to Tommy and wobbled up to him. It looked up at Tommy's face and then lowered its head forward and gave this hugging motion on Tommy's legs as if it was loving on him. Tommy could tell it was being sweet and thought how nice and gentle this little guy is. The chicken creature turned and flapped its wings then flew off. "Hey, where are you going? We just got acquainted?"

Again, Tommy is walking and thinking, and a while later he is crossing the path of another man. This man is dressed like people did in ancient civilization, his clothes are funny looking. Tommy wonders to himself, 'why is this guy dressed so funny? He is coming towards me and looks like he is walking specifically to see me. OK, this must be someone else I need to talk to so let's see where this goes.'

"Hi there," Tommy said. "It appears that I am lost but obviously I am on some mysterious journey, are you here to see me?" With a deep strong voice, "Yes, as a matter of fact, I am here to see you, Tommy."

"And how did you know my name is Tommy?"

"Tommy, I was given a gift, God gave me powers to see into the future, to interpret dreams and tell of their meaning. God gave me the ability to understand dreams and visions of all kinds, I have seen you in one of my dreams."

"OK. Are we going to walk anywhere or just stand here and talk?"

"We will walk." He said.

"Let's go then, by the way, I had this adorable creature following me, I really like him and curious if you know anything about it?"

"Yes, he is a Cockatrice. His purpose is to be a path guardian, like how an Angel is your guardian on earth. He will come when danger is imminent and has the power to kill the serpents and evil devouring creatures that would hinder your progress or take your life away while you are on this path. Count your lucky stars he was with you.

Back to who I am. My ability to interpret dreams was leading me through this kingdom where I lived. In the second year of his reign, something troubled King Nebuchadnezzar about a dream that he could neither remember nor interpret. His magicians and astrologers could not interpret his dream, much less didn't know what the dream was. The king decreed that all the wise men, including me and my companions, would be to death. However, after I sought God in prayer, the mystery of the king's dream was revealed to me, and they took me to the king to interpret it. Immediately I attributed my ability to interpret dreams to the one true God since he answered my prayer. The key feature of the dream, as I told it to the king, was that one day there will be a kingdom set up by God that will last forever, and it will destroy all previous kingdoms known to man. With this, I was honored by King Nebuchadnezzar and placed in authority over all the wise men of Babylon. At my request, they also placed my three countrymen in positions of authority as administrators of Babylon. In time, King Nebuchadnezzar built a huge golden statue and decreed that all his people bow down and worship it at the given signal. His decree said that whoever refused to bow down to it would be thrown into a blazing furnace, ouch, that's extreme! Word reached the king that Shadrach, Meshach and Abednego my three countrymen were not worshipping his gods or the statue, and so they summoned them to Nebuchadnezzar's court.

Faced with being thrown into a blazing furnace, the three faithfully announced that their God could rescue them from the fire, but even if He did not, they would not bow down to the image. The furnace was so hot, seven times its normal heat that the king's soldiers were killed while putting the three into it. Then Nebuchadnezzar saw that there were four men in the furnace, completely unbound and walking about and that the fourth figure looked like he was of God. When the king called them out of the furnace, he and his governors were amazed to find that it had scorched not a single hair of their heads, nor was there even the merest smell of fire about them. King Nebuchadnezzar had a second dream, and not for the first time, he acknowledged that I had the spirit of the holy God within me and could interpret his dream. My interpretation of the dream was fulfilled, and after a period of insanity, Nebuchadnezzar was restored to his kingdom, and he praised and honored my God as the most-high.

Nebuchadnezzar's son, Belshazzar, became the new king, and during a banquet, he ordered the gold and silver goblets that had been stolen from the holy temple in Jerusalem to be brought out for use. In response to the defilement of such holy items, Belshazzar sees a handwriting on the wall. Once again, his astrologers cannot assist him in its translation, and so I was called upon to interpret the writing. As a reward for interpreting the writing, King Belshazzar promoted me to the third highest position in the Babylonian kingdom. That night, as I had prophesied, the king was slain in battle, and his kingdom was taken over by Cyrus the Great, and they made Darius the Mede a king. Under the new ruler, I excelled in my duties as one of the administrators to such a degree that King Darius was contemplating

making me head over all the kingdom. This infuriated
the other administrators so much that they looked for
a way to bring me down. They encouraged Darius to
issue a decree forbidding his subjects from praying to
any of their gods for the next thirty days. The penalty
for disobeying was to be thrown into a den of lions.
However, I continued to pray so openly to God that
they could see me at my bedroom window doing so.
With much regret, the king gave the order for me to be
thrown into the lion's den, but I said a prayer to God
to rescue me. The next day when I was found alive and
well, I told the king that God had sent an angel to shut
the lion's mouths, so I remained unharmed. This
resulted in King Darius sending out a decree that all
his subjects were to worship the God that answered
my prayers. And I continued to prosper throughout
King Darius' reign. Tommy, I saw the coming of Jesus,
I told these hundreds of years before he was known
and wrote it down for the future that when he came,
my prophecy would have come true. I also seen the
final end time, technology was moving so fast and I

could see things like people watching each other in a split second of doing something from one nation to another nation, people are communicating with small boxes by their ears listening to another person, explosions that ripped up miles of earth, birds that fly faster than imaginable that carries humans in their bellies, there will be wars, grasshopper looking birds with spinning overhead wings shooting what looked like stars with trails of fire off their arms, then one final war which Gods chosen people, or might I say the people who choose God will not have to witness. The lesson from my life is that I exercised great integrity and in doing so, received power to interpret dreams, a gift and favor from God, and I got the respect and affection of the powerful rulers I served. However, my honesty and loyalty to my masters never led me to compromise my faith in the one true God. Rather than it being an obstacle to my success, my continual devotion to God brought me the admiration of the unbelievers in my circle. When delivering interpretations, I was quick to give God the credit for

my ability to do so. No matter who we are dealing
with, no matter what their status is, we are to treat
them with compassion. As Christians, we are called to
obey the rules and authorities that God has put in
place, treating them with respect, however, as you see
from my example, obeying Gods law must always take
precedence over obeying men. I see you Tommy as a
possibility to tell people my story. I see that one day
before time is to end the Country that was blessed
with milk and honey will be misled by the ruler of
darkness. He will lead astray many more people in
this powerful nation than some continents have a total
of people combined. He will arise a leader that will be
in power for eight years then he will lead the people to
a negative debt that can't be paid back in the matter of
time equal to the Savior's resurrection till the time in
which you are standing. There will be two separate
parties representing power in this nation. People will
love this leader of the party blind to sin as he pulls in a
number above reality to follow him, he will bring a
movement that will allow the growth of sinners into

the destruction of the holiness of that nation which was once chosen by God to help and feed other nations. A man of God who is forgiven of his previous life as was Paul will be brought forward to lead the nation. Having a four-year span, the opposing people will grow exponentially and cause many roadblocks to hinder his ability to prosper back the nation and reduce its sin while the sinning party's crimes and sins will be ignored. The opposing party will increase immorality till this nation fails miserably. He is known by multiple names, the antichrist, the man of sin and the false prophet, this religiously confused power will play a prominent role in the deception of mankind prior to Christ's return.

Tommy, I hope you make time to tell my story, it would be nice to know that my work is alive, and people can know what to look for before they dwindle away to an eternal death of torment. It's time for me to continue down this path we are standing on, you should do the same."

"Good luck to you, I seem to keep running into these different people, I hope you don't have to deal with all these odd people like I have been encountering." Tommy turned, walked away and never looked back.

Soon after he is approaching his next encounter. The little chicken creature returns, "Hey little guy, good to see you! You walk with me?" Little chicken creature gives Tommy a wink as to say yes and wobble beside him and off they walked. A while down the path he feels a sprinkle fine mist, this is the first time his body has felt any physical sensations since he's been on this path. He walks by a tree called a weeping willow, this one is very tall with the longest limbs ever seen on one of these, and the leaves are omitting a wetness that is so refreshing it brings him back to a real-life feeling.

Drawn to this tree he walks up with the little chicken creature and there is this man sitting under it. "Hey there mister. You OK?" The man wouldn't talk he was weeping. Tommy asks, "Is this mist I am feeling by any chance your tears? I noticed you are weeping and ironically it happens to be under a weeping willow tree."

"No Tommy, the mist is not me, but you are close, it is a representation of my sadness."

"Sadness? What are you sad about? Are you lost too? I am becoming sad because I don't know if I am dreaming or if this is my final destination, and how do you know my name?"

"Tommy, I am the worst person in history, no bad person is a match for my crime. Not even Attila the Hun, Hitler, Osama Binladden, nobody has my treacherous fate from being the worst human ever. The reality is those people are good compared to me. I shouldn't be placed in that list of terrible people because I followed and learned from the most-high, Jesus. As our savior was about to take away the cause of death from all of us with his powerful love and was on his way to die, I knew he was our God, I walked with him, I witnessed all that he did to prove he was of Heaven and I knew he was paying it all by allowing himself to be executed, a price that no other person of this earth would have to go through to save mankind, it was his life he was willingly giving.

His mission was to die in place for all of mankind, so we could beat death, meaning eternal death and to give us life, eternal life. You might not understand but I did and was a greedy worthless dog! I sold him out, my lust for money caused his death, I guess something planned it that I would be the one, stupid me I didn't even think to ask for forgiveness which was right there for me to have. I was the one in charge of our group's money bag and sometimes stole from it, a disloyal thief. Even though the other apostles deserted Jesus and Peter denied him, my greedy butt went so far as to lead the temple guard to Jesus at Gethsemane and then identified Jesus by kissing him. I made the greatest error in history. What you need to know is an outward show of loyalty to Jesus is meaningless unless we also follow Christ in our heart. Satan and the world will try to get us to betray Jesus, so we must ask the Holy Spirit for help in resisting them. Although I tried to undo the harm I had done, I failed to seek the Lord's forgiveness. Thinking it was too late, I ended my life in suicide. If we are alive and have breath, it's never too late to come to God for forgiveness and cleansing from sin. Sadly, I was given the opportunity to walk in close fellowship with Jesus, I completely missed the most important message of Christ's ministry. The non-believing people wanted Jesus dead, I went to the chief priests in charge of the man hunt to find Jesus and asked him, "What are you willing to give me if I hand him over to you?" So, they counted out thirty silver coins. Can you believe I sold God for a measly pocket full of coins?

I approached Jesus to kiss him, it was how I could alert the group that came to kill Jesus who he was without pointing directly at him, but Jesus asked me, "Judas, are you betraying the Son of Man with a kiss?" He knew I was his betrayer.

When I the one who had betrayed him, saw they condemned Jesus, I was taken over with remorse and returned the thirty silver coins to the chief priests and the elders. I threw the money into the temple and left. Then the torment of deceiving my master was agonizing, I went away and hanged myself. Tommy, if you are ever offered a chance to receive forgiveness and the pleasure to experience Jesus, please do it! I feel my doom is near as the end of time as we know it is about to take place. Well Tommy, I know my fate is doom, do you know yours?" Tommy did not have any respect for him, he took it upon himself to leave this miserable, pitiful man. "What a loser!" he said aloud, and he and the little chicken creature walked off.

Tommy is walking confused and disoriented, he turned and looked back as many times as he could till he could not see Judas any more. Each time he looked back all he could see was Judas gasping for air as he was crying out loud and so hard he was losing his breath. What a sight to see, a grown man weeping as

much as a busload of women whose children just
died.

Tommy is coming to another clearing, it looks like a
dead end. What now? He is nearing the end and there
is a small river. He walks till the path ends at the river.
The river is clean! "Wow! I never seen a river so clear
that I could see the bottom." There by the shoreline is
a small boat. The boat is serenading him with the
most beautiful sound, it's not music but in the same
form as a music sound, but way more spiritually
soothing. The music is the same way Satan's voice was
when talking to Tommy earlier in the path, it was
entering his body instead of hearing it through his
ears. Well, enough of this mesmerizing himself with
the tunes coming from this boat, it's obvious he needs
to jump in, the path ended and nowhere else to go.
"Hey little chicken creature, I really enjoyed your
company, you are a bad-ass! I found out that you were
here to protect me, and you did a very good job! I have
no idea what is about to happen here, there is this
boat and I know I must get in and float to where ever

it takes me. So, are you ready to take a ride with me in this boat.?" The little creature stared directly at him, again it gave him a one-eyed wink, but this time a tear dropped out of its eye. Tommy knew that meant no. "I really will miss you and always remember you." The same way he could hear Satan talk through his body he heard this, "I love you, where I come from it's easy to love, nobody has anger and all us creatures are kind to each other. We will see each other again Tommy, just do the right thing and when we see each other again we will have a feast under a weeping willow tree that has tears of joy! See you on the other side, with love and respect for you."

This brought about an empty space in Tommy like he was hollow, that bird left him feeling very sad.

Tommy jumps in and the boat automatically departs from the shore. He thinks to himself, this is so strange, this whole trip seems like a month of walking, but, it is like I just got here. Am I losing touch with time? Am I even part of time? What is time? Oh man, that's it I've gone crazy, I am insane, I lost my mind.

This is not real it's a dream, NO! I am lost in a time warp! Oh God please tell me what this is! Just as he was in the midpoint of figuring whether he was crazy or what this madness was, he looked at the shoreline and saw the first person he met on the path. Passing by in this floating boat he can see the handsome Devil of a man that gave him his first speech on this trip. The man is waving and behind him no light only darkness. Tommy waves back and noticed the music paused, it was so quiet, it was as if he became deaf and was without breath like he just suffocated. He did not like this, it was creepy! He knew that man had some nasty power that caused this. Was he trying to tell Tommy something? Tommy is about to be all the way past him then there was light again and the serene music played again, the man was gone. Floating in peacefulness he is wondering where next? What next? Then there is Sarah by the shoreline. He saw her standing at the river's edge, a bit far for him to yell out so He waves at her, she is waving back, and he could see by her expression; she was laughing as if she just told herself a joke. He remembers her joy and sweet laughter and he is laughing with her as he is reminiscing about his conversation with her. While he is enjoying his thoughts about her, he passed right by and she disappeared.

Continuing to float along this clear serene river he is waiting to see where this voyage will end. He is passing a new place, this is unreal with beautiful scenery, it's like nothing anyone can imagine. He can see another person by the shore, there is Paul waving and smiling. Tommy waves back remembering Paul's story and how much he trusted in Jesus coming to save mankind from the guilt of sin and the punishment of eternal torment. He has all this logged in and embedded in his mind, and all the stories told him from the different characters on this path are memorized. Tommy is waving at Paul while he passes by and there on the other side of the river is Daniel. In his mind he is saying, Hello Daniel, no words are being exchanged, it's all visual with no words needing said. This floating on the river is reminding him of the time he went to Disney world as a child. They have a ride there called, "It's a small world." On the ride you float in this little boat in an animated fake river and pass all the different countries of the world, and each scene is a picture of what that country would be famous for in landscape, if it was Norway there were mountains, Egypt has pyramids... Each country has little children characters dressed how they would be in that country and they are waving at you as you pass them.

He passes Daniel and sure enough Daniel is waving. Tommy remembers the power of his ability to interpret dreams and see into the future. Then there is Judas. Passing him there isn't any waving or smiling, oh boy, he is still crying, and how terrible his life must be. Tommy remembers what Judas said about betrayal and feeling so much pain and suffering. He really remembers the part about selling Jesus right before giving his own life to save people from eternal death. Tommy waves at him with pity as he passes. All he can see is Judas looking down, Judas never waved.

Tommy figures his torment must be so powerful that he did not know what was going on around him. For some reason Tommy said to himself, 'I will pray for him.'

TOMMY MEETS THE ROCK,

THE CORNERSTONE

Now something must be happening to Tommy because after passing Judas Tommy thought to himself to pray for another person. Drifting further down the river with his spirit being serenaded by the serene sounding music Tommy remembers all these people he met on this path so far. He comes to grip with the fact they all had an important message to tell in their own way and that they had a moral designed just for him. "I feel like I am getting something out of this journey so far." He is listening to this music and thinking to himself, then out of nowhere, Boom! He hit a very large rock, it was solid like a wall. It snapped him out of this thought process and makes him wide alert as he's trying to catch his balance. He reaches out to grab the rock to steady himself, so make his way out of the boat. Just as he was reaching to grab the rock a hand grabbed his hand, and with the power of a crane it lifted Tommy up and placed him on the ground. "What in God's creation is this?" he asked himself. When the hand yanked him out of the boat he was blinded by a bright light, it was so bright it took him about three minutes to see again.

As his vision is coming back, he can see this man standing in front of him. This man looked so clean, he was profoundly white, and his clothes were so bright white it was as if they were underlined with electricity. Tommy felt a presence unlike anything this journey had to offer yet.

This man overpowered him with pure majesty! Not able to speak, he lost his ability to talk, Tommy had no choice but to follow his instincts. Feeling an intense fear and a deep amount of shame Tommy fell to the ground and put his face directly on the ground, he hid his face from this man. For whatever reason he knew he should not look at him, he was feeling shame, but more than shame was total fear. A voice spoke that had a powerful sound, and when the first words came out it was so loud it sounded like he was two feet away from a thunder and penetrated through his entire body, but oddly it felt like a mildly strummed harp had begun to play serene music. "Tommy, I am the rock that you thought the boat hit. I am the means for the transition to eternal life which is the opposite of eternal death and has a different meaning after death. I want you to walk with me as I explain what that really means. You need to pay close attention, I have so much to tell you! It's vitally necessary you understand everything there is to know about the important things I am about to educate with. You have much to remember, and this will take a long time to explain. First let me explain my purpose for you and all mankind alike. God made a man; his most special creation and he was happy with the creation of man. That man may as well have been his child, he was particularly dear to him. He did not spend all his time with his creation. He didn't want him to be lonely and thought it would be nice to create again another living being for that man to have a partner to share life with, thus creating what they would pattern marriage after for all the earths time. But one problem existed with these two. A culprit that would cause them to fail from keeping a simple request of their creator. That bad culprit influenced them to turn against their creator's design of innocence. It was a guy you might remember having met already on this path you journeyed on today. He is the archangel Lucifer since known by many names but to name a few, Satan, Beelzebul and Apollyon, any of those names sound familiar? God created Satan as the head of the Angels. He was at one time the most powerful, intelligent and beautiful angel in heaven. He was second only to God Himself. But, because of his desire to be like God, Lucifer rebelled against God, and God kicked him out of heaven along with one-third of the angels. Satan is the leader of the Fallen Angels (Demons). His main name means our chief adversary. Satan is so powerful that even Michael the archangel did not oppose him personally; Michael attacked him in the name (with the power) of the Lord. Lucifer was the first to sin against God and the first to break His laws. Satan has since influenced the world to think that mankind was the first to sin. Adam and Eve, Gods first two human creations sinned, but they weren't the first to sin. Satan had already rebelled against God and was waiting there in the Garden of Eden to plant his lies in their thinking. Satan cannot create matter, he can only manipulate it. Just like a box of Legos; though we can make something, we did not manufacture the Legos! Satan is not omnipresent or omnipotent that is, he is not all knowing, all present, and all powerful, only God is! Because of all of Satan's entourage (demons), it may seem like he is all that and he will do what it takes to have you believe that he is. He gives people what they want, so it fulfills what he wants. He deceives people by subjective truth and human reasoning that sounds appealing but it's a trap! So, he caused Adam and Eve to sin and as a result, God no longer held them on a pedestal and because they sinned God granted them death which is eternal.

What is death? It is eternal by endless separation from God, first getting cast into hell. How did we get to the place that God built a Hell? It happened when Satan was thrown out of Heaven. Until he rebelled against God, all the "Heavenly realm" drew its life, existence, and strength directly from God in a perfect relationship, and when Satan rebelled that went away. God cast Satan and the 1/3 of the Angels out of heaven then God prepared the relentless fire for him and his angels, and then Humanity fell. It separates all of human-kind from God due to the act of sin by the first created humans, Adam and Eve. Thus, you are all under the curse or the guilt of sin which is death and are incapable of rejoining God in what once was a perfect state, God's judgment and wrath are now with us.

So, the question now becomes, is this fair? Maybe, maybe not! Adam and Eve represent all of humanity, they are the original humans who set the path to how everything would be there after from the decisions they made! Thus, you all take the blame! You, as humans, have the bullheadedness to go your own way which is the wrong way paved with undeserving pride and arrogance! Consider this; was it fair for One Man (Jesus), who was guiltless to pay a penalty for all humans of a death that He did not deserve? Not fair indeed! God gave Adam and Eve true happiness and perfection with only one rule; do not eat fruit from the tree of knowledge, they did, yielding everything they should never have known.

Adam and Eve did not respect who makes the rules, and they took it upon themselves to determine what was good or bad. Ultimately, they sought themselves over God, to act as their own God in charge of where they were. They also agreed to be swayed and misled by Satan when they already had the rules set in place, first by Satan, then by each other.

This selfish behavior entered man's mindset which gave birth to sin and corrupted everything in creation, people, animals, the earth. As a result, people inherited the guilt and shame of being apart from our Creator thus forcing us to either try to seek Him in vain attempts or persue our self-interests which causes people to be separated from God and His glory.

God was not without mercy. His first act was to cover Adam and Eve with clothing, so they would not feel shame! Then He promised one day he would make a way to save them. Eventually, this was through a savior that would be his highest sacrifice, his son. So why the wrath of God over all this? What is the Wrath of God? If God is love, why is He angry at you? The wrath of God is to be taken seriously, and seriously by those who reject Him. You need to understand God's Righteousness. He is entirely Pure, Holy and without sin and never existed in its presence which explains his absence from you on earth. While you are full of heinous sin and no matter how good you try to be, you cannot exist in person with him.

God is a God of judgment; He has the right, the authority, and the power to judge you and then to determine what to do with you as His creation. And you have no excuse to reject him or his ways because God has placed this instinct within your consciousness. Thus, when you reject God and follow your own needs and ideas, you are in fact inviting His wrath and judgment upon yourselves. You cannot think or say at the time of your judgment, "Hey, how could I know," because you do know and do have access to a wealth of information to learn from! So, if the thought enters your mind and you wonder about God, and you decide not to research him, then shame on you and what a loss.

There is no being right in his eyes, neither by the Law or earning righteousness with deeds! Just by being born all have sinned; it condemns all life! If all you do is live for yourselves, you miss out on what life is about and on relationships that honor God. So, the answer to why God has wrath upon you is because sin made God angry! When Adam became a sinner, the Spirit left him not gradually but immediately! Sin is real, all wrongdoing is sin, even the smallest seeming so innocent affects all people; you must beware not to ignore this.

There will be an accounting for you all, a judgment!! Beware not to live for the creatures and the created while ignoring the Creator! The Wicked suppress God's truth and His character which makes them evil! Pay attention! You have no excuse; God revealed Himself through His creation alone. You also need to beware that your rationalizations and intellectual arrogance will convince you Hell is not real! Tommy, LISTEN to me very carefully! What I am about to tell you is what I told you I would explain to you when I first talked to you, it is very important that you tell people what I am about to say if you ever get the chance! I told you that there is eternal life, and there is death. Eternal life results from accepting the free-gift I gave with my death, it freed people, which I will explain my death later, right now you must understand death. What is death? Death came from Adam and Eve's sin. Sin results from Satan persuading Eve to deceive God. Satan is doomed for Hell which was made specifically for him and his followers and anything that cannot exist in Heaven with God, all which will be cast into hell. It is eternal by endless separation from God. How did it get to the place that God had to build a Hell? God is pure in every way, he cannot exist in the presence of sin. When man sinned he then became unable to be with God allowing himself to be cast into hell with Satan.

What is Hell? HERE IS THE BIG WHAMMY! You better store this information in your memory!

 There will be a certain point in a time when the righteous people who accepted the free-gift of my death will be instantly changed into immortal beings. That time is still coming, it's in the future. It occurs when I return, and the last trumpet sound takes place, then I resurrect and bring back to life the bodies reuniting them with their spirit.

Nowhere in the plans for heaven will the wicked and non-believers be transformed in this manner. It's as well because they won't have eternal life, they are not reborn which is receiving the gift that Jesus gave his life in place of our sins and believing in his resurrection from death.

It is inconceivable and unreasonable to fabricate such an event. As stated in my last speech on earth, "The soul that sinneth, it shall die." No matter what we understand a soul to be, let's accept the evidence that it will die and must die because of sin. If the wicked live eternally in fire, then they have the same thing as the righteous which is living forever but in a different place. So, how can hell be eternal? Who could give them eternal life but Christ? Christ only exists in Heaven so how could there be an eternal place without Christ. Those who do not believe in the only begotten son Jesus and accept his gift of dyeing in place of sin, they will die again, that death will never end, and they will disappear eternally... It's an endless eternal death because it is an endless, eternal punishment. The second death is an eternal death from which I will never raise them, the only ones raised are the only ones going to Heaven.

Tommy, what is unquenchable Fire?" "Sir, I am not sure."

"Someone may raise this question: What about the unquenchable fire that burns the wicked? God describes the fire in hell as Unquenchable. Doesn't that mean it will never go out? NO, it doesn't. To quench means to extinguish or put out. No one can put out the fire of hell. That is the strange fire made from God. No one will be able to escape from it by extinguishing it. Isaiah says of that fire, "Behold, they shall be as stubble; the fire shall burn them; they shall not deliver themselves from the power of the flame: there shall not be a coal to warm it, nor a fire to sit before it." After it has accomplished its work of destruction, that fire 'will' go out. No one can deliver themselves from its flame by putting it out because the flame dies by itself, and finally, not a coal will burn because nothing will remain from it including a person's spirit or soul. Unbeliever's spirits will be wiped out for eternity, and before the flames die out they will have eliminated the body, soul and spirit, disintegrated, vaporized, invisible, never to be seen or remembered again.

Jeremiah prophesied that Jerusalem would burn with a fire that could not be quenched, and it burned down to ashes. Understand the word "quench." It does not mean fire that will never go out. It only means what it is, "Unquenchable." It can't be quenched. Tommy, think about it, when you build a fire, and when anything catches on fire what happens to the object that burns?"

Tommy was afraid to answer wrong but replied, "It turns into ashes?"

"Yes, it does not continue to burn, ashes are the remains of the fire! The same when a person's soul is cast in the lake of fire, it will eventually turn to ashes, the lake of fire ends up devouring everything in it. People think that in the worst-case scenario if they live in heat forever then they are living forever and that gives them a second chance sooner or later, right? No, not true, hell is not forever it's the death that eliminates sin, Satan, and a person's existence of ever having a life. Remember ever hearing the term eternal darkness? That's what this is, when there is nothing left after an object has burned away it will never know light again because it won't exist in order to be in light.

So, Tommy, the alternative you should desire is Heaven! It is forever! The fact is that theology has made an ogre out of our great God of love. God has been portrayed as crueler than Hitler. Even though Hitler tortured people and experimented with them, he finally allowed them to die. They will argue that God will keep these deathless souls alive for the sole purpose of seeing them suffer and scream throughout eternity, God would then be evil, how can evil exist in Heaven? But non-believers do not realize that by saying this they are accepting the idea of a God."

They kept walking and Jesus continued to lecture Tommy who was preoccupied with Jesus' brilliance and absorbing his speech and understanding this powerful message.

Jesus went on to tell Tommy, "God's Justice is Vindicated? Not only is such a picture misrepresented of God's love, it also distorts His justice. Think for a moment about the implications of a doctrine that would consign every lost soul to an immediate, never-ending hell at the time of death. Suppose a man died 10,000 years Before Adolph Hitler with only one sin in his life. His soul would go instantly into the fire to be tormented for eternity. Then picture the death of Adolph Hitler, who supervised the deaths, torment and suffering of millions of people. According to the popular doctrine, his soul also would immediately enter hell to suffer eternally. But the man who was sent to hell because of only one sin, will burn 10,000 years longer than Hitler. How could that be just? Would God deal in such a manner? It would contradict God's statement that each one must be punished according to his deeds.

"Accordingly, God said there will be no more sorrow, pain, crying, or death. In order for no more pain to exist, there cannot be eternal hell existing either! Get it? The two things are mutually restrictive of each other. We should thank God every day that His plan will finally bring an end to suffering. No one will be sent to Hell because he sinned, because everyone has sinned. No one will be left out of heaven because he lied, stole, or committed adultery. The only reason anyone will be cast into Hell is because he refused to turn away from his sin and into the arms of a loving Savior who stands ready to pardon and cleanse him or her from all unrighteousness, sin, and death. For God so loved the world that he gave his biggest sacrifice, his only begotten Son, and whosoever believe in his purpose to die in place of sin will have everlasting life, and not perish, which is going to Hell to be eliminated forever.

Now who am I? I am Jesus. I will tell you what makes following me different than other religions giving reasons to believe in their version of God.

You can literally read and learn from the Bible. The Bible book is not a story of fables and methodical characters, it's a thorough book with documented history and even better yet a very accurate list of historical events. Tommy, do you believe in George Washington the so called first president in the land of milk and honey?"

"Milk and Honey? I believe in George Washington the president of the U.S.A."

"Why Tommy?"

"How can I not believe in him we have history books documenting his whole life story."

"Bingo!! That is how you know the Bible is entirely true! It is also a factual and complete book of history with more historical events listed than any single history book you can find including famous names you can recognize like Augustus and Tiberius Caesar, and such as Pontius Pilate that you can cross reference with non-biblical books. Check yourself to see if I am correct in this statement, if you look in one of today's current history books this is an example of what it would say about Pontius Pilate." (Pontius Pilate's date of birth is unknown. He is known to have rained from the Samnium region of central Italy. Pontius Pilate served as the prefect Judean from 26 to 36 A.D. He convicted Jesus of treason and declared that Jesus thought himself King of the Jews, and had Jesus crucified. Pilate died 39 A.D. The cause of his death remains a mystery. An artifact found in 1961 proved his existence.)

"There now! My time on this earth is documented by non-biblical books, that should say enough! There were eye-witness accounts of my life, all the things I did were legitimately seen by thousands of people who then wrote down and accurately documented the information the same way the history of George Washington's and Augustus Caesar's life was documented in non-biblical books up till this very day.

So, what happened with me? What did I do that was so important? After sin was birthed into life, people had to be saved from it and needed to be forgiven. Thousands of years earlier it was written in the Bible and predicted that I would come. I went to incredible dimensions for you by giving my life on the cross; I didn't just suffer and die as a metaphor; it had to happen! It was either people die, meaning they would be eternally separated from me because of sin, or I die, then you have life eternally. The people forced me to die, after they established that I breathed no more because I lost almost all my blood and my heart stopped they confirmed that I died. After I died, 3 days my body stayed in a tomb, I arose back to life and thousands of people physically seen me with their eyes after my death and documented this. My death was so it could forgive you of the sin you were forced to be born into, thanks to Satan, and allowing you to know and be with me eternally. It required my death to do away with sin. If there wasn't sin, there wouldn't have been a need for my death and shedding my sinless blood. By being born into earth like you were, I became sin, so I could beat it for all of you! Because sin is the violation of God's existence, it requires a price to be paid from the wages of sin brought on by Adam and Eve following Satan.

Death is eternal separation from God. Without some payment for that awful penalty of eternal death, human beings would face oblivion through death with no hope beyond the grave. At one time it was mandatory for people to sacrifice the best living thing that was dear to them, generally their prize animal, the show quality one worth more than any other sheep or cow in the herd. If the people were poor and only owned one animal it was automatically as good as a prize animal because it had more value, about like only having one dollar to your name would be like a million dollars. It had to die to save the owners family from condemnation of their sins. But, I took on sin and sacrificed myself once to take away the sins of many people forever; paying the price for you. I will appear a second time, not to deal with sin, but to bring salvation to those who are waiting for me to go to Heaven. I paid the price, me, and you cannot earn it through anything you do because you cannot do what I did, it is impossible for you to arise after death on your own.

If you talk to another man and he tells you that only so many people will inherit the opportunity to go to heaven, and then he tells you that you must earn your place in heaven, that man is a troublemaker. You can't earn Heaven by doing good deeds. You need not knock on doors to tell people about me to earn a spot in heaven, you do that from the joy of knowing me and what I did for you, and it makes you want to share that information. Heaven is not something you can earn! I paid for you to be there. But, I do want you to share what you have learned, knock on doors and tell people what gift they have waiting for them, so people can know there is a place waiting for them in heaven. Then you will earn something better than anything that can be bought, or pride can give you, it will bless you to help the spirits of other people live eternally.

Tommy, I paid the price, but beware. I will tell you a tale and hopefully after hearing this you will understand when you accept my gift to be in heaven eternally, you still need to continue to turn from sin. So here it is, this is a tale of little Tommy, 'Tommy's big catch of the day.' Tommy was a good-looking young boy who lived in the Deep South. His summer days are filled with walking through the woods, playing with friends, and fishing in the pond down the dirt road. Fishing was by far his favorite thing to do. Almost every other day during his summer vacation, he would dig up worms and take off with a fishing pole in his hand to go fishing for the day.

This one steamy hot day, like most others during Tommy's summer break, he woke up early and could hear the pond calling him to come fish. Tommy quietly walked out the front door, grabbed his spade and worm pail from the porch then walked into the woods to search for bait. He turned over old stumps and dug under leaves hoping to find worms. Under one old stump he hit the jackpot. The ground was squirming with big healthy live bait. In two minutes, he had all the bait he needed, and in 15 minutes he was at the pond.

Reaching into his bait bucket, Tommy pulled out one of these big worms. He double hooked it and tossed it into the water. He noticed a stinging in his hand, brimming in the thrill of the moment he paid no attention to it. Within 30 seconds, Tommy had a strike and pulled in a nice big mouth Bass. 'Wow' he thought, a fish in the first minute. This is unbelievable!

He put the catch on his stringer, hurried to re-bait his hook and tried his luck again. Once again, he felt a stinging sensation in his hand as he threw his line into the pond, so what he didn't have time to worry about was stinging sensations. Within just a few seconds, he caught another huge fish. No time to waste, he fumbled as he hurried to bait his hook, his hand felt numb and stiff. But Tommy was too excited about catching another big fish to give it much thought.

At the end of only 45 minutes of fishing Tommy had caught eight large fish. This was by far his best fishing day ever. He was so proud of his accomplishment that even though there was plenty of day left to fish, he threw the heavy stringer of fish over his shoulder and dashed down the dirt road toward home to show off his catch to his mom and dad.

The local sheriff drove up alongside Tommy and seen the big catch, he congratulated him on his catch of fish. With a smile and a victory hoot, Tommy held up the stringer to show him. The sheriff gasped, parked his car and ran out to Tommy. His eyes hadn't deceived him, Tommy's arm was red and swollen to about twice its normal size. The sheriff asked Tommy, hoping to not hear what he thought might be the answer, "Exactly what bushes have you been around and what bait did you use to catch all those fish?"

Tommy boasted, "No bushes or brush just the wooded area where I found some huge worms under an old stump sir. These worms are strong and really wiggle hard and they make such a big movement in the water the fish went crazy," the boy answered as he was holding up the bait bucket to show the Sherriff. After a close look at the worms, the sheriff went into emergency mode. Securing the bucket in his truck, he then scooped Tommy and his stringer of fish into the backseat of his patrol car. Spinning a U-turn on the gravel road, he sped off to the hospital sending a message for Tommy's parents to meet them there, but Tommy did not make it, he died on the way.

What the sheriff had discovered was that Tommy had been fishing with baby copperhead snakes. Tommy's deadly bait brought him a good morning's catch but cost him his life. If Tommy had stopped fishing after that first sting and thought something was not right from it, it would have saved him. One bite from a baby copperhead won't kill a person who gets treatment in time. But Tommy was having fun and didn't bother himself with the signal from the small voice of pain in his hand. As his hand grew numb, something silenced even that small voice.

Playing around with sin is like using baby copperhead snakes for bait. Sinning seems harmless to people who don't think something isn't right and don't recognize the sin and its deadly consequences. The more sin you get into, the number you become to its sting. In the excitement of the moment, you ignore the still small voice of God warning you of danger and encouraging you to choose life instead of death.

Did you understand that Tommy?"

"I sure did, it was an interesting analogy. But I feel like all this could be a dream and none of this is real. Maybe when I wake up I will remember that."

"Tommy, do you know that you were created to live forever? Life, the universe and humans are created, and that you were created to be with me in heaven." Jesus already knew what Tommy thought but was baiting him for another topic. Tommy replied, "Created to be with you? Created? Yah right, good luck if you believe in creation, let me tell you what I know! You ever heard of energy exploding, I believe in the physics that scientists have researched and proved. We are the aftermath of enormous energy. The energy was so intense it exploded into the universe as we know it today."

"Yah, exploded into perfectly round planets strategically placed in the universe. Wow Tommy, that sounds good but not the way I heard it from scientists. Answer this Tommy, where did life come from?"

"You should already know this since you know so much. Evolution! An organism recreated itself into many microorganisms. All the other microorganisms developed from those later. Here is the fact, it has to do with Biology. The first one went into water and became a fish, then they eventually crawled out of the water growing legs and as time evolved, the creature kept recreating and became many creatures with legs and that's how all the animals got here." "Superb! But I must disagree and here is why. There purely is no evidence of a species mutating into an entirely different kind. Something cannot evolve from nothing! Life according to evolutionists began when different chemicals under the right circumstances came together and formed a more complex unit which ultimately developed into an organism. Then it took millions of years for life to begin because of the ideal kinds of chemicals combining. Originally, they didn't know they were right for each other until by chance under some arbitrary circumstances they finally met and made a match. Then it required millions of more years for organisms to co-mingle and become transformed into complex creatures.

The key factor in the theory of evolution is that the right elements came together under arbitrary circumstances. It would have to be that way because if the elements were put together in a planned or predestined or systematic way, there would need to be a force directing them. The life forms that resulted would then have been, "created." If they were created, then something greater than it would have already been there to help it form, right?

And if humans came from monkeys then why are there still monkeys? If humans were once monkeys wouldn't they have evolved out of existence?

Have you ever seen an explosion?" "Yes, I wasn't born yesterday," Tommy replied.

"What did the item that got blown up look like after it exploded?"

"Well a big pile of dust and pieces!" "O.K. Tommy, the explain how the planets around the earth where you live became perfectly round, wouldn't they be oddly shaped? How do you explain them sitting in midair not moving just floating never moving from the spot they are in, wouldn't they fall or hit something or move? How do you explain only two planets moving and circling each other? Doesn't that mean the rest of the planets should still be moving? How do you explain those two planets not colliding with any other planet? And what about gravity? If the planets are the result of an explosion wouldn't they have blown away and become dust? When you look up into the night sky, you catch a glimpse of the same universe ancient stargazers saw. Even the few thousand stars visible to the naked eye can evoke awe and wonder.

Since the beginning of time until this time you live in now, scientists still see the universe as undreamed of even with the tools of modern astronomy. While the full extent of the universe remains unknown to humans, astronomers are advanced in science with the ability to see multiple billions of lightyears into the universe. Within the known universe there may be as many as 10 sextillion stars, a 1 followed by 22 zeros, you don't even have a calculator that can store that many numbers, and that's only the universe where you came from Tommy!

The size of some of those stars is also mind-boggling for you to fathom anything about. The sun that lights up the earth is huge from your perspective, about 109 times the diameter of the earth. Yet some stars are more than 1,500 times the diameter of the sun! If a star that size was placed at the center of your solar system, it would extend from earth beyond the orbit of

Jupiter. This is only the beginning of what a microscopic molecule would look like on a ball the size of the Sun compared to what is imagined of how far the universes distance can be measured.

How about this Tommy, why does the earth consist of water and life, but the rest of the planets do not? Shouldn't all planets contain life since they all came from the same explosion? Shouldn't the same pattern for life exist throughout all of them?

I can ask you three hundred of these questions to every answer you give Tommy."

Even though Jesus had clear and precise facts, Tommy is feeling like he is wise and will beat Jesus with this answer and told Jesus, "Physics! Physics does not lie."

Then Jesus presented a simple question to Tommy.

"OK Mr. smarty pants, if you know physics let's see if this is correct. The number one law of physics is energy cannot be created nor destroyed, if so where did all this energy known as a universe come from?

Did it just magically appear out of nothing? The number two law of physics is everything runs down meaning it becomes less not more complex like the extinction in animals instead of them evolving further. The genes of plants, insects, and humans are continuously becoming defective, riddled with disease, and mutating cancers are not improving.

The law of thermodynamics proves that organization cannot flow from random chaos. So, you tell me Mr. Genius, how is it we have huge complex structures like galaxies, galactic clusters, and the very non-random universe? And then tell me if this is correct, another law of biology is that life cannot come from non-life. A creature cannot create itself. So then, where did all this life on the earth come from? Another law of biology is creatures can only create creatures like themselves. For example; a dog cannot give birth to a cat. So then, where did all this life diversity come from? Not evolution! I should tell you a fact, there has NEVER been an experiment that showed something evolving into something else even though scientists have been trying to prove it using the theory of hundreds of thousands of generations of fruit flies and E. Coli.

Also, fossil records do NOT show a clear evolutionary path, but they show that certain species did not exist before some other species. Most paleontologists face a situation where there were only gaps in the fossil record, with no evidence of transformational intermediates between documented fossil species.

Are you commencing to understand me Tommy? Do I sound like I know something about this stuff? Maybe I had something to do with this?"

All this knowledge this still has not impressed Tommy, and he is sure he got him now, he laughed with pride and asked Jesus, "I don't mean to laugh but O.K., where did God come from? No way you can answer that now, can you? Ha-ha gotcha there!" Tommy is so smart, right?

A noise like an atomic boom sounded, it took Tommy's hearing away. Trumpet sounds blast so loud it felt as if his head blew into pieces many directions. Then complete silence.

"You are a fool! Foolish pride is the death of every man! God didn't come from anywhere. God is entirely self-contained. God has always been, and there would be no reality without him. Your question appears to be tricky because it sneaks in the false assumption that God came from somewhere and then asks where that might be. If there was "something" before God, then that something would have to be God creating God! God is the First Source and Center of everything. The answer to that question is, it does not even matter. It is like asking what does blue smell like? Blue is not in the category of things that have a smell, so the question itself is flawed. In the same way, God is not in the category of things created or caused. God is uncaused and uncreated. God unconditionally exists, infinitely before you and eternally after you.

How do we know this? We know that making something from nothing cannot create anything. So, if there were ever a time when there was absolutely nothing in existence, then nothing would have ever come into existence from nothing! But things do exist. Therefore, since there could never have been exactly nothing, something would have always existed. That ever-existing thing is what we call God. God is the uncaused Being that caused everything else to come into existence. God is the uncreated Creator who created the universe and everything in it. Only a God based on love could always have existed. But since you humans do not yet have perfect love, you carnal humans still have difficulties fully understanding that. But when you are only a spirit in heaven, you will be intelligent in a way to know distinctly. Do I need to tell you all I know, or will you finally accept that I know all?"

Tommy dumbfounded by all the answers coming in so fast is feeling like he is in a war zone. "Um, I think that will be all that for now, sir."

Jesus went on to tell Tommy about how he informed people of times to come in his last speech on earth before ascending into the sky. These things were documented and written down, later applied to the book. Things were forecast and written before their events happened, and most of them have come and passed. These events are visible and accurate events proving truth to the Bible's printed documented history. And, that he revealed the ending of the earth to come in the same speech which meant that Tommy should listen carefully to what he is enlightening him about.

"Tommy, think with me about what I am doing here. I want you to wake up, so I can show you there is more to life than you know. Neither your life is an accident, nor this path you are on. I want you to open your eyes to a probability, and that would be what happens to you after you die if you are not dead right now."

Tommy interrupts, "Dead? Am I dead already?" "Yes Tommy, are you dead?"

"No, this is a dream, isn't it? Am I really dead?" "You figure it out when you get the chance Tommy. I want you to listen to this last fact! Your thought like most atheists concludes that you die and get buried, then that ends all life and existence for any mortal. I want you to know there is another sector, the afterlife. What do you think that is Tommy?" Tommy shrugs his shoulders, "I don't know, apparently rotting six feet under the ground." Jesus went on lecturing as they are walking and said, "What happens after you die depends on what happens before you die. It is appointed for men to die once, but after that comes judgment. This is an appointment no one will miss. As people have recognized, the statistics on death are appalling, one hundred out of one hundred people will someday die. All people are all terminally ill with a disease called "about to be dead!" Soon enough you get your end to life and a seat in the highest court system there is! There will be the saved people who are those that trusted my coming and teachings as Lord and Savior, and accepted my death for saving them from sin, and believe that I arose back from the grave. Then, there will be the lost, they are those who haven't trusted, believed in me or accepted the existence of God. For my followers their spirit goes to be with me in heaven, and their body is buried until the day of resurrection when I return to the earth. Their bodies will be raised imperishable with a body that is perfect in every way, free from the suffering of death and decay. In life your bodies wear out, like a clock continually running down, but when you are raised from the grave, it will be with bodies that can never decay, never wear out, never suffer injury, never grow old, never get sick, and never die. Isn't that something to look forward to? Let me explain more, there is one similarity between the fate of the saved and the lost. At the moment of death, the body is buried in the grave while the spirit enters a new realm. For the believer in me, the moment of death brings him into the personal presence of his new home, Heaven. For the unbeliever, they have permanent death because the unsaved are then cast into the lake of fire where they encounter their final death. Do you remember what being cast into the lake of fire involves Tommy?"

"Yes, you vanish into nothing forever!"

"Fantastic my son, eternally separated from the presence of Almighty God. Death begins the definite ending of the removal from time, to be forgotten eternally and never remembered. God eliminates those that do not need him or want him and do not believe in me. This is the final destiny of those who do not know Jesus Christ. To make it more personal, it is the final destiny of your friends and neighbors, your loved ones, your parents, your brothers, your sisters, your children. I will know them personally if they believe in me and if they look up to enter the kingdom of heaven. Without believing in me, I will reject them and say I never knew you. And Hell is their destiny if they die without me, including you. Let that thought linger in your mind. The reality of hell is more than just a theoretical doctrine. There is a place reserved for you in the lake of fire Tommy. They once thought of you but no longer remember you." "What? What do you mean? What the hell did I do to deserve Hell?" "Tommy, no matter how bad you are you do not deserve hell, it's the whole point I am trying to make, it is not about how good or bad you are, good people are born into sin as well and have the same destiny, if you do not accept my death beating sin, there is no way out, remember what I told you about sin? All men are born into it and have its nature no matter what! The only way out is faith in my death and resurrection back to life to prove that I am who I said I am! I am the resurrection and the life. He who believes in me will live even though he dies an earthly death; and whoever lives and believes in me will never die. Do you understand this? Do you believe this?" Tommy is grasping who this Jesus really is and is facing the fear of permanent separation from existence. "I want to believe, sir. I do not want to be thrown out of existence, please." Jesus is making progress with the self-made wealthy genius geek. "Well then, know I laid my life down for you, for all people that ever existed, and I Love you, that's why I came down to earth, I could not stand to see all mankind torn away from me and cast into hell to vanish forever. You are

my precious love, my children. I want you to tell
people this story of your journey. I want you to tell
them everything I told you! Time is near the end of
what is now known as the earth, it is time to move on
to better things. I foretold this in my instruction book,
the Bible which most people believe is just a
storybook. You can know it is true based on the
factual evidence of the history told in it. I warned
people about the ability of self-annihilation.
Humanity has had the capability for self-annihilation
for more than 75 years since both the United States
and the Soviet Union developed and stockpiled
hydrogen bombs and the world had to learn to live
with "mutually assured destruction." Look at
Hiroshima, Japan. Precisely a definition of what I am
telling you. It could not fulfil this prophecy until man
had the potential for self-extinction through weapons
of mass destruction. Again, just this last century did
this happen to prove it is real. With all the nuclear
powers in the world it is likely that someone else can

perform this action other than Hiroshima to use this deadly force for evil destruction.

Next, what sign will there be when these things are about to take place? I foretold that Jerusalem would be the central focus of the political and military upheavals that would immediately precede my return, as written in the Bible, quoting me, "But when you see Jerusalem surrounded by armies, then know its desolation is near. For these are the days of vengeance that all things which are written may be fulfilled."

I foretold the rebuilding of Israel right before my return and here is what is happening, in 1948 Israel became an independent nation for the first time since the Babylonian takeover in 606 BC, more than 2500 years. In the 1990s around half a million Jews have returned to Israel from the former Soviet Union.

Hebrew, the language of the Old Testament has been revived. By 300 BC the language of the Jews had changed from Hebrew to Aramaic and Greek. Hebrew had remained an unspoken and dead language until recently. Dead for about 2200 years, in 1948, it was proclaimed the national language of Israel.

Today there are around 5 million Jews in the land of Israel, about one third of the estimated total number in the world. There are still about 5 million in the United States and about another 5 million scattered around the rest of the world, but predominantly in the former Soviet Union where there is still a steady stream of Russian Jews returning to Israel as you can see on television with several Christian stations seeking help with donations for this cause.

Next, I spoke in the Bible In Revelation 13:16-18 about the Anti-Christ, referred to as the beast, "He causeth all, both small and great, rich and poor, free and bound, to receive a mark in their right hand, or in their foreheads: and that no man might buy or sell, save he that had the mark, or the name of the beast, or the number of his name."

For the first time in 1900 plus years since someone wrote this book, the Bible, you now have the technology to do this. They could place a tiny computer chip under the skin of one's hand that contains identification plus medical and financial records. If so, purchases would be made by electronic transfer without the use of cash. In addition, this could serve as a global positioning device, allowing tracking of one's position to within a few feet anywhere on the planet. The idea is looking evident by the way people are living now. A cashless society could virtually eliminate muggings, the drug trade, and tax evasion.

Now Daniel, whom you have had the pleasure to meet here on this path foretold this prophesy, of an advancement in technology, and that is an absolute fact you are living in it today and you can see it with your own eyes. 150 years ago which is only a blink of an eye and a second in time, people used candles for light, rode horses for transportation, worked the field to provide for the family, girls got married and started families at the early age of 13 years old, and people did not have a social fear for such simple things such as, are you ready for this Tommy, something you can relate to is people could fart in public, and you what, it was not funny or offensive it was just considered what you did when your body had to do it. In the shortest period you went from horse carriages to cars for transportation, then came flight for transportation. The rapid advancement of technology in the 1950s and 1960s brought television and the space age flying into the heavens and then came computers. In outer space there are satellites that transfer visual news from one country to another across the world in a matter of seconds. Now, do you think from many thousands of years of existence this stuff happening now is a coincidence if it was written and foretold 2500 years ago? Tommy, this is proof I am on my way back soon. Remember this and tell people that I am the true vine, meaning giver of life eternal, my Father is the vinedresser. Every branch in me, meaning you and all people, that do not bear fruit, meaning doing good towards other people and telling the good news how to go to heaven, he takes away. And every branch that bears fruit he prunes it, that it may bear more fruit, meaning if people are tested with troubles and it feels like pain, and their faith in me delivers them from it, I will advance their life to a higher level. If you are tested and it feels like punishment, then it's me correcting you to be in a better place. Abide in me and I will abide in you. People as the branch cannot bear fruit themselves unless they abide in the vine which is me. I am the vine, you are the branches; he who abides in me and I in him bears much fruit, also meaning prosperity, love, true happiness and health, and eternal life; for apart from Me you can do nothing. If anyone does not abide in Me, I throw him away as the branch and he dries up and dies; and they gather them and cast them into the fire, meaning hell and it burns them, meaning destroys them, and they are forgotten about. If you abide in Me and My words abide in you ask whatever you wish, and I shall do it for you, by this My Father is glorified that you are bearing much fruit and so prove to be My disciples.

Just as the Father has loved Me, I have also loved you; abide in My love.

If you keep My commandments, then you will abide in My love; just as I have kept My Father's commandments and abide in His love. These things I have spoken to you, that My joy may be in you, and that your joy may be made full. Apart from me, you can do nothing. Tommy, when you went from being a fun-loving guy to a pure geek filled with expert knowledge, that wasn't you being a genius of your own doing, it's no different from the seed I planted in Einstein for the theory of relativity, I planted a seed in your brain for a purpose, for you to fulfill my work. I planted the wisdom in your mind to create a way for industries to prosper so you also would prosper and become sought after by intellectual people, then one day when you have the spiritual intellect you can educate people that did not believe my existence.

If given another chance, it is vitally important that you witness to all your geeky, nerdy, and evolution believing acquaintances and any non-believing atheist people, and the community who thinks with a scientific mind. I love you Tommy, I love every one that was given the free choice to accept me or not.

I want you to understand what life's timeline is by this theory. Pretend you are an hour glass. It gives you and every human so much sand to start your life with. Some have about one pound which could be the equivalent to 103 years of life, some have a half a pound which could be fifty years, and then some only get an ounce or two. You might live seventy-two years, if so how much sand do you have left in your hour glass? We know you have used at least over one half of it so if this is the case you could conceivably live another twenty years. Maybe you have used one hundred percent and life is done for you as we speak. Some people believe they have fifty percent to go, but really, only have two percent. But the one to concentrate on is the amount of sand that you have left, the question is what are you going to do with your time in that one to thirty-three percent left in the hourglass? How are you going to live the rest of your life? Are you going to chase money? Are you going to work till you are seventy-two then die having made your whole life about work? Will you retire then count your dollars as you play golf and watch over your possessions? Will you spend the amount of sand-time resting or maybe caring and showing love to your family? Maybe you would consider living good by spending that time differently and helping people. Do you think it could be volunteering or maybe telling people what you learned with me so far? Either way your hour glass runs out of sand and you face death, which way you go from there depends on what you did while you had sand in your glass. Tommy, my last message then we will stop walking and talking. I want you to have eternal life. Here is a shortened version of eternal life and use it to inspire people how long they can have freedom with no suffering and plenty of happiness.

Take a bird that has a drop of water on its foot, it flies to a chrome ball the size of a baseball and touches the chrome ball with its foot leaving the drop of water on the ball. It does this once every one-hundred years. Take the amount of time those drops of water rusts the ball away into nothing, countless millions of years! Then take a ball the size of the earth and duplicate that bird dropping water every one-hundred years again until the earth sized ball rusts away. Billions upon billions of years and more like trillions! Now after you have eliminated those two balls, do this again with a ball the size of the sun... ... ... Tommy, when the ball the size of the sun rusts away, that will only be a second in infinity!

I hope to see you on the other side my beloved friend." Jesus extended out his arms to hug Tommy, and he's overwhelmed with his heart pounding, "I can feel my heart beating again!" Tommy reached back and hugged Jesus, and then cried real tears.

"Yes Tommy, let it go, your tears are not that of sadness but happiness, you certainly understand."

At this part of the journey music began playing out of nowhere, it's Rod Stewarts song, "Have I Told You Lately."

The music is playing, and these words are what Tommy is listening to,

Have I told you lately that I love you, Have I told you there's no one else above you? Fill my heart with gladness, take away all my sadness, ease my troubles that's what you do! For the morning sun in all its glory greets the day with hope and comfort too, you fill my life with laughter and somehow you make it better, ease my troubles that's what you do! There's a love that's divine and it's yours and it's mine like the sun, and at the end of the day we should give thanks and pray to the one, to the one. Have I told you lately that I love you, Have I told you there's no one else above you? Fill my heart with gladness, take away all my sadness, ease my troubles that's what you do! There's a love that's divine, and it's yours and it's mine like the sun, and at the end of the day we should give thanks and pray to the one, to the one.

And have I told you lately...

FINISHING THIS JOURNEY

Tommy tells Jesus, "I can hear my heart beating. I haven't even thought of or felt my heart beating until this moment Jesus, it's like I am alive and it's thanks to you!"

The sound of Beep Beep-Beep, Beep-Beep, is going off in his head. "What the heck is that noise?" Beep-Beep, Beep-Beep, Beep. "Jesus, what's that noise?" When Tommy asked the second time it was warped with an echoing sound. "Jesus, what's that noise?" He hears his words in a slow-motion speed and this time his head was spinning and he was dizzy, he blinked, and Jesus was gone. Tommy is feeling weak in his stomach; this experience has been nothing he could've ever dreamed he would experience, and if it is a dream, for it to be so vivid. Blinking his eyes because they were scratchy with blindness, Tommy can see an elderly lady motioning to him to come her way, "Oh boy, just what I need, another path character, I guess I have to go talk to her now." He walked over to her and she was pointing and said, "Go over there, do as I say as we trade places, go, git, go-on, go there now, and remember to accept Jesus' death!" She pointed towards an opening in the trees then motioned for him to go that direction. He wasted no time; maybe this journey was coming to an end?

He felt a complete change like a metamorphosis into another body. Tommy went over to the wooded opening where there was a sandy blustery wind followed by a whistling train sound, similar to a tornado but much quieter, it was cloudy and hard to see through and his vision was disappearing, but he kept walking with trust. He lost his vision and then he heard Beep-Beep, Beep-Beep, Beep. He yells, "Stop! Stop with the noise already!" Beep-Beep, Beep-Beep, Beep. Tommy is trying to talk but is being shushed to silence, "Shhhhhh, relax and be quiet!" He can see more clearly as his vision is coming back. His eyes are weak but focusing and there it is, he's awakening in a hospital and can see a doctor with a small group of people standing over him. He heard the doctor announce, "He is alive and maintaining a steady heartbeat, put the oxygen on regular flow now!" Tommy cannot talk, he is observing the whole situation. The doctor walked up to Tommy and told him, "Sir you were in a terrible accident. We revived you several times and looks like this time we got lucky. We will take you to intensive care where you will have time to heal and get better. Take care of yourself and I will have a Doctor check on you in a few hours."

Tommy has not yet got the fact he died and is in the Hospital due to his motorcycle wreck. He needs more time to gather his composure and find out what all this is about. Tommy's journey was nothing more than a vision he seen through his death process. Later Tommy is reminiscing about this path he walked down while recovering in his Hospital bed. He is playing it over and over still living in this incredible journey he was on. The hora from this trip is numbing his entire body as it totally absorbs him, it's making him feel good like this numbness is a healing process for his body heal from the wreck. The next morning the doctor went to greet Tommy and check him out. "Hello there. I am Doctor Leavings. I am going to check you out and see how you are doing."

"Doctor, what is going on, why am I here?"

"I wouldn't expect you to know what happened this soon so let me tell you. From the report we got you were in a motorcycle accident, an old lady pulled out in front of you and you hit her. They brought you in announced dead, but one intern noticed your eye twitching and called the ER doctor on duty at the time over to check you out. He sees signs of life, then he called me over and we administered CPR, you came in and out of life several times, we worked on you for over fifteen minutes then ultimately you awoke yelling at us to stop! But we kept you alive and here you are."

"Wow, I can't believe I am here, it feels like I shouldn't be here and in the wrong place." Tommy said.

Doctor replied, "Why not believe it? Are you not happy to be alive?"

"I am not sure, I feel weird!"

"Weird, let me tell you what is weird, your body doesn't have half the scrapes or bruises you had yesterday. It is like you just fell off your bicycle instead of getting in a motorcycle wreck."

"Speaking of motorcycle wreck, what happened to the old lady's car I hit, was she mad at me for hitting it?"

"No Tommy she is not mad and seemingly never will be." "Oh good, did her car get much damage, do you know anything about it?" "I am sure it got a little damage and I do not know what happened to her car, but she also arrived here with you in another ambulance, the only thing left to say is you hit her on the driver door, your motorcycle penetrated her window as it threw you over the car." "So, she is here too? How is she?" "Tommy, she died. And I clearly remember her, as she was giving her last breath she mumbled something out loud, it sounded like she was talking to someone telling them, "go over there." She repeated this a couple times and was talking out loud. She was giving instructions for someone to go to a place by some trees and something about believing in someone's death and trading places with her. We were all listening to her because she seemed coherent and adamant about what she was saying. Not sure what she meant but it seemed as if she wanted to die. About that time, we were working on you, then she died, and you woke up. I affirm she must be in a better place now by her facial expression as she passed on. We will never know what happens after we die." Tommy looking at him with a sure thought tells him, "I believe I know, and I think you should know! I have a good idea where the old lady went and let me tell you, we are not a mistake! You, me and all these people on earth are not an accident that evolved from an uncreated rock that magically appeared out of nothing then creating life, get where I am going with this?"

Tommy went on to witness to Doctor Leavings about his magnificent journey and all he learned. He had the doctor sitting down and listening with amazement while he told the story about his incredible journey. Within a fifteen-minute time frame the doctor was already amazed with his story in a way he did not want to stop listening. And guess what? The doctor accepted this Jesus and believes in him and decided to use him as his way out of this earth when he dies. The story got around the hospital after the doctor went out and told other staffers about this man's death experience in room 777. One by one for several hours people stopped by and Tommy told his story. At one time he had as many as seven people standing in his room listening very intently. Tommy was also amazed, not at himself but the desire these people had to listen to him. At the end of the day it was time for Tommy to get some shut eye, he said out loud, "Jesus, your words must have some magic to them, I told many people today about my journey and what you told me, they listened like they were being told how to become millionaires. Some people probably did not believe me, but to be able to tell your story and have people listen so attentively to what I said inspired me." Clearly, Tommy heard a voice in his head, "Yes Tommy, those people were listening to you like you had the next million dollars get rich quick scheme. You gave them something that sounded like a million dollars but it's not anything millions of dollars can buy. You told it with conviction and lovingly. That is what I wanted from you, see you soon Tommy!" Tommy is lying there about to go to sleep when a bubble popped in his brain, "What, fifteen minutes? Do you mean all that happened in fifteen minutes, well I guess the ambulance has to add another 15 minutes, but still that seemed like a week?" Talking about his incredible journey and how long he was knocked out dying.

Several months later Tommy reconstructed his life. He quit working so much with big corporations and has enough revenue from the software he designed that he easily pays his bills and lives comfortably.

Many big organizations that use his software still want him for consulting Six sigma, but when they call him what they get is twenty minutes of consulting telling them about his journey. The new companies that call him for software get an additional twenty-minute sales pitch about Jesus.

One day he is sitting in his home feeling something is wrong. Not sure what to make of it, he remembers Jesus telling him about the Vine and the branches on the vine. Thinking to himself about the meaning of it and how Jesus clearly said, "Abide in me." The feeling is overwhelming to him, then he thinks back to the people in the hospital and how they were listening so intently to his story. It brought a sense of joy to his heart. At that point he realized he must go out in public to tell people about this journey. So, he does. He leaves out and randomly picks certain people in public to tell. Soon enough he gathers a following. Tommy is out every day in different places drawing small crowds to hear his story. You can imagine it looking like when Jesus himself would walk through little towns telling people about the true meaning of life, he drew a crowd everywhere he went. At the end of his speeches some people stay and pray with him to receive this gift from Jesus and others laugh at him like he is a crazy guy just needing to tell a crazy story. A several months into Tommy's speaking to others about his journey, someone approached him, he's a preacher that sat at a distance one day listening to his speech about the journey.

"Excuse me sir, I could not help but to be in love with your story. I believe you and feel you need a different platform to tell this story." Tommy, "O.K. What do you mean by that?"

"Well, my name is Roy Hope, I head up a church here in town and we also have a TV ministry. I would like to have you as a guest on my show if you would consider it." "Consider it? Are you kidding me?" Roy looked at him nervously and said, "I am sorry, but no I was not kidding, and I meant nothing bad by asking, I just thought...."

Tommy interrupts him, "Heck yah! It would honor me. When can I come?"

It relieves Roy that Tommy said O.K. because he thought Tommy was getting mad from the way he replied to him. Roy replied, "Lets exchange phone numbers and I will set up a day we can make this happen."

They parted ways till a week later, Tommy got the call and Roy set up a day for Tommy to come speak. Sunday came around and Tommy is getting nervous. He gets to the church and meets with Roy and he took Tommy to the stage and showed him where each of them would sit for the cameras. About an hour later the time came for the congregation to be seated. While people were trickling in he could see them at a distance all looking at him. The longer he waited and the more those people stared at him he became more nervous. Roy introduced Tommy to the congregation. "People today will be a memorable day for you like none you had before. I had the pleasure to listen to this man tell a story that is almost hard to believe, but

the almighty God works through people and Tommy
is one of them. He has a wonderful story! And with
that said, Tommy let this congregation know how you
met Jesus!" Tommy hasn't ever been in this type of
surrounding with cameras and TV crews. His
nervousness was growing, and he had stage fright so
bad at first, he couldn't talk. He sat there, and
everybody sat patiently in the audience, there was no
noise around the room and he remained sitting with a
closed mouth. Roy caught on about Tommy's stage
fright and started talking, He asked Tommy some
questions and he answered with a very shy voice, then
out of nowhere you will never guess what happened?
Boom! A wet wobbly trumpet sound came rumbling
out the back side of Tommy. Instantly the whole
congregation was profoundly quiet. Then from the
crowd a little girl shouted out, "Mommy that man
farted!" Like she really had to be the anchor man
telling the news. Then the one by one the people in the
audience laughed, No one knew if it was about
Tommy farting or the innocent little girl alerting the

world that Tommy was living one of his life's most embarrassing moments on live TV at its best. The TV audience did not hear the fart at first, but if it weren't for the camera guy speaking to the studio room through his headphones, maybe the TV audience would not have known. What the TV audience heard was the camera man ask, "Did he just fart?" The people in the studio room were motioning with their hands at the camera man with a slicing across the throat motion and covering their mouths for him to stop talking. No one knows what the TV audience did in the privacy of their homes, but I am sure they found the camera man's statement amusing.

So, a couple minutes of laughing and giggling Tommy began talking, "Breaking news! The fart is out of the bag. At my age you sort of fart your way into a speech. I apologize for the trumpet sound my backside felt necessary to embarrass me with, it's what happens when I develop a leak. I have the gift of giving that one little musical note in public when I am nervous, and it always clears the air, get it? I'm not here to blast my way to embarrassment but to tell you what Roy heard me talking about. He thought it was necessary to bring me here and tell all of you about an accident I had a while back. I encountered the most incredible experience, I died and came back to life. I did not encounter the beating and humility Jesus did but share a similar experience."

While he was talking, he gained confidence from the look in the eyes of the congregation as they were like everyone else that heard his story, they looked at him with amazement. When he finished speaking he got a standing ovation. This special TV episode brought many ratings into the media ministry of Preacher Roy that week. Roy asked Tommy to come back several times. After about three times at Roy's church another TV preacher heard Tommy speak and asked him to come speak at his Church. That began a domino effect that had Tommy making his way around to many places, and he became popular. He had one person ask if they could tell his story and write a book about him.

Now that Tommy has a ministry talking to people and witnessing his story he is living what he feels is the real deal about life. One day Tommy is at the park walking and absorbing life. It makes him happy when he meets people around the park and some recognize him from his speeches and others are just taken away by him approaching them to tell his story and by his happy attitude. While Tommy is walking, he sees this lady who is standing alone with a very old dog. He noticed that the dog was so old it looked like it was about to croak. It was so old and run down if it were a human it would be in a wheelchair. Tommy is smiling at it and loving its attitude and it's will to live longer. He walked up behind the lady and made a few jokes about the dog. Her back facing Tommy, "Excuse me Miss, how many times do you have to call him before he remembers his name?" The lady never looked back she just froze and stood there. Tommy was feeling a bit frisky, her not responding opened the door for more jokes.

"I think he answered me, and it sounded like he said, "I might not remember my name because my memory's not as sharp as it used to be, and my memory's not as sharp as it used to be, also my memory is."

The lady is still standing with her back to Tommy, maybe she is insulted and hopes he moves on or maybe she is laughing silently and wants to hear more.

"What's that, what are you saying this time little guy? Are things coming back to you? Things are starting to click for you, Your knees, your elbows, your neck."

The lady never acknowledges Tommy. Continuing to talk to the dog Tommy said, "Hey little guy, I bet you didn't know it, but you didn't stop barking because you grew old, you grew old because you stopped barking." No response, O.K. this puts Tommy over the edge! This lady is way too cool to not be bothered by his jokes and has no response in any way! Well watch out now, Tommy is feeling young and frisky and it's like he ate a reversal of aging pill and it made him go straight into teen Tommy mode. So here comes the big whammy for this lady, if you ignore him then he will give it to you good and here he goes.

"OH, what's that you say poochie? You never know what day of the week it is, but you know on the day the big newspaper comes if you did not get dressed up and jump in the car you missed church."

"Miss, your dog looks like he has bounced back from cancer, heart problems, hip surgery, blindness, and even a stroke. WOW! Oh, what's that you say little doggy?

Geez lady, through all those problems he kept his sense of humor. You know what he told me? He asked me, "Do you know what kills me? Apparently, nothing."

"Miss, maybe we can talk about other things if you are ready?" Still no answer, it looks like she is giggling.

"OK. It looks like you leave me no choice but to continue.

You know your dog is old when he stops searching for the meaning of life to focus on searching for pain relievers.

You know he's old when his secrets are safe with his friends because they won't remember them.

You know he is old when his joints are more accurate than the meteorologists.

> Looks like he doesn't want to achieve immortality by going to heaven, he wants to achieve it by not dying. Did you say something poochie? Yes, he did, he said, "This is the oldest I've ever been and at my age, flowers scare me."

Well, I guess we might want to give him a break from talking to me, he'll need the energy to walk home."

She is still standing with her back to Tommy, the lady can't help it, she is giggling a little. She turned and said, "OK, enough with the elderly dog jokes." After she turned around Tommy immediately started rambling on about his journey. "Miss, I was just having fun, I wanted to lighten up the mood, so you would let me tell you about this incredible journey I encountered. I was in an accident and had the opportunity to be blessed with finding out some very critical information that all people need to know, and I must tell you! Did you know there really is an afterlife? You will be so glad to know that there truthfully is a Jesus."

This lady is staring at with amazement before he ever delves deep into his story! He thinks she is in awe of him talking since most people usually are. Tommy is talking, and she shushes him to be quiet. "Shhhhhh."

"Excuse me." He said. She put her finger over her mouth and shushed him again. So, Tommy holds back and awaits the reason for this slight interruption, he is wondering if she is insulted by my dog jokes and just now waiting to tell me off? Is she not interested in my incredible journey? What is it? She said, "Look at me!" He looked at her and waited. She said, "Is there anything special about me that you see?"

"Yes, you are pretty, you have nice eyes and a good smile, now can I finish my story?" Tommy was so focused on his story he has no sense of what this lady is after. "Look at me." She said it again. Tommy is not getting it. "O.K. I am looking. When do I get the surprise?"

"You must have a terrible memory!" she said.

"Yes, like I was telling you I was in an accident and hit my head so hard that I died, and because of that I do have serious memory issues, probably not as bad as your dog, but yes I am a slightly forgetful."

"All right then, you don't realize where this is going so if you don't mind let me show you something. Here, hold my dogs' leash." Tommy grabs the leash then the lady went on to make a failing attempt to walk on her hands, after trying and falling several times Tommy is clueless, he thinks this lady is out of her mind. She stands up and said "Enough of the fancy footwork! Does that ring a bell?"

"Not really, but I will make a bet that if you practice when you are wearing a pair of jogging pants, not only will you find it easier to do and get better at it, but you surely won't show your panties."

She is not laughing, "O.K. then, you must know this, let me sing a little tune to you and see if this rings a bell." Tommy became very excited about this and is having fun with it. She started singing, "Misses Brown you got a lovely daughter." Tommy is getting a feeling from this and he keeps looking at her as she is becoming more familiar to him. "Again mister, listen and think along! I was trying to walk on my hands and I was singing to you the Beatles song, Misses Brown you got a lovely daughter. Was there ever a time in your life that these two things might ring a bell to you?" Finally, after his extreme focus on telling his story gets lowered to a pay attention focus. He studies her, and he finally gets it, he sees what the missing link is, it's Wendy! Oh wow! What a huge coincidence.

"How on this awesome earth did I miss that? I am so sorry! I haven't seen you in so long I almost forgot what you looked like. Your hair is way shorter, and you have obviously matured to some degree, and..."

"Shhhh! Enough said, now you know who I am. How have you been Tommy? I see you have not lost your sense of humor." Tommy is a little embarrassed from not recognizing her and feeling somewhat shameful for his long absence from her and Athena, he told her, "Wendy, after that accident I lost some of my memory and that is partially why I did not recognize you right away. But for some reason I do remember my journey and it's etched in my brain like a hard drive on a computer. And so far as a sense of humor, I lost it a long time ago but thankfully I met a lady named Sarah. Sarah is part of the story I must tell you. I hope you will give me a chance to tell you what happened and catch up with you at the same time. First thing I would like to say is I am truly sorry for my past life and the way I treated you, disrespected you, and how I deserted you. I know I opened the door to Satan and allowed him to steal our lives away from each other. I'm asking you to forgive me if you can find it in your heart. I have too much to tell you and cannot wait to hear what stories you might have in store to tell me. So, what do you say?"

"It's my pleasure to forgive you! I can't wait to hear this story and you have one other person who will be more than happy to hear your story also."

"Well, I guess I started this off talking to the dog, I see no reason why he can't listen too."

"No, not him silly boy, Athena, your daughter! I know she is going to be so happy to see her daddy."

Weeks later Tommy and Wendy have repaired what was once a volatile relationship. They are spending most of their days together and resuming a much-needed relationship with each other. This time around they have something in common, both are mature and spiritually in tune with Jesus and seek Gods kingdom. It is her desire as well as Tommy's to tell his story and spread his message about Jesus to the entire world. Also, Athena gets to share in their rejuvenation and got to know her father again. It is to Tommy's greatest delight to find out Athena is devoutly connected to Jesus also. Tommy and Wendy eventually fall in love again. "Wendy, I think that time apart was good for us, if I hadn't endured all I did and went on that incredible journey we could not be as happy as we are now, and I have never been this happy, ever!"

"Likewise, my big funny, genius, and loving Christian man!'

The End

It took me around 3 years to write this story between working and living. At the part where Tommy meets Jesus I struggled to make sure I applied accurate information, so I would not lead people astray. What I mean by that is I told Jesus' story the best way I could and that you should not hold all that was said by Jesus in my Novel as gospel fact, and it wasn't written for debate, but to inspire you, so do your homework, and use my novel to consider, "Where will you be seated after death, smoking or non?" Those of you who liked this story and read this to the end were obviously intrigued enough to finish reading it. I hope that after reading this story you consider all that was said by Jesus about eternal life and the doom of burning into a vapor from Hell. You are not committed to believing the story of what Jesus said but I hope most you consider it and think about your destiny.

Like Tommy, I also had a journey to travel down and it was writing this Book-Novel. I felt led by God to tell this story. One day while I was sitting in church, the idea was planted in my mind in a vision with the entire story outline already in place. I am trusting this was God telling me to tell the world of his existence and I am obeying his wish. Also, I believe that in this story there is a message for all people, Christians and Atheists who have an open mind to, "What If, Heaven and Hell? Do we turn to dust and blow away or are we going to a Heaven waiting for us?" Take your pick and good luck with your decision. For me I choose Jesus, at least we know he is real and have proof of his existence! With thanks and love for all you, I hope this blessed you and you enjoyed the story, have a wonderful life on earth and I will see all you believers on the other side.